Who Were You?

Irene Lebeter

Kind Regards

Irene Lebeter

Also by Irene Lebeter -

Vina's Quest
Maddie
The Clock Chimed Midnight

Who Were You?

By Irene Lebeter

Published by Author Way Limited through Amazon
Copyright 2020 author

This book has been brought to you by -

ISBN: 9798612298342

In memory of my parents, Jimmy and Greta,
with gratitude for their love
and example of how to live

For Jane

Irene Lebeter

CHAPTER ONE
New Zealand
2016

I stand in the doorway and stare at the empty armchair. You chose that floral chintz material to match the pale pink walls. Sunlight streams in through the bay window and bathes your chair in an aura of light. In my mind I hear your voice. 'How was your day, sweetheart?'

Curling myself into a ball, I lean my head against the chair's wing and breathe in your favourite scent, 'After the Rain', made on the Scottish Island of Arran. Aunt Viv in Dundee sends you a bottle every Christmas, and only the other day I found last year's bottle, half full, on your dressing table.

My thoughts roll back until I'm fourteen again. You and I are on the ferry going over to the South Island. How excited we both are when the Aranui docks in Picton, to the raucous calls of the gulls and the lapping of the water against the ship's keel. Even at that time in your middle sixties, you had the wonderful gift of remaining a child at heart. The memory of that day brings a lump to my throat and I wipe away a stray tear. 'How will I go on without you?' I whisper, the words wrung out of me as the silence closes in.

It hits me then that you never spoke about your

life in Scotland before you came to New Zealand, and I know nothing about your childhood. How I wish I'd asked you more, but it's too late now. You've gone and taken your secrets with you.

I drag myself into the kitchen to make some dinner. The food is tasteless, and I simply push the pasta and salad around on my plate. The past three weeks have been hard, but this is my worst day yet. Elva warned me that this would happen when the initial shock wore off.

Must write to Aunt Viv. Should have done it by now. It's going to be hard to find the right words, but she's your best friend and needs to know. I return to the living room and take an airmail letter out of the desk drawer. Then, pen in hand, I start to write.

2nd November, 2016

Dear Aunt Viv

I hope you still remember me, Ros Mathieson, although you haven't seen me since I was a small child. This is the hardest letter I've ever had to write. I've put it off for the last three weeks, but I can't do so any longer. I must let you know what has happened ...

CHAPTER TWO

Despite sleeping poorly, I waken before my alarm. I shower, dress and eat breakfast in record time. Then I put out food and water for Smoky and he meows his thanks, before climbing through the cat flap on the kitchen door to go and explore the big outdoors. There are no major hold-ups on the drive into work and I stop off at the Post Office on Cuba Street and drop my letter to Aunt Viv into the overseas mail-box.

When I walk into our office on the twentieth floor of Alston Tower, Ted Downie gives me a smile. 'Hi, Ros, how're you today?'

'Fine,' I say, even though my head is all over the place. I hang up my jacket on the ancient coat stand, which resembles the Leaning Tower of Pisa. I watch the stand swaying under the weight of my light cotton jacket and hold my breath, certain that one of these days that stand's going to topple over. When it remains upright, I go to my desk which adjoins Ted's, our laptops positioned back to back.

'I see our new reporter is already in with Charlie.' I nod towards the outline of the two men, visible through the vertical blinds covering the glass partition, which separates the editor's room and the main office. I've always found Charlie Nunn an approachable boss, and encouraging to young staff like me.

'Yep, he was here when I got in, must have arrived at the crack of dawn.' Ted, who misses nothing, peers across at me over the top of his specs. 'Are you sleeping alright, kiddo?'

I make do with a nod. Despite wearing eye make-up, I guess the puffy, red eyes are a dead give-away. But I say nothing; I hate crying in front of others, preferring to keep the proverbial stiff upper lip.

Elva says I bottle things up too much and I guess maybe she's right.

Ted is our senior crime reporter, and he's been kind to me as a young trainee. Almost like a dad. He's known for his habit of poaching other people's ideas, but I'm sure he doesn't think my work is worth poaching. I've found him to be the real deal, and genuinely concerned about how I'm coping following my bereavement.

Keen to get our conversation ended before I burst into tears, I'm glad when Matt Armstrong comes into the office. 'Morning,' he says, and drops his backpack on to the floor, then throws his jacket and baseball cap over the back of his seat. As second in line to Charlie, Matt has been selected as my mentor, and I must submit my articles to him for proofreading.

Matt heads over now with one of my manuscripts in his hands, his pencilled scrawl visible in the margins. 'This is the piece you showed me yesterday, Ros. It's fine apart from the few alterations I've suggested.' He stands close to me as he's speaking, and I discreetly draw back from him. I'm never sure what food Matt consumes, but his breath stinks and makes me feel nauseous. I'd like to speak to him about his problem, but bad breath isn't an easy subject to discuss, is it? Think I'd need to have a few glasses of wine to be brave enough to broach it.

Just then Charlie emerges from his office, with the new guy in tow.

'Let me introduce Simon Leggat, ex Christchurch Herald,' he says.

On first glance, I reckon over a metre and a half tall, inky black hair tending to curl at the ends, and piercing blue eyes. Even before he reaches us, I feel overpowered by the reek of after-shave, as if he's thrown half the bottle over himself. Strikes me at once that he looks very confident and self-assured. Lucky devil.

Charlie turns to Simon. 'You and Ted have already met. And this is Ros Mathieson and Matt Armstrong.'

'Welcome to the team,' Matt says, holding out his hand to the newcomer.

Simon shakes hands with each of us in turn. 'Good to meet you guys, although I apologise in advance that I'll probably get your names mixed up.'

Ted shrugs. 'No worries, unless of course if you call me Ros.'

When the laughter subsides, Charlie directs Simon to the empty desk. 'Everything you need should be in the drawers or your filing cabinet. Once you've sorted yourself out, Matt can show you where Personnel is, so you can fill in any necessary forms. We need to make sure you're on the payroll before you do any work.' Laughing at his own joke, Charlie returns to his room.

The silence is punctuated only by phones ringing as we concentrate on our various tasks. Trawling through the messages that have been left for me, I see that Charlie has assigned me to run a report on a house fire that occurred over the weekend in an inner-city suburb. Two family members died, while two others are in the Burns Unit at Wellington Hospital. I type out a first draft, using the sketchy material Charlie has given me.

When he hears me sigh, Ted takes off his specs and looks over at me. 'The boss said he was going to put you on to the weekend's fire story. Having problems?'

'There's so little to go on. Think I might go over to the hospital?'

Ted rubs his nose and stares down at the keyboard for a moment. 'Don't think they'll tell you much but it's worth a try.'

I get up and put on my jacket. 'Anyone need anything while I'm out?'

Matt holds out a five dollar note. 'A sandwich please, Ros, anything but egg mayo.'

***

'I'm Ros Mathieson from The Wellington Post,' I tell the receptionist in the Burns Unit, holding out my ID badge. 'I was hoping to have a word with the patients from the Coburg fire.' My eyes latch on to her earrings, which remind me of giant curtain rings.

'I'm afraid not. The police are here waiting to speak to them.'

'Can I at least have a try?'

She shrugs, her earrings swinging around. 'Okay, but I wouldn't hold out much hope. Turn left and it's straight down the corridor.'

I only get a few yards before I'm stopped by a big, burly policeman. 'Whoa, and where do you think you're going?'

My reply is to once again take out my reporter's ID from The Post. 'I'm keen to get a word with the injured from the fire.'

'No way. They aren't even well enough to speak to us yet.'

I turn on my best pleading look. 'Can you give me any information?'

His eyes smile warmly, but I'm unsure if he's being pleasant or feeling sorry for me.

'You can print that no reason has been found yet for the blaze and that the two people rescued from the building are being looked after in hospital. That's as much as I can give you.'

Aware it's as much as he's going to give, I say thanks and leave.

Back at the office, I place a cheese and chutney sandwich on Matt's desk, and beside it the change from his five dollars.

Ted looks up as I approach my desk. 'Any joy?'

I shake my head. 'No more than what we already know.'

***

At midday I sprint along to The Lavender, our usual haunt, where my best friend, Elva Kahui, is seated at the table. I return her wave and weave my way over.

Elva and I have been besties since we started as 11-year-old pupils in the first grade at St Serf's Girls' Grammar in Wellington. Our close friendship has continued, and we meet for lunch a couple of times a week.

Situated here on Cuba Street, The Lavender is conveniently close to both Alston Tower and Wellington Hospital, where Elva is secretary to a cardio-thoracic surgeon. The café lives up to its name with lilac and white gingham tablecloths and lilac frilly blinds.

'Sorry I'm late. Matt wanted to discuss the current piece I'm working on. He always picks the time when I'm getting ready to go for lunch.' I squeeze the words out between breaths, before I take my seat.

'No worries. Calm down before you bring on a heart attack. I passed the time replying to some texts.' Elva switches off her mobile and pops it into her handbag.

'Speaking of Matt. Is his halitosis still as bad?'

'Yep. I almost said something this morning but don't want to offend him. I suppose we should order before we begin chatting?' I pull out a couple of menus from the wooden stand on the table and hand one to Elva.

Leigh, our usual waitress comes over. 'Hi there, guys, and what can I get you today?'

'Think I'll have the prawn pasta,' Elva says, and closes over the menu.

I look up at Leigh. 'John Dory for me thanks.'

Leigh brings us two glasses and a carafe of

water, the ice cubes inside jingling as she lays it down.

'What's your morning been like?' Elva asks me, while she fills our glasses.

'I've been over to the hospital,' I tell her. 'Charlie asked me to report on that dreadful fire over the weekend.'

'It's claimed two lives already. We discussed it at our mid-morning tea break.'

'I spoke to one of the police officers on duty but didn't get much from him.'

Elva changes to a brighter subject, 'Mum and her friend, Violet, are going on holiday to South Australia near the end of this month. Their trip will clash with my painting weekend in Masterton.'

'Oh, I forgot about your weekend away.' Elva's a keen artist and goes on an annual painting retreat to Masterton each November.

'Mum's worried sick about Nikau being left on his own in the house; she's sure he'll throw wild parties while he's got the place to himself.'

'What did you say to her?'

'I said he'd be too busy watching all the rubbish programmes on television, with nobody there to argue. But, to be honest, I'm sure once his mates get to hear that he's on his own they'll be swarming into the house tout suite.'

When Elva's dad died, he left Mrs Kahui to bring up Elva and her young brother single-handedly. Elva's part-Maori blood shows in her olive complexion and black hair, while Nikau is fairer skinned like his Austrian mother. The family home is in Brooklyn, one of the inner suburbs, handy for shopping and public transport.

'I'm amazed how well your mum has recovered from the ischaemic attack last year.'

'I know, it's fantastic. There's no stopping her. Sometimes I think she forgets she isn't a teenager any longer.'

'Your mum has a wonderful spirit. I know lots of people younger than her who act like they're eighty.'

Elva sits back as Leigh brings our meals to the table. 'So how about the new reporter?' she asks, when Leigh moves away again.

'Not sure, it's his first day. I'll reserve my judgement meantime.'

'Doesn't sound like he's made a good first impression.'

I cut into my fish and the wafer-like flesh billows out. I take a mouthful before replying. 'Delicious. I'm glad I picked it. Right, back to the new guy. He seems very sure of himself, slightly arrogant even. But, early days yet.'

'You don't usually have problems getting on with people.'

'True. Maybe I'm not giving him a chance as I'm feeling a bit lousy today.'

'Yeah, you look a bit down in the mouth right enough. Are you sleeping okay?'

'Ted asked me that when I got into work this morning. I said I was fine, but it isn't strictly true. No matter how many hours I sleep at night, I wake up tired each morning.'

'Maybe you should consult your doctor. Perhaps you're depressed. A bereavement takes it out of you. And you were very close to your gran.'

I yawn and cover my mouth to try and stifle it. 'Yeah, it's true, I don't seem to be dealing with Gran's death too well.'

Elva eats the last of her pasta and pushes the plate to the side. 'Ros, please don't take this the wrong way, and I promise I'm not trying to criticise, but do you think you might benefit from some bereavement counselling?'

'What, go and see some weirdo who wants you to open your heart to them?'

Elva laughs and shakes her head. 'They aren't weirdos, they're properly trained counsellors who know how to help. Your GP would refer you if you ask.'

'I can speak to you.'

'But it's much easier to offload to a stranger.'

'You seem to know a lot about it.'

A shadow passes over my friend's face. 'Mum had to get help after Dad passed away and left her with two young kids to care for. It really made a difference to her.'

'I'm sure you're right but I'll leave it for a bit yet. If I can get back to a normal sleeping pattern, it should help.'

Once Leigh clears away our used plates, we order a dessert with our coffee, chocolate fudge cake for Elva and blueberry cheesecake for me. On leaving the café, Elva and I share a hug. 'See you on Thursday,' she says, and we go our separate ways.

Irene Lebeter

CHAPTER THREE

'Right guys, I'm off, see you on Monday?' I push my empty glass into the centre of the table while I'm speaking. The Green Man, an Irish pub in downtown Wellington, is our Friday night haunt after work and usually our cars are left at the office and we go home by taxi.

Ted glances at his watch. 'I'll need to go too. Anne has invited some of the neighbours round to ours this evening.'

'Do you want me to drop you home?' I offer, knowing Ted has downed a few lagers. I'm on soft drinks at the moment, because alcohol is making me weepy, no doubt due to my recent bereavement.

Ted drains his glass and gets to his feet. 'Thanks, Ros, that'll keep Anne's face straight if I get home before the folks arrive.'

We say our goodbyes to the others and head out to my Toyota.

'Thanks a million,' Ted says, as we pull up at his house.

'Say hi to Anne for me,' I call out to him as he closes the car door.

Smoky greets me on my return home, rubbing himself against my leg. I feed him and settle down in front of the telly with a microwave meal for quickness.

At the end of the programme, I look for the key to the desk drawer, something I've been meaning to do for days now. Gran always kept that bottom drawer locked and I've no idea where she's hidden the key. After a long search, I find it. Inside the drawer are several souvenirs of Gran's, and I lay them out one by one on the top of the desk.

The red leather diary, its covers scuffed and rubbed, seems to have been started when Gran first came to New Zealand in 1972. It's a five-year diary but, as it's the only one in the drawer, I guess she must have stopped writing a diary after that.

Inside the diary I find a dried-up leaf, once red and yellow veined, now discoloured and fragile enough to disintegrate at the touch. It occurs to me then that Gran once told me about the holiday she and Grandad had in New England in the fall, so I guess the leaf is a souvenir from that trip.

I recognise Mum from the school photograph of a girl's netball team in 1988. Mum is standing on the back row, on the left. The other photograph is of me with Mum and Dad when I was a toddler. I put the picture down quickly when I feel the tears welling up.

This is the first time I've seen Grandad's Gold medal for sprinting that he appears to have received when he was a teenager in Glasgow. In the box with the medal, is a newspaper cutting with his death notice dated 10th April, 1997. I see from the notice that the funeral service was held in the Presbyterian cathedral in Wellington, followed by a burial in the cemetery in Johnsonville. I was five when he died, so a neighbour or friend probably looked after me while my parents and Gran attended his funeral.

The final item is a silver coin dated 1942. I recall Gran showing this coin to me years ago, and she said it was worth two shillings and sixpence, commonly known as a half crown. I'm not sure why she kept one from 1942 but it obviously must have meant a lot to her.

I smile down at this treasure trove, looking on it as Gran's legacy. Since I started attending the writing group, I'm always looking out for stories. I have to email something to my writing colleagues for next month's meeting and, looking at these items, I'm sure I can get a story out of them, or at least some of them.

'Thanks, Gran,' I whisper to her picture sitting on the desk, 'you've come up trumps, as always.'

***

'Elva, do you want to have your shower before dinner?' Heidi Kahui asked her daughter when she came home from work that evening.

'I will Mum. The air conditioning was out of commission today and the office was like a sauna.' Elva hurried into her bedroom, pulling her sweat-soaked top over her head before stepping out of her jeans.

Heidi was carving the meat when Nikau sauntered into the kitchen. He sniffed appreciatively and dropped his dirty work clothes into the laundry basket. She was pleased that he seemed to be enjoying his work as a plumber. After the problems he'd given her when he was at school, it was a relief that he'd at last settled down.

She watched him draw his fingers through his

fair curly hair, inherited from her. He resembled Karl, her brother who died aged 9. Tears welled up at the thought and she was glad to be distracted when Nikau spoke again.

'How long till dinner, Mum? I'm meeting the lads in the pub at eight.'

'We'll be ready to sit down in five minutes, Liebling,' she promised. Even after living in New Zealand for thirty years, Heidi still reverted to her native German tongue when using endearments to the kids.

Elva appeared, her hair gleaming and wearing fresh clothes.

'Good timing,' Heidi said, smiling at her pretty daughter.

'And did you see Ros today?' she asked, when they were seated at the table.

'Yep, this was a Lavender day.' Elva spooned some veg on to her plate and slid the dish along to her brother.

'And was she well?'

Elva took the gravy boat from her mother and poured some over her meat. 'I don't think she's got over her gran's death yet. Says she hasn't been sleeping too well.'

Heidi shook her head. 'No, of course she hasn't, it will take time for her to recover from the shock. Is she still doing well in her job?'

'Yeah, she likes working at The Post.'

'No wonder the poor girl's struggling, since she's lost so many family members.'

Heidi had known Ros' parents and her gran since Elva and Ros first met at school. With her parents dying young, it was understandable that Ros had been desolate when her gran passed away recently.

'Are you in a rush or what?' Elva asked Nikau, after he'd bolted down his meal.

'Yep,' he replied, pushing back his chair and getting to his feet. 'Sorry Mum, I need to get off now.'

'But Nikau, what about dessert? It's your favourite, sherry trifle.'

'Leave it in the fridge for me and I'll eat it when I come home.' He dived out of the room and a minute later they heard the front door close behind him.

'What's he like?' Elva said after he'd gone. 'Always rushing around somewhere?'

Her mother smiled. 'Boys will be boys. And talking of boys, how are you and Adam getting on these days?'

'I like him, Mum. He's great company and fun to be with, but don't go getting ideas of us settling down together. We're just good friends.'

Heidi stretched over and laid her hand on top of her daughter's. 'As long as you're happy, Liebling, then I'm happy.'

'I'll do the washing up, Mum. You sit down and watch your programme.' Elva knew that her mother had become hooked on a new quiz show.

'Okay, thanks.' Sinking down into the soft cushions on the settee, Heidi picked up the remote control.

CHAPTER FOUR
Scotland

The rattling of the letterbox wakened her. She heard the postman's feet crunch over the chips on the path. A quick glance up at the clock above the fireplace told her he was a couple of hours late on his round today.

She got up from her armchair, stiff from sitting so long in one position. On her way through the hall, she glanced into the brass-framed mirror, a wedding gift from their best man. Running her fingers over the unblemished skin on her face, she winked at her reflection. 'Not bad for nearly 78, old girl,' she murmured. Still her own teeth, albeit with fillings and a few crowns, and a good head of hair, even if silvery white by now. With the aid of her stick, her slight frame stooped down to pick up the mail and she carried it into the living room.

Junk mail, apart from the New Zealand letter. She wasn't wearing her glasses but knew it was from her long-time friend down under.

She stuffed the other envelopes into the wicker waste-paper bin and went into the kitchen to make a cup of coffee. While waiting for the water to boil, she stared out of the kitchen window at the sun glinting on the river. No wonder it was known as the silvery Tay, she thought, humming quietly to herself. From her upstairs bedroom, she could even catch a glimpse of the road bridge that transported travellers over to Fife. She and Dave had lived in this house on Farington Street for forty years, following Dave's redundancy from his job in Glasgow.

Since Dave's death seven years ago her neighbour, Jenny, phoned every morning to check if she needed anything from the shops. Sometimes Jenny's nosiness was annoying, but she had to admit that the woman was an excellent support.

She carried her coffee into the living room and sat down to read her letter. It wasn't until she put on her reading specs that she noticed it had been written by an unknown hand. A feeling of foreboding surged through her, but she shrugged it off and slit open the letter.

2nd November, 2016
Dear Aunt Viv

I hope you still remember me, Ros Mathieson, although you haven't seen me since I was a small child. This is the hardest letter I've ever had to write. I've put it off for the last three weeks, but I can't do so any longer. I must let you know what has happened to Gran. As you know, she was very fit for 77, and often used to joke that she'd live until 100. 'They'll have to take me out and shoot me,' she would say.

Since my parents' tragic deaths, Gran and I have stayed together in the family home at Lyall Bay. I did leave a couple of years back, when I shared a flat with my fiancé for a few months. When that relationship ended, I returned to Gran's house. We were very close and often had outings together at the weekends; usually just the two of us but now and again my friend Elva would join us.

Three weeks ago, I was at work when I received a call from Wellington Hospital. Gran had fallen down the stairs leading from our back door into the garden. Her cleaning lady, Freda, found her shortly afterwards and phoned an ambulance. Gran had fractured her hip and later in the day was taken to the operating theatre. She appeared to be making a good recovery, and I was even beginning to relax again, when she developed pneumonia. Despite the best efforts of the hospital staff, she passed away within a few days. I was in shock at first, denying it had happened.

I'm glad to have her cat, Smoky, with me for company. He misses Gran too, and constantly goes into her bedroom to look for her, but we have settled into our new life together.

I'm still trying to get my head round what has happened in such a short space of time. This is why it has taken me so long to write to you.

I'm sorry Aunt Viv but I can't write any more at the moment although I promise to contact you again soon. I know this will come as a great shock, and I wish there was an easy way to tell you, but there isn't.

Meantime, take care of yourself.

Love from Ros

x

By the time Viv got to the end of the letter, the writing was smudged by her tears. Her friend's last airmail, dated two months' ago, was full of joy and bustling activity, with no sign of anything amiss. How could it have happened? And the end so quick?

Oblivious to the growing darkness outside, Viv lost track of time. The curtains remained open, her usual routine having deserted her. She leaned forward to place the letter on the table and her hand bumped against the coffee mug, its contents long since gone cold. The mug toppled over and a river of coffee streamed across the surface of the table and dripped down on to the carpet. Lacking the energy to clean up right now, she stemmed the tide with a wad of tissues.

There was a knock on the front door. Viv ignored it, but she should have known better, and a few minutes later the knocking became a loud banging, and Jenny's voice called to her through the letter box.

With a sigh, Viv lifted her head out of her hands and, using her stick, moved slowly towards the front door.

CHAPTER FIVE

After another restless night, with Gran featuring in my dreams, I waken at 8.30 and immediately begin to panic. I throw the duvet aside and race into the shower. It's only when the power of the water wakens me fully that I remember today is a public holiday, our last one before Christmas. Frenzy over, I slip on my wrap and go into the kitchen. The idea of a cooked breakfast begins to form in my head. I grill a few rashers of bacon and crack an egg into the frying pan, while watching the early morning news programme.

I gobble down my breakfast, hoping I will still have some appetite for lunch. Elva's boyfriend, Adam, is working today so she and I are going with her mum to Masterton for lunch. We've booked a table at a popular fish restaurant there, which Elva discovered when she was at her painting weekend recently.

I rinse through my breakfast dishes and leave them on the draining board. After I'm dressed, I pop along to the corner shop to buy some milk. It's when I'm heading home again that I get a strange feeling that someone is following me. I stop outside the butcher's shop and look round. The road behind me is empty, but the sensation persists. I continue until I reach the gift shop, where I pretend to study the items in the window, allowing time for the person to pass me by. No-one comes, but the distinct thought that I'm not alone doesn't leave me. It's spooky, but I straighten my shoulders and walk on.

A couple of hours later Elva and her mum arrive to pick me up. 'Be good,' I say to Smoky, having filled his dish a short time earlier.

Elva releases the lock on the car door, and I step into the back seat behind her.

'How lovely to see you, Ros.' Elva's mum turns and flashes me her beaming smile.

'It's great to catch up.'

Mrs Kahui is beautiful, and she must have been a real stunner in her younger days. I find it easy to imagine her coming from a titled family in her native Austria but, according to Elva, that isn't so.

'Elva keeps me up to date with how you are,' she says, turning back to face the front.

Once I've fastened my seatbelt, Elva indicates and moves away from the kerb. The traffic is lighter than expected for a public holiday and soon we reach the freeway towards Masterton. Mrs Kahui and I keep up a steady stream of conversation during the journey.

'We've some time to kill. Let's have a walk in the park,' Elva suggests, once we find a spot to leave the car.

We stroll around, admiring the exquisite blooms and water features. 'D'you remember you used to bring us here as kids?' Elva reminds her mother when we reach the miniature station, where the children's model train begins its circuit of the park.

Mrs Kahui laughs. 'You and Nikau used to start talking about riding on the train the moment we left Wellington. As soon as we got into the park, you were off like the wind racing towards the ticket office. Happy days,' she says, and I hear a slight catch in her voice.

The hum of happy conversation from other diners and the mouth-watering smell of food welcomes us to The Dolphin. We are shown to a table in the conservatory, looking out on a duck pond, the windows framed by brightly coloured hanging baskets. 'It's such a pretty place this,' I say, pushing my sunglasses up on to my forehead.

'Elva tells me you enjoy working at The Post,' Mrs Kahui says, during our meal. 'It's good to have the company of your colleagues now that you're alone in the house.'

I pull some crabmeat away from the carcass before replying. 'Yes, I do find it very lonely without Gran. And yet in some ways the house is a comfort.'

She fingers her pearl necklace and nods. 'I always think it is foolish to move house too soon after a bereavement.'

She breaks off to take a drink of water. 'You're doing very well, Ros, and my advice is to take things slowly before you make any important decisions.'

'I know Gran would want me to carry on with my life and not brood on her death.' A sad little laugh escapes from me. 'Easier said than done though.'

Mrs Kahui doesn't reply but simply leans across the table and squeezes my hand. 'Elva was saying you have a new member of staff at The Post,' she says, changing the subject.

'Simon Leggat. He used to work at The

Christchurch Herald. Comes across as a bit of a know-all but hopefully he might grow on me.'

She nods wisely. 'Often people put on a front when they start a new job.' She looks over at her daughter. 'Will we order coffee now, Liebling?'

Elva signals to our waitress and the conversation returns to more general subjects.

It isn't until I'm back home in Kiwi Crescent that I remember my sense of being followed this morning and I feel a chill running through me.

***

Simon removed his gear from the boot and carried everything indoors. With today being a public holiday, he'd joined some mates for a round of golf and was pleased with his performance. It had been hot out on the golf course and he was glad to reach the nineteenth hole and quench his thirst. Taking a can of Foster's out of the fridge, he pulled back the ring top and heard the welcoming fizz. He drank almost half of the contents in one gulp, then burped loudly.

His thoughts went to Ros. In the four weeks he'd been at The Post, she'd been quite hostile towards him. He knew he could sometimes come across as arrogant, but people close to him were aware that this was a front to ward off his fear of rejection. Maybe he'd been too pushy in trying to flirt with Ros, and perhaps taking a step back would be best.

Yet he couldn't get her out of his mind. They had both applied to attend the same course in Wanganui in February so perhaps the rivalry hadn't helped their relationship.

Unable to think of cooking on such a hot night,

Simon rummaged in the kitchen drawer for a menu from the local Chinese take-away. Once he'd placed his order, he went off to shower. He'd dressed in clean shorts and t-shirt when he heard a ring at the doorbell. Grabbing some notes out of his wallet, he padded along the hallway. The smell of the black bean sauce hit him the minute he opened the door, and he sniffed hungrily.

He spooned the soft noodles on to a plate and put the beef dish on top. Opening another can of Foster's, he settled down to watch a T.V. documentary about saving the planet, a subject close to his heart.

***

Simon was in a deep sleep when something disturbed him. He wasn't sure what had wakened him, but the digital clock showed ten minutes after twelve. When he stood out of bed, he felt the room swaying.

'What the hell,' he muttered. Surely to God he hadn't drunk so much as to render him dizzy. It wasn't until he saw the items on the dressing table shifting about that his sleep-drenched brain realised it was a quake. Wellington often experienced tremors, so he stood there until the shaking subsided before trying to get back to sleep. Still awake at half past twelve, he got up and went into the living room. He switched on the television and heard the report that an earthquake had hit Christchurch around midnight, the second quake in five years to strike that city.

Simon watched the horror unfold on the screen, and rang his parents at their farm in the South Island. He felt sure they were far enough away in Dunedin to remain unaffected, but he needed to know they were safe. The number rang out for a long time before his mother's sleepy voice answered. 'Hello,' she mumbled.

'Mum, sorry to phone so late but wanted to check all was well at Lime Tree.'

'Of course, it is, Son,' she said, her voice less sleepy now. 'Why did you think it wouldn't be?'

Relief surged through him. 'That's great, Mum, but there's been another quake in Christchurch. If you switch on your telly, they're speaking about it right now.'

'Okay, Son, since you've wakened me up, I might as well check it. Simon says there's been a quake in Christchurch and it's on telly at the moment,' he heard her say to his father, who'd obviously also wakened.

'I'll phone you again tomorrow, Mum,' he promised, and hung up, happy that his parents were safe.

CHAPTER SIX
2017

Leggat sidles up to me, coming so close that his cheek almost touches mine. The only thing in his favour is that his breath doesn't stink like Matt's.

'Hi Ros, heard you got a scoop yesterday. Quite a feat, interviewing the big man himself.' Leggat's sneer is evident in his voice as he sweeps past my desk. In his chauvinist eyes, how can a woman be successful? I'm Rosalind to you, only my friends call me Ros, is what I'd like to say but I'm not brave enough and ignore him instead.

When he moves away to pester the young boy who is with us for work experience, I go over to the coffee machine. But his jibe still angers me while I watch the water gushing into the polystyrene beaker. 'Ouch,' I yell, and pull my hand away when it overflows and boiling water spurts out, but not before it scalds the back of my hand.

Back at my desk, I watch Leggat go into Charlie's room, no doubt giving our poor editor the benefit of his superior knowledge. At least I'm not alone in my aversion to Leggat; a girl who works in the print room tells me he's ruffled a few feathers in that department.

I chew the end of my pen and try to concentrate on the piece about Wellington Hospital's extension that

I'm writing for tomorrow's column. But after a few minutes I throw the pen down in disgust, inspiration having deserted me in my current disgruntled state.

My phone rings at that moment. 'Hello, you're through to Ros Mathieson from the Wellington Post, how can I help you?'

'Good afternoon, Ros, Sheila Carter speaking. I wondered if we could fix up a time for you to come to our office.'

Sheila is my contact at the Community Trust, and we have agreed to meet so that I can write an article about her work with homeless and disadvantaged people.

'Yes, of course we can. Let me see, would next Monday at eleven o'clock be convenient for you, Sheila?'

'Yes, that's fine. I could introduce you to some of the clients who attend our groups here. For the sake of privacy, we only use their first names.'

'I understand that, and of course, I'll check that you're happy with what I write before it is published.'

'Perfect.'

'Fine, Sheila, see you then. Bye.'

When I hang up, I write the appointment in my desk diary and also key it into my mobile. Then I sit for a moment staring out of the floor-to-ceiling window at the view over the Wellington skyline. It's one of the benefits of working on the twentieth floor, the downside being when the lifts are out of action, something that's happened a lot recently.

I see that Leggat is laying it on to Charlie. Only

two and a half months with us and already he's acting like he's the boss. With Charlie's attention taken up, I decide now is a good time for me to escape, the urge strong to finish my article at home, along with a restorative glass of vino. I promise myself I'll get up at the crack of dawn to ensure that my piece makes it into the lunchtime edition. Decision made, I come off the laptop and put my notebook into my handbag. As I leave the office, Ted raises an eyebrow but says nothing. I'm pretty sure he's aware that I'm still not coping too well with the loss of Gran.

'Goodnight, Harry,' I say to the security guard, a retired policeman, in the foyer.

'Night, Ros.' He winks at me as I go towards the revolving door.

Driving along the coast road towards Lyall Bay I think how lucky I am to live near the beach. Gran and Grandad bought the house at Kiwi Crescent when they first came to New Zealand in 1972. My mum, born in that house in 1973, was their only child and nineteen years later it was my turn to see the light of day in Kiwi Crescent.

That thought brings on a warm feeling.

I slow down when I come into Lyall Bay. An army of schoolchildren are waiting at the pedestrian crossing, so I stop to let them over. They make their way across, jostling to beat their friends to the other side. The crossing patrol man has a benign face, like a kind grandpa. I can barely remember my grandad, as he died when I was 5-years-old. I have a faint recollection of sitting on his knee while he read me a story before bed and that he always smelt of pipe tobacco.

The driver behind toots to remind me that the crossing is clear again. I give him or her a wave of thanks and move off, recalling the feeling of devastation I experienced when Mum and Dad were killed in that train crash in London. I was a teenager at the time, and I've lost count of the number of times since when I've used the 'if only' words. 'If only they hadn't gone on that holiday, they'd still be here', 'if only they'd travelled to Windsor the following day, they'd still be alive'.

I'm stopped again at the next set of lights. 'I guess it's because you lived longer than Mum and Dad that I became so close to you, Gran,' I murmur, over the soothing tones of Debussy's 'Au Clair de la Lune' coming from my car radio.

When the light changes through amber to green, I move from neutral into first, then second gear, and put my foot back on the accelerator. I turn right into Dolphin Road and near the brow of the hill take a left into Kiwi Crescent.

Running my Toyota into the driveway of No 18, I turn off the engine. I bought the dark blue hatchback just under a year ago and, so far, it has given me good service and little trouble. I sit behind the wheel for a few minutes, staring into space. In my mind I see Leggat's face in front of me.

That darned man is a pest, constantly invading my privacy. I close my eyes, trying to block out the image of his face and it's then that a thought drifts into my mind.

Is Leggat as bad as I paint him? Has my break up with Don left me bitter towards all men? But I shake my head vigorously. No, Don was the biggest ratbag that ever existed but Leggat is still a pain.

When I come out of the car, Smoky is sitting at his usual place on the front room window ledge waiting for me. By the time I go inside, he is behind the door; he purrs and rubs his fur against my leg. He was a rescue cat that Gran took in and she named him in keeping with his colour.

'Hello there, boy, I can always depend on a welcome from you, can't I? Even if it is just cupboard love.' I stroke him as I'm speaking and when I go into the kitchen, he pads behind me to wait while I replenish his food and water. I also leave out a saucer of milk for him.

CHAPTER SEVEN

Next morning I waken up, sobbing and calling her name. It's that dream again, the same one that keeps recurring. Even though I understand its meaning, it's nonetheless distressing. I raise my head off the sodden pillow, perch on the side of my bed and take deep breaths.

After a meagre breakfast, I set off earlier than normal, as I want to give my article to Matt. Halfway along the shore road, I switch off the engine and open the car window. It's peaceful at this early hour; a calm sea, some birdsong and no traffic to disturb. The pohutukawa trees are blooming along the shoreline. I've always loved their bright red flowers; they lift my spirits when I'm feeling down. And I surely need them lifted today. I allow myself a few more minutes to enjoy my surroundings, then I re-start the engine.

Once in Cuba Street, I turn into the lane at the side of the Wellington Post, leading to the car park at the rear of the building. Apart from Charlie's place, there are no designated parking spaces and the system runs on a first come, first served basis. With only two cars this early on, I'm spoiled for choice.

'Morning,' I say to Harry when I come into the main foyer from the back entrance. I turn towards the lift and he calls after me. 'Sorry Ros, lift's broken down.'

'Again? But it was only repaired two days ago.'

Harry shrugs 'I know. Think they need to rip it out and start again. The engineers are on their way but I'm afraid it's got to be the stairs at the moment.'

I let out a most unladylike word, then Harry and I exchange a smile.

After a long slog up to the twentieth floor, I'm out of puff, my breathlessness showing I definitely need to lose weight.

I go into the ladies' staff room, where I draw a comb through my hair, moving my head from side to side, pleased with the sheen my new shampoo has produced. On closer inspection though, I notice that my auburn highlights are needing done again.

In the office, I hum to myself as I make a coffee, happy that Leggat will be out on assignments all morning so I won't have to put up with his snide remarks until after lunch at the earliest.

The caffeine boost helps me do yet another edit of my article. A tweak here and there, then I leave the final version on Matt's desk. As a trainee journalist, I'm given a fairly free rein but important articles, such as the present one, has to be vetted by Matt. When he's satisfied, he'll pass it to the printing section for insertion into either today or tomorrow's edition of the newspaper.

Shortly afterwards, Ted appears in. 'Morning, Ros?'

'Hi. Did you and Anne have a good meal last night?' He'd told me yesterday that he was taking his wife out to the Chameleon restaurant in the city to celebrate their wedding anniversary.

He gives me a thumbs up. 'The meal was superb. A wide selection of food and the portions were massive. You should try it sometime, Ros.'

'Definitely will. Might suggest it for our next girls' night. The restaurant's in Customhouse Quay, isn't it?'

'Yeah, at the corner of Panama and the Quay.'

When Ted's phone rings, I turn my attention to the next article I'm working on about the Wellington Harbour Trust.

***

Elva and I arrive at The Lavender at the same time, walking from opposite directions.

'How's your article about the hospital extension going?' Elva asks me, after we've given Leigh our lunch order. Being employed at the hospital, she's interested, especially as her department will be moving into the extension when it's completed.

'I finished it this morning. Matt vetted it and he passed it to the print room before ten o'clock.'

'Great, I'm looking forward to reading it.'

'Should make it into tomorrow's edition at the latest.'

'What's happening about Matt's bad breath?'

'Just the same. He's a lovely guy but I have to turn away when he speaks to me as I can't stand the smell. Don't know if it's due to the food he eats or stomach trouble but it's horrible. Wish I could say something to him, but I'd hate to hurt his feelings.'

'It's a difficult one. You'd think one of the other

guys in the office would give him the nod about his problem?'

I shrug. 'Maybe I'm the only one who notices.'

The café is quieter than normal, and Leigh is back in record time with our starters, along with the usual jug of water.

'I had that dream again last night.'

'The one where your gran appears?'

I nod. 'In the dream Gran smiles and calls to me. She looks so happy and I race off towards her but as soon as I get near, she's surrounded by a thick, smoky mist and I'm left, sobbing and out of breath. It happens a few times during the dream and I'm always determined to get to her and touch her, but the mist stalls me. When I waken up, my pillow is sodden.'

I finish my starter first and rest my arms on the table-top. 'So, how was the wedding?' I ask, wanting to change to a brighter subject.

'Shona was magnificent, and her sister made a stunning bridesmaid. I'll show you.' Elva brings up the photos on her phone and hands it over to me. 'That's Shona and her sister.' She stretches over and draws her finger across the screen. 'And there's the bride and groom outside the church.'

I hand the phone back once I've trawled through all the pictures. 'Was it a big affair?'

Elva lays the phone down on the table and twirls her fork between her fingers while she thinks about that. 'I guess there were around 80 guests and quite a number of us from the hospital had been invited.'

'Where did the happy couple go for their

honeymoon?'

'They've gone on a four-week cruise, taking in Los Angeles and San Francisco. Lucky devils, we're all so envious. So, how is the bold Simon this weather?'

'The same as ever. Sometimes I think my relationship with Don has made me distrust all men.' Don and I had our wedding arranged and, finding him two months before our big day in bed with another woman, wasn't easy to recover from.

'But, after all he put you through, I can understand it leaving you like that.'

'Gran never liked Don. I should have listened to her.'

Leigh brings our mains. I squeeze some lemon juice through the little muslin bag on to my fish. The muslin doesn't stop my fingers getting wet, so I lick them and dry them on my serviette. 'How has your morning been?'

'Mr Hamilton has returned from the surgical conference in Japan, full of ideas of how to improve the working of the department. My fingers ache from racing over the keyboard to type the new forms that he wants to introduce. By the way, are you doing anything on Saturday, Ros?'

'Nothing in particular. Why?'

'Do you fancy coming with me to the races at Trentham?'

'Since when have you taken an interest in horse racing, Elva?'

'I haven't. But I've got a couple of free tickets for the Members' Enclosure at Trentham on Saturday.

It's the Wellington Racing Club's January Meeting.'

'Tell me more.'

Elva sits forward and rests her chin on her clasped hands. 'I got the tickets from Adam Barclay when we were at the nightclub last Saturday.'

'You seem quite struck on Adam,' I say, giving her a knowing look.

'We're just good friends but yes I have to admit he's quite special. He fitted in well at the wedding last week when he came as my partner. Anyway, Adam's brother owns a racehorse called Dandy Boy and he's racing it at Trentham on Saturday. The tickets Adam gave me would let you and I sit in the enclosure and have lunch in the Members' Dining Room.'

'But would Adam be happy to have me tagging along with you both like a spare part?'

'Adam won't be there. He left yesterday for America where he'll be working for a couple of weeks in Chicago. Sent there by his company, all expenses paid.'

'Excellent, so we'll be left to our own devices. Right, count me in.' I sit back when Leigh arrives with our coffee.

'We can place a bet on Dandy Boy and see if he brings us luck. I'll drive us to Trentham. And by the way Adam said there is a strict dress rule on race days.'

'What does that mean? I don't have any fancy hats.'

'No need to go to that length. Just dress smartly and wear good footwear. No shorts or jandals allowed. What's so funny?' Elva asks, when she sees the smile on my face.

'My gran never spoke about jandals. She always called them flip-flops. She spent the first thirty years of her life in Scotland so didn't adapt to some of our Kiwi words. Some of her Scottish sayings were a hoot. Often, I didn't have a clue what she was on about; it sounded like a foreign language to me. I think I got more used to her accent when there were just the two of us living in Lyall Bay.'

Elva nods. 'I suppose it would have been difficult for her to adjust to the new words after living in Scotland all that time. I loved your gran's Scottish accent and she was always so kind to me when I came to Kiwi Crescent. Anyway, back to the racing. I'll do the driving.'

'Trentham is quite close to Upper Hutt, isn't it? How long do you reckon it will take us to get there?'

Elva taps her fingers on the table. 'Traffic allowing, I guess we'll drive there in just under half an hour. The tickets also include free car parking at the course.'

'It gets better by the minute. Think I should get back to the office.'

'Yep. Same here.' We drain our coffee cups and signal to Leigh, who brings over the bill. On exiting the café, we hug and say our goodbyes.

CHAPTER EIGHT

By the time I'm ready to leave on Saturday, Smoky's already outside in the garden, so I leave some food and a saucer of milk for him in the kitchen close to the cat flap. I'm pulling on my pale blue cotton jacket when I hear Elva toot her horn.

'Hi, you look great,' she says, as I get into the passenger seat of her red Kia.

'You're looking pretty swish yourself.' I return the compliment when I see her cream silk trousers and black top with sparkly beaded design on the front.

'Fancy some air?'

I nod and she slides open the car roof before we zoom off in the direction of the highway, enjoying the light breeze. When Elva switches on a CD, the two of us sing along to some Abba hits.

Arriving in Upper Hutt, Elva reduces speed and stops at traffic lights outside a large department store.

'How much further?' I ask, looking over at some ladies' outfits displayed in the shop window. The clothes are in green, brown and tangerine shades, so I guess they must be getting ready for the autumn season already.

'We should be at the racecourse in about ten minutes.' Elva stretches over for her bag sitting on the back seat. 'Could you get the parking permit out of my bag, Ros?' she asks, when she finds she can't reach it.

'Sure'. I lift the bag on to my lap and rummage until I find the permit.

At the racecourse, an official looks at the permit. 'Anywhere over to the left,' he tells us, pointing to the spot.

Once parked, we link arms and head off in the direction of the clubhouse. 'Will we place our bet first?' I sidestep a large hole in the path as I'm speaking, shunting Elva a little to her right.

'Yes, and then we can have lunch in the Members' Lounge. Our horse runs in the three o'clock race.'

We stop to admire the flower beds near the main entrance. I bend down and run my finger-tip along the edge of a slipper orchid. 'Beautiful, aren't they? And so delicate.'

Elva points to a large bush, beside a clump of multi-coloured lupins. 'Remind me of the name of that bush, the one with the bright lemon flowers.'

'Leucodendron. Don't you remember we saw loads of them on our school trip to Tasmania years ago? They grow in profusion over there.'

'Yep. Just couldn't recall their name.'

We move on into the racecourse proper and Elva nudges my arm. 'Look over there. I think there's a race about to start.' We watch the twelve horses, one to a stall, standing ready. A couple of the horses are becoming restless, using their feet to churn up the ground. The jockeys, each wearing a different coloured outfit, stroke the horses' manes and pat their sides, in an attempt to keep the animals calm and relaxed while waiting for the starting pistol.

On the other side of the fence from us some of the officials and Committee members are lined up, along with the sports media, their telescope lenses poised. In the far away field, a short distance from the horse stalls, are four blue and white planes belonging to a private club. Hopefully they won't take to the air during the race.

I jump when the gun goes off. We feel the vibration from the pounding of the horses' hooves. The punters in the viewing stands go wild as the race nears its end, with the two front horses neck to neck. Either one could win until the very last few yards when the black horse overtakes the light brown one.

We bypass the touts calling out for business and go straight to the betting booths. 'Five dollars each way on Dandy Boy in the three o'clock,' Elva says, pushing a ten dollar note through the gap at the bottom of the window, as though she does this every day.

Marvelling at her confidence, I follow her example when placing my own bet.

'Right let's go and eat,' Elva says, as we move away from the booth. We climb the hill to the clubhouse overlooking the course. It's a substantial red brick building, with terraces around it. The tables on the terraces are jam-packed with excited punters, laughing and calling over to friends at other tables.

Thankfully it's cooler and quieter when we go inside the clubhouse. The Members' Room is all we'd expected. A smell of beeswax wafts up from the wooden floors and furniture. Some expensive-looking chandeliers hang from the ceiling, alternating with Raffles-type fans. Tasteful floral arrangements sit on the wide windowsills and on the occasional tables placed around the room. In general, there is a feeling of opulence throughout.

We find ourselves a table and order lunch. We finish our meal with gigantic desserts. Later we're served coffee in fine white china cups and saucers. Our waitress leaves the silver coffee pot on the table to allow us to refill our cups. We munch on petit fours while studying the race enthusiasts around us. Many are dressed flamboyantly but others are in more simple attire, similar to our own.

It's when we're drinking our second cup of coffee that I hear my name called. I turn my head towards the speaker and freeze. When I finally force myself to look at him, I'm aware my face is stiff and unsmiling.

'Hello Ros, what a surprise to see you here.' Doubt flickers across Simon Leggat's face, almost as though he's expecting a rebuff.

It takes a kick from Elva under the table to remind me of my manners. 'This is my friend Elva,' I introduce her, and say, 'Simon Leggat, a colleague from The Post.' I'm aware of how ungracious my words sound but find myself unable to be polite to him.

Leggat is dressed in casual slacks and wearing a black leather jacket over his blue checked open-necked shirt. I must grudgingly admit to myself that he is quite handsome.

'Mind if I join you both?' he asks and sits his

pint of lager on the table, without waiting for a reply. 'Can I get you ladies a drink?' he continues, shrugging off his jacket and draping it across the back of the chair.

I'm about to say 'no thanks' when Elva replies. 'I'd like a gin and tonic thanks.'

'The same for you, Ros?' he asks, and I nod, dumbstruck.

'Must visit the little girls' room,' Elva murmurs to me, getting to her feet as Leggat heads over to the bar.

On her return to the table, I lash her with my furious eyes. 'Why on earth did you accept his offer? Now we'll be landed with him for ages.'

She punches me gently on the arm. 'He seems pleasant enough and I thought it would give you a chance to get to know him better. You know, out of the office.'

'I don't want to know him better. I see enough of him at work.' The words explode out of me and I throw my best friend a thunderous look.

She gives me an infuriating smile. 'A lot of people are different outside of work. Perhaps you've misjudged him, Ros.'

I'm about to slate her further for encouraging him but Leggat arrives back with the drinks, leaving me no chance to respond. Ignoring my rudeness, he sits down in the chair nearest to mine. 'So, what brings you two girls to the races? Don't think I've seen you here before.'

'Are you a regular then?' Elva chips in, to save me having to answer.

'I come quite often with my cousin, he's a Member. Not sure where Gavin is right now, he vanished somewhere in the grounds.' He gives a shrug. 'We'll catch up later.'

I'm not surprised he lost you, bet he did it on purpose, are the words I'm saying in my head, wishing I had the courage to voice them.

'Do you live in Upper Hutt, Elva, or are you from Wellington?' Leggat's obviously tired of trying to converse with me so he's chatting up my friend instead.

'I'm from Wellington. Ohiro Road, Brooklyn.' Elva's tone is maddeningly sweet, in fact if I didn't know she was keen on Adam, I'd say she was flirting with him.

'I live near Ohiro Road, I have a small unit in Honeysuckle Crescent.'

I remain silent during their conversation. I'm staring stonily at the table-top when Elva looks at her watch. 'Oh Ros, it's nearly time for our race to start,' she says, getting to her feet.

I'm up from the table in a flash. 'We better move to get a good viewing space.' I don't even try to mask my joy at leaving Leggat.

'What horse are you betting on?'

I leave Elva to reply. 'He's called Dandy Boy, he's owned by a friend of mine. Thanks for the drink,' she finishes.

'You're welcome. Good luck with the race.'

'Thanks,' I say, without smiling. Normally I would be ashamed of my behaviour but I'm still furious at his intrusion, spoiling what had been a pleasant lunch.

'What are you playing at?' I hiss at Elva as we make our way down to the enclosure to find a good vantage viewing space.

'Oh Ros, you were a real misery guts up there. The guy can't be all that bad. Don't you think you're blowing everything out of proportion?'

Knowing she's right makes me even angrier.

'You don't have to work with him,' I shout back at her and then suddenly I burst out laughing. 'Yes, I did behave appallingly. I don't know what it is about him, but he seems to bring out the worst in me.'

Elva squeezes my arm. 'Well let's forget about him and concentrate on Dandy Boy. Is that him in No 7 stall?'

'I think so.' I take my small binoculars out of my bag, but they're designed more for theatre viewing than a racecourse.

When the gun goes off, we begin to shout for Dandy Boy. The horses thunder past us and by the time they reach the touchline we're hoarse. Our horse hasn't won but he has given a good account of himself, coming in fourth. By the time we return to the car, my bad mood has vanished and neither of us mentions Leggat's name on the way back to Wellington.

***

Simon stared after Ros, admiring her confident stride, even though it felt like she'd kicked him in the guts. He liked the shade of blue she was wearing. He continued to watch until she and Elva reached the top of the stairway and disappeared from view.

Only then did the questions flood into his mind. What on earth was that all about? She was so hostile, he thought, but her friend seemed fine. He wished he didn't fancy Ros, but he'd fallen for her on his first day at The Post and the more she rejected his advances, the keener it made him. Did she really find him so abhorrent or was she simply playing hard to get? He wished he knew the answer.

Shaking his head, Simon made his way back to the bar and sat on one of the high stools facing the gantry. 'A pint of Foster's, mate,' he said to Bruce, the barman, laying a five dollar note on the counter. I might as well get bladdered, he thought, depressed by how little progress he'd made with Ros.

Bruce put the pint down in front of Simon, spilling a little as he did so. He got a cloth and wiped it up and dried the bottom of the glass. 'What's got into you today, mate? You're not your usual brimming with life chap?'

Simon grimaced. 'Woman trouble,' was all he said.

Bruce laughed. 'You're better off without them. By the way, Gavin was in here looking for you a while back.'

'Yeah, we got separated in the crowd. Think I'll stay here and wait for him.'

Bruce grinned. 'Good thinking, I'm sure he'll gravitate back here eventually.'

Getting a signal from another customer, the barman went off, leaving Simon to stare into his glass and wonder how the hell he was going to get Ros to return his feelings. But one thing was sure, he was smitten by her and he wasn't going to give up yet.

When Bruce came back to his end of the bar, Simon ordered another Foster's and a neat whisky. He downed the whisky in one go and asked for another. Then he carried his drinks over to a table in the corner near the window, where he continued to brood on his failure to win Ros over.

When Gavin came into the bar over an hour later, he spotted his cousin straight away. Slumped in his chair, Simon looked up and waved to him.

'So, this is where you've been hiding,' Gavin said, as he sat down opposite Simon. 'You missed a couple of good races although the horses we bet on were simply out for a stroll today. Don't think they've come in yet.'

Simon had downed a fair amount of alcohol since Ros left and he now saw his cousin through a bit of a fog. 'Had a few jars,' he mumbled.

'So I see. Would have offered to buy you a drink but by the look of you, you've had enough. It's good I decided to do the driving today.'

'Itsh Rosh's fault,' Simon protested, slurring his words.

'Rosh? Oh Ros, the girl from The Post? The one you fancy? Was she here in the bar?'

Simon nodded and hung his head in defeat. 'It ishn't rechip …. rechiproc ….' he stammered to a halt.

Gavin grinned. 'Reciprocated. Difficult word to say even when you're sober, mate. How do you make that out?'

Simon shrugged. 'Didn't want to know me. Her pal was friendly enough.' He spread his arms out on the table and supported his head on them.

Bruce came over to collect the empty glasses from a nearby table and picked up Simon's empty glass at the same time. 'So, you two have finally met up.'

Gavin smiled at the barman. 'We have, Bruce, and now we're heading home. I've got evening surgery later.'

Bruce nodded. 'See you guys later,' he said, and carried the empties over to the bar.

Gavin helped Simon to his feet and hustled him downstairs. Out in the car park, he bundled him into his car, praying that he wouldn't vomit over the cream leather upholstery.

Simon fell asleep on the way back to Wellington and Gavin turned on the radio. He deposited Simon at his unit in Brooklyn and made him some strong black coffee.

***

As Gavin was driving to work his thoughts were on his cousin. It was a long time since he'd seen Simon so drunk and decided he must have it bad for this Ros female. Girls usually succumbed quickly to Simon's charms but, with this new one, his cousin appeared to have hit a brick wall.

When Gavin drew into his space in the surgery car park in Hobson Street, he immediately forgot about Simon's problematic love life when he saw the queue of people waiting with their sick animals. The majority of the people brought cats and dogs but now and again the patients were rabbits or hamsters.

'Evening, Gavin,' his receptionist, Flora, greeted him when he went into the surgery. 'Looks like we're in for a busy session, especially with Linda having the night off.'

Gavin shrugged. 'Sod's law,' he said. His colleague, Dr Hanlon, was attending her college friend's wedding today.

Taking off his jacket, Gavin slipped his white coat over his shirt. 'Give me five minutes and you can send the first patient in,' he told Flora, going over to scrub his hands.

CHAPTER NINE

As I round the corner, I glimpse Leggat's face through the half open lift door. I turn away quickly, but he sees me and presses the button to open the door again. Silently I curse my bad timing and step into the lift beside him. The doors close and we begin our descent.

He tries to make pleasant conversation. 'The lift seems to be more reliable these days, doesn't it?'

I reply with a nod of my head and look straight ahead, finding it impossible to disguise my dislike of him.

'Have you had any word of your training week?' He's obviously overheard Charlie speaking to me about the week's course in Wanganui next month, which I'm keen to attend.

'Not yet.'

I'm spared from any further conversation when the lift stops on the seventh floor and a woman wearing a well-tailored suit joins us. The doors close again and we continue downwards. The lift finally comes to a halt on the ground floor. The woman hurries out and I follow her, with Leggat a few steps behind me.

'Hi, Ros,' Harry passes me in the foyer and, inclining his head towards Leggat, gives me his usual wink. Although he's never voiced it, I'm certain Harry dislikes Leggat.

Leggat trails me out to the car park. 'I'm off to

interview school kids about playground games,' he tells me, raising his eyebrows. 'Wish me luck.'

Using his key fob, he switches off his car alarm and swaggers over to his four wheel drive. Sitting in my Toyota, I watch him in the mirror and, only when he has driven out of the exit, do I switch on my ignition.

***

Twenty minutes later I drive into the grounds of The Tui Inn, early for my meeting with Sheila Carter from the Community Trust. This will be our second meeting; on the first occasion I visited their offices in Wharf Road and met some of their service users. We should have had this second meeting weeks ago, but Sheila has been off work on sick leave for over a month.

Above the doorway on a wooden board there is a picture of a Tui. To my mind the Tui is probably the most colourful of all our New Zealand birds. Entering the dimly-lit interior, I spy the only vacant table, well away from the bar counter where we can talk in peace. It takes a few minutes for my eyes to adjust to the darkness after the bright sunshine outside. There are drink mark rings on the wooden table top and a strong smell of beer pervades the air, making me glad that we aren't eating here.

Avoiding a sticky patch, I place my folder on the table and get out my notebook and pen. A few minutes later Sheila walks in. Her navy blue coat is unbuttoned, as though she'd thrown it on in a hurry. I raise my hand to her and watch her wending her way to our table, all the while admiring her pendant with the New Zealand greenstone. Out of habit I get to my feet and shake hands with her, even though we've met before. 'What would you like to drink?' I ask, as she settles herself down, facing me across the table.

'A soda water and lime, please. No alcohol for me while I'm driving.'

'Sensible lady. Same goes for me.' Pulling my purse out of my bag, I make my way over to the bar, where the barman leaves off drying some glasses to serve me.

'Two soda water and lime, please.'

By the time I return to the table, Sheila has taken off her coat and draped it over the spare chair.

'Pretty crude establishment, isn't it?' I comment, as I sit down.

'Yep, not very inspiring but at least it's handy being close to the city centre. So, how about your report?' she asks, raising her glass to take a sip through her straw. 'As I told you at our last meeting, confidentiality for our service users is imperative.'

'Yes, I remember Sheila and for that reason I've kept the people I mention in the report anonymous.' As I'm speaking, I slide the manuscript towards her. 'Let me know if there's anything you disagree with and I'll change it.' At our first meeting we discussed why I wanted to write the report about the setting up of the Trust and the valuable work it did to support homeless and disadvantaged Wellingtonians. At that time, we both agreed that my report would help to advertise the work of the Trust and perhaps bring them more volunteers and funds.

While Sheila is reading over my article, I study the punters around me. I enjoy watching human behaviour, which will be useful if I achieve my ambition of writing a novel one day.

'That's excellent,' Sheila announces, when she gets to the end. She downs some more of her drink. 'Just the sort of publicity we need. Thank you.'

'Great. When I get back to the office, I'll pass the article to the print room staff.' While I'm speaking, I gather up the sheets of paper and push them back into my folder.

Our chat becomes more general as we finish our drinks and we shake hands once more before parting company in the car park.

***

After dinner, I carry my mug of coffee over to the laptop, ready to email Aunt Viv. She describes herself as computer illiterate, but I think she's much better than she gives herself credit for. It's wonderful at her age how well she has taken to 21st century technology. I must try and persuade her to go on to Skype and then we can talk face to face. Maybe her grandson, Daryl, would be able to set up Skype for her.

In my email, I tell her about the trip to Auckland that Elva and I are planning and attach a couple of pictures taken at Trentham racecourse. By the time I press the send button, it's after nine o'clock, by my reckoning mid-morning in Scotland. Emails are so much quicker than letters.

***

Simon brought the drinks over to the table; their usual one was occupied but Matt had claimed a smaller one beside the window for them. The Green Man was busier than usual tonight as later on there was a football match on telly. Many guys preferred to follow the game in the pub with their mates rather than watching alone at home.

Simon had worked at The Post for almost three months and he enjoyed his Friday evenings in here, where they pontificated over a lager. Or two. Or three.

'Think we'll be making tracks as soon as the match starts,' Simon suggested, when he sat down facing Matt. 'It'll get too noisy with the crowd in here.' Neither of them were interested in football; cricket and rugby were more their thing.

Matt took a long swig of his lager. 'I needed that, it's been a busy day.'

'Same here. Both my assignments took longer than expected, especially when I spoke to the school kids about playground games. Honestly, some of them would make good television presenters, the confident way they speak.'

'Yes, I heard you telling Ted about them when you returned to the office. The place was quiet with just Ted and me there.'

'Did you also hear me complaining about how rude Ros was in the lift this morning? She's a moody cow that one.'

Matt shook his head. 'I don't find her moody. And she's a very good writer. I think in time she'll be a real asset to the paper.'

'Ted said as much too. I seem to be the only one she treats like the enemy.'

He fell silent for a moment. 'God knows what I've done to upset her. I'd go out with her in an instant, but it doesn't seem like she's interested.' He looked across at his colleague. 'What about you, Matt? Are you currently in a relationship?'

Matt shook his head. 'I did have a girlfriend years ago, but she decided to go to London on a working holiday and didn't return to New Zealand.'

'Too bad, mate.'

Simon put his fingers to his ears when someone at the next table turned up the volume on the television. Another group of football fans had come in and were at the bar stocking up their supplies for the game.

He grinned at his colleague. 'Will we go now before the match starts?'

Matt nodded and the pair of them slipped out of the pub, leaving their table for the football fans.

***

'How was your day, love?' Ted asked Anne, when they were having dinner that evening.'Good,' she said, adding another spoonful of carrots on to her plate. 'The fayre was a great success. As usual the home baking stall was sold out within half an hour of the opening, but both the book stall and the craft stall did well too.'

'Which one were you manning?' he asked, as he re-filled his wife's wine glass. 'Can't remember which you said.'

She sighed, aware that Ted only listened to half of what she told him. 'I was on the book stall. They sold well but as usual I've come home with more novels than what I donated.' Anne had been a member of the local conservation trust for many years now and she took great satisfaction from the money-raising projects they undertook.

'You look great in your new outfit, love,' he said as they were clearing the used plates from the table. 'The rose-pink colour suits you.'

She laughed. 'Oh Ted, what are you like? I've had this for years, sure I've worn it to a couple of social events we've been to.'

Ted made a face. 'Have you? Well I guess that's me in the dog-house once more.'

Anne brought a pot of filter coffee to the table, along with a plate with two gigantic fresh cream meringues on it.

'Wow, they look yummy.'

'Yes, Monica Blyth's meringues are famous. I had to buy them just before the fayre opened or there would have been none left. I know what a sweet tooth you have, Ted.' She stretched out and caressed his hand.

He smiled and patted the bulge in his middle. 'You really shouldn't encourage me.'

'Rubbish, you're fine the way you are.' She and Ted enjoyed a happy marriage, their only regret that they hadn't been able to have children. They'd tried IVF a few years back but without any success. By now they'd accepted that it was not to be.

'How were things at The Post today, Ted?'

'Fairly routine. Charlie was away at a meeting most of the day and Matt and I were holding the fort in the office. Both Simon and Ros were out on assignments. Ros was meeting with her contact from the Community Trust. She's been doing a report about homelessness in Wellington and met some of their service users. Seems to have done a good job and Matt told me he didn't have to suggest many changes to her manuscript.'

'You're fond of Ros, aren't you, Ted? I know by the way you talk about her.'

'Yes, she's a lovely girl and she's not had it easy, what with losing her parents at a young age and, more recently, the grandmother she lived with. Think she's finding it hard to deal with her bereavement.'

'You should invite her for dinner some night, Ted? I've only met her that one time when you left your keys and I called at the office with them. I found her very easy to chat to.'

'Good idea, love. I'll do that. Will we leave the washing up meantime and see what's on the gogglebox?'

'Yes let's.' Anne moved over to the sofa and started to scroll through the list to see what programme she fancied. 'This looks an interesting documentary, starting in five minutes,' she said and pressed the appropriate channel.

Ted brought their glasses to the coffee table and sat down beside Anne, putting his arm round her shoulders. 'Ros and Simon don't seem to be hitting it off,' he laughed, 'Simon was telling me today that Ros cut him dead in the lift this morning.'

'Perhaps he isn't her type. From the way you've described him he does sound a bit of a know all.'

'Don't think he's as confident as he makes out. Right here's our programme now,' he said, turning up the volume on the remote and sliding closer to his wife.

CHAPTER TEN

Thank goodness Daryl got me on to the internet, Viv thought, as she double-clicked her google icon and opened her email account. She didn't even have to use her password to sign in as her grandson had arranged that the password stayed in place permanently.

Daryl was a clever lad, employed as a carpenter by a well-established Dundee firm, but Viv was sure he'd soon start up his own business. The lad was good at anything he turned his hand to, and especially adept at explaining things about computers to an oldie like her. She smiled when she recalled him saying to her, 'Grandma, we really need to teach you to be computer literate. It's time you moved into the 21st century you know.' His hazel eyes sparkled with mirth and they'd both burst out laughing.

She looked over at the framed photograph sitting on her desk. 24-year-old Daryl was in the centre, with his sister Pamela, two years his junior, on one side of him and the youngest of the siblings, Norma, on his other side. The girls were turning out to be stunners; Pamela with her long black hair, while Norma's curly mop was fairer. Pamela already had a steady boyfriend and Viv was sure Norma, with her pretty face and kind nature, would soon find a sweetheart too.

Now she had an email account, communication had been quicker and easier between herself and Ros in

New Zealand. Ros was a bonny young girl, a few months older than her Daryl. Viv daydreamed for a moment that the two of them met and fell in love. She laughed and chided herself for her matchmaking. It would be nice though.

Today the laptop was on a go slow but at last her in-box opened showing the email messages she'd received. She was pleased to see that there was a message from Ros. Viv tapped her fingers on the desk as she waited for the message to open. Following the shock of receiving a letter from Ros last year, bearing the news of her gran's death, the girl had promised that she wouldn't lose touch and she'd kept her word.

Hi Aunt Viv, the message began, *I hope you are well and enjoying your activities. You seem to have interesting events with your Evergeen Club - love the name!! It's great that you have supportive neighbours.*

I'm attaching a few photographs I took when I went with Elva to the horse racing at Trentham last month. If you click on the picture it should open up. I'm sure if you have any difficulty, Daryl will help you.

Elva and I have booked a trip up north at the beginning of December. The holiday is a long time off but it's nice to have something to look forward to. Our base will be Auckland and we plan to travel to some interesting parts of the Northland. Two places interest us. First is The Waitangi Meeting House, where the Maori chiefs signed a Treaty with the British in 1841. The Treaty House, known as 'the Residency' was the home of James Busby, the British government's representative in New Zealand. The second place is the

Movie Set from The Lord of the Rings and The Hobbit trilogies. This area, once beautiful farmland, was transformed into The Shire from Middle Earth.

We will spend time in Rotorua on our way home. There is a large Maori settlement in Rotorua and the area is famous for its boiling mud pools and geysers. Elva is part-Maori so she's keen to see where her ancestors lived. We'll be back home in Wellington two weeks before Christmas which gives us some time to get organised for the Christmas party season.

All is going well on the work front and I'm still enjoying my job as a trainee journalist. I write lots of articles for The Wellington Post and hope soon to get a column of my own.

I think of you often, Aunt Viv, and enjoy hearing about Daryl and his sisters.

Love from Ros xx

Viv tried to open the pictures Ros had attached to her email, but nothing happened. She tried another couple of times with no success. She sighed, this was yet another job she'd have to leave to Daryl. Just as well her grandson was so patient with her.

A glance at the clock sitting on her desk reminded her about meeting Nora, her friend from the Evergeen club, for lunch at 'The Cherry Tree' in Nethergate. Her taxi was due shortly, so she'd need to get her skates on. She closed her laptop and whispered 'be back soon' to Ros who, although on the other side of the world, was only the click of a mouse away.

CHAPTER ELEVEN

Ted was alone in the office on Monday morning when Simon walked in. He stopped beside Ros' desk. 'Where's her Ladyship?' he asked Ted, nodding to the empty chair.

'She's in with Charlie,' Ted answered, inclining his head towards the editor's office. 'You and our Ros don't seem to get along too well,' he added, with a grin.

Simon shook his head. 'She snaps at me every time I try to speak to her. And, as I told you last week, she was so rude to me in the lift. I haven't a clue what I've done to her.'

Ted held his hands up in front of him. 'Don't worry about it, mate. It's hard to know what goes on inside a woman's head. I've been married to Anne for thirty-nine years and, although we've been very happy together, I'm still at a loss to follow her logic at times.'

Ted's phone rang and he lifted the receiver before it switched on to voice mail.

Simon was left wondering what Charlie was discussing with Ros. He suspected it might be about the seminar in Wanganui and felt a bit miffed that the boss had decided to send Ros instead of him.

***

Charlie tapped his fingers on the desk as he watched Ros fill in the application form for the seminar. She was a pretty girl, with her shiny auburn hair and good quality clothes. The thought flitted through his mind that Ros and his son, Malcolm, would make an attractive couple. His matchmaking was interrupted when his youngest employee broke into his thoughts.

'Think that's everything, boss.' Ros pushed the form across the desk.

'Thanks, I'll countersign it and send it off.'

His office door closed behind Ros with a gentle click. Charlie looked down at the application form; her printing was very neat, just as he'd expect from such a well-groomed lady. He was pleased she'd agreed to attend the four-day course in Wanganui, which he'd assured her would help further her career. Charlie knew the lecturers and rated them highly.

Simon Leggat had put his name forward to attend the course, but he'd decided to send Ros instead. Simon was a good journalist, but Charlie had found him on occasion to be a tad too sure of himself. Giving the place on the course to Ros would help bring Simon down a peg or two.

Charlie yawned and stretched, then poured himself a coffee before returning to his paperwork.

CHAPTER TWELVE

My journey up to Wanganui is smooth and there are no hold-ups with roadworks or traffic jams. I listen to music from the radio while I drive up through Otaki to Levin, where I stop for a coffee and a muffin. Then it's on to Palmerston North. Much of the way the road follows the course of the Wanganui River, the country's longest navigable waterway and often called New Zealand's Rhine. My newly acquired sat nav brings me into the town at Purnell Street and from there it doesn't take long to get to The James Cook in Alma Street.

'You're in room 254, Miss Mathieson, on the third floor.' The hotel receptionist, Colette I see from her name badge, hands me my keycard. 'The lift is over there beside the stairway,' she says, smiling at me while she indicates to the opposite side of the foyer.

'Thanks.' I return her smile and head over to the lift.

I'm hit by the mixed smell of furniture polish and air freshener as I enter my twin room. Inside it feels cool and welcoming and, for a few minutes, I stand at the window and gaze out at the mountain scenery surrounding the hotel. I open the window wide and breathe in the fresh air. Although rugged, the mountains don't look barren but are covered in green vegetation. A thick, overhanging mist obscures the mountain tops; the long fingers of mist that run haphazardly down the mountainside remind me of soft icing on a cake.

I think the mountain I'm looking at is Taranaki but Mount Ruapehu and Mount Tongariro are also in this area and I'm unable to identify which is which. I give up and retreat to the centre of the room. Leaving my case on one bed, I kick off my sandals and throw myself down on to the other, stretching out on top of the duvet cover. The pink painted walls tone in well with the lilac and pink shades of the drapes and bed coverings.

I close my eyes and next thing I know twenty minutes have elapsed, so I guess I dozed off for a time. Feeling refreshed, I get up and start to unpack. My mobile rings in the middle of my task and I stop to press the green button.

'Hi Ros,' Elva's voice comes over the airwaves, 'how did your journey go?'

'Great. Only took me about two and a half hours.' While I'm speaking, I lay the hanger holding a couple of my t-shirts on to the bed and sit down beside it.

'And what about the hotel? The James Cook isn't it?'

'Yep. It's a large hotel, with about seven floors. My room is to the back, bright and airy, with a view of the hills surrounding the hotel. The receptionist on duty was extremely helpful; her name was Colette and she had such a lovely smile. Pretty name too.'

'It is, don't think I've ever met a Colette. Sounds French? Wonder what the food in the hotel will be like?'

'Won't know until I go down for dinner. How're things with you?'

'I'm going out for dinner with Adam tonight,' she informs me, excitement ringing in her voice. 'We're going to The Dolphin in Masterton, where you and I went with my mum. He's picking me up at seven.'

'Fantastic. Enjoy yourself.'

'Have you met up with any of the others on your course?'

'Not yet. I fell asleep when I first got into my room and now I'm unpacking my case.'

'Right, I'll sign off and let you get on with it. Enjoy the course. We'll catch up for lunch on your return.'

'Sure, bye,' I say and switch off.

***

When I go into the dining room that evening, ceiling fans whir overhead, making it comfortably cool. At a window table a woman leafs through a magazine. My first instinct is to choose a different table, but then I change my mind and go over to where she's sitting. 'Do you mind if I sit here?'

When she looks up, I see she's about my own age, with strawberry-blonde hair and deep blue eyes. Her smile is welcoming. 'Not at all, I'll be glad of the company. I'm Jill Paterson.' She lifts her clutch bag off the table and places it down on the floor at her feet.

'Ros Mathieson,' I introduce myself and take the seat facing Jill. The room looks out on to a well-cultivated garden, its greenery lush despite the hot weather. A fountain with a nymph on it stands in the middle of the lawn and the tinkle of water is clearly audible in the quiet dining room.

'Which paper are you with, Ros?'

'The Wellington Post. With me being a trainee journalist, my editor thought this would be a worthwhile course for me.'

'Same here. I've travelled down from Auckland. I work with the Gazette up there.' We chat quietly about our respective publications while other people begin to file into the room.

'I'm going up to your neck of the woods at the beginning of December,' I tell Jill. 'My friend and I are going to base ourselves in Auckland and travel around from there.' I glance around the room and notice that the tables are almost full by now.

'You'll love it, there's so much to see and do up north. I hope you're going to visit the Treaty House at Waitangi, lots of history there,' Jill starts to say, when a voice interrupts her.

'This seems to be the only empty seat, so do you ladies mind if I join you?' I turn to the man at my side. He is very tall and looks to be in his forties. Bald on top, he has a band of hair around the back of his neck and sides of his face, giving him the appearance of a monk.

'No problem,' I tell him and indicate to the seat next to mine.

'Thanks,' he says, and his smile encompasses us both. 'I feel a bit like a fish out of water among all you young people. After teaching English for twenty years,

I've only recently changed career. Hence my attendance on this course.'

Jill stretches out her hand across the table. 'I'm Jill Paterson from the Auckland Gazette.'

'Trevor Beggs.' He shakes hands first with Jill and then with me. 'Just call me Trev.'

'Ros Mathieson,' I say, 'I work in the Wellington Post. Which paper are you with, Trev?'

'The Christchurch Herald. I came over to the North Island on the early morning ferry from Picton. I brought the car with me and drove up here from Wellington.'

The conversation halts while we give our order to the waiter. 'Will you ladies share a bottle of wine with me?' Trev asks, to which we readily agree. 'Chardonnay,' he says to the waiter and glances at us to get our approval of his choice.

Once the wine arrives and our glasses are filled, I put the question to Trev that I've been dying to ask since he told us where he worked. 'Did you know a Simon Leggat at the Christchurch Herald?'

'I've never met Simon, but I've heard he's a good journalist. Come to think of it, didn't he go to Wellington to work with your paper?'

'Yes,' I say, nodding, 'he works in the main office where I am.' I decide not to give my opinion of Leggat since I don't know Trev, and gossip goes round swiftly in newspaper circles.

'Do you know anyone from the Auckland Gazette?' Jill asks him.

'No, I don't.' Trev looks round and rubs his

hands. 'Here comes the food. Don't know about you two, but I'm ready for some.' He stops speaking when the waiter brings our starters.

'Silver service, no less,' Jill says, once the waiter has moved on to another table. 'I bet the charges in this hotel are too steep for my pocket.'

I nod and spread some liver paté on to my biscuit. 'Just as well we're on expenses. So, how do you like working for the Christchurch Herald?' I ask, turning to Trev again.

'Very much. My colleagues are supportive and, although it's a complete change of occupation for me, fortunately I'm a fast learner.' While he's speaking, he stretches out for the pepper dish sitting on the table. After offering it to Jill and me, who both decline, he shakes some on his own starter. 'Mind you,' he continues, spearing a couple of prawns with his fork, 'it was a bit of a culture shock taking orders again after being in charge for so many years.'

'Yeah, I guess it would be.' I put down my cutlery, aware that if I eat any more paté, I won't be ready for my main course. 'Were you living in Christchurch last year when that second earthquake struck?'

'Yes. A few months before the quake my wife, Cheryl, and I had moved into a new house in Hoon Hay, not too far out of the city. It was terrifying.'

'Did you have much damage to the house?'

'No, we were very lucky, and our home was spared but our friends nearby weren't so fortunate, and they were out of their house for two months.

Thankfully neither of them suffered serious injury. Some people are still living in temporary accommodation.'

'There were some fatalities though, weren't there?' Jill put in.

Trev nodded.

'Even in Wellington we could feel some shaking,' I tell him. 'I didn't know what it was until the newsflash came over the television that Christchurch had been hit by an earthquake once again.'

When the main courses arrive, we fall silent for a time. Soft music plays in the background during our meal. I try to recall the name of one of the tunes, but I can barely hear the words due to the buzz of conversation around the room.

Jill and I order a dessert and Trev opts for biscuits and cheese. We're at the coffee stage when the course organiser gets to her feet, smiling at us all. 'I'd like to welcome everyone to Wanganui.' Her dress, a coral shade and made from a floaty sort of material, looks stunning against her olive complexion and black hair. 'Most of you have come from the North and South Island but we're also pleased to welcome delegates from Australia and one lady joins us from Japan,' she says, smiling at a lady seated near the back of the room. 'From the chat during our meal it sounds as if you're enjoying one another's company and making new friends which is wonderful.'

She then goes on to introduce the two people sitting with her at the top table. These two will lead the course events over the next two days; Jason Hughes, a pot-bellied 50 something, who will hold workshops on interview techniques, and a rather plain, mousy looking lady called Susan Armitage, who is to give us talks on research and fact-finding.

After dinner, we are left to our own devices for the remainder of the evening. The course proper will start with our first workshop after breakfast tomorrow. Jill, Trev and I drift towards the bar where we join a few other delegates and enjoy a nightcap before retiring to our rooms.

CHAPTER THIRTEEN

'Isn't that a magnificent Kowhai tree?' Jill says, when she and I are relaxing on a bench in the hotel garden during a break between our morning and afternoon workshops. The tree at the side of our bench is weighed down with its mass of yellow flowers, suspended like fingers from its branches. 'I can fully understand why we look on the Kowhai as our country's national emblem.'

'It's lovely, yes, but I think our emblem should be the Pohutukawa. We have some growing along the esplanade at Lyall Bay and their crimson colours are spectacular.'

Jill presses down on her stomach and breathes out. 'I'm so glad I stuck with a small portion of food from the buffet table.'

'Same here. I wanted to keep space for our big meal tonight. They certainly feed you well in this hotel.'

I lean back and close my eyes, listening to the birdsong above our heads. I've almost drifted off when Jill breaks the spell. 'How did you get on at the workshop this morning?' Jason, who led the session on interview techniques, put us into pairs to conduct pretend interviews.

'I thought I'd prefer being the interviewee rather than interviewer but in fact the opposite was the case. Mark, who I worked with, is a hoot and so easy to interview as he likes telling stories.'

Jill laughs. 'I was paired with Tony, you know the guy from The Melbourne Age, and he just loves the sound of his own voice so I'd no trouble either.' We carry on sharing our thoughts on the workshop until Jill glances at her watch. 'Oh heck, we'll need to shift it, Susan's session starts in two minutes.'

'Can't believe how quickly the time has passed,' I mutter, as I gather up my clipboard and folder and hurry indoors after her.

Susan begins the session a couple of seconds after Jill and I slip into our seats at the kidney-shaped table in the Conference Room, us at the top end while Susan sits at the narrow end on her own. Trev is a few seats down from me on my right and, when I catch his eye, he smiles and points to his watch face, mouthing the words 'late again'. Remembering I'd just made it to the morning session on time, I return his smile, enjoying the easy banter with him. It occurs to me again, as it did at dinner last night, that he must have been a popular teacher, who would get the best out of his students.

'We're going to discuss research this afternoon and I'll give you tips on how to go about it,' Susan tells us. In contrast to her mousey appearance, Susan's voice is strong and confident. I decide she must be one of these people who is confident when talking about a subject near to her heart but who isn't interested in small talk. I concentrate on her words for the next hour and she uses a white board and black markers to draw up a list of do's and don'ts when undertaking research.

Afterwards, when she opens up the session to questions, my hand shoots up first.

'Ros Mathieson from The Wellington Post,' I begin, as we've been instructed to do.

'Yes, Ros?'

'You've given us various bodies, research libraries and so on that we can use in our work, but can you tell us how much these places charge for their services? Even though our respective employers will foot the bill, we'll need to prove to our editors that the information we receive justifies the cost.'

Susan nods. 'Good question, Ros, and yes it can be a fairly costly business as you often have to pay for a day's session in the Records Office. But you'll gradually get to know which avenues yield the most useful information. Many concerns, such as libraries, don't charge anything as you yourself do the hard work. The librarian will point you in the right direction and supply the books and papers you require for your research, and then leave you to it. The one item you will need to pay for is photocopying, but I guess that's understandable.' Susan has been looking around the group as she's speaking but now she turns back to me. 'Does that answer your question?'

'Yes, thanks,' I reply, and she takes the next question, which comes from the man sitting next to me.

'Can you enlarge please on what you said about checking for copyright?' he asks, and Susan starts to give us a fuller explanation than she'd done previously.

'I have some handouts here,' she says, and lifts a pile of paper from the table. 'You can pass them round and each take a copy,' she goes on, handing half the pile to one side of the room and the rest to the opposite side.

'That was a good session on research, wasn't it?' Trev remarks in the dining room that evening. 'Should be useful to us all in our work as journalists.'

'And Susan's right about not putting too much reliance on Wikipedia,' I say, 'we're always hearing how unreliable the information is. Just really people's own ideas, biased sometimes, and often without any real substantiation of the facts.'

'You need to be so careful that you don't ruffle any feathers in what you say, don't you?'

Jill's question remains up in the air when the waiter comes over to check what we want from the extensive dinner menu and the conversation changes to food.

CHAPTER FOURTEEN

'It's been lovely to meet you,' Jill tells me, when we're having breakfast before travelling home from the course. She hands me a slip of paper. 'That's my phone number and email address in case you and Elva have time to look me up when you're in Auckland at the end of the year.'

'That would be lovely. Can't remember the name of our hotel in Auckland, but I can email you when I get home.'

'I live in Papakura, not too far from the city, but I work right in the heart of Auckland. So, I could either meet you after work in the city or pick you up at your hotel.'

I'm surprised to find myself feeling quite emotional at saying goodbye to my new friend. We've become quite close while we've been here. 'Great, thanks. Elva and I will definitely contact you,' I promise, and put the paper with her contact details into my diary.

We've finished breakfast and are ready to leave the dining room by the time Trev arrives at the table. 'Think you're too late, Trev,' I say, 'the waiters have cleared away the food from the buffet.' I can't resist touching my watch face. He gets the joke straight away and laughs.

'No worries, Ros. I decided to lie longer this

morning as there was no workshop. I'll just grab a coffee before I leave. When I get to Wellington, I'll have a meal on the ferry.'

Trev hands one of his business cards to each of us. 'Enjoyed your company, girls, and if you're over in Christchurch any time do give me a ring. Cheryl and I will be pleased to welcome you to our home.' He gives us both a peck on the cheek and saunters over to the coffee machine. 'See you around, guys,' he calls over his shoulder.

Jill and I collect our cases from our rooms then, after handing our keys to Colette on the reception desk, the two of us say our final farewell in the hotel car park.

The journey south takes longer than it did on Monday because I'm held up a few times with road works. During the long spells I'm stationary, I listen to the car radio to help while away the time; I enjoy the stirring sound of the 1812 Overture and hear one of my favourites, The March of the Hebrew Slaves. It's almost two o'clock when I drive into Wellington. I stop at the milk bar in Cuba Street, near The Lavender, and pick up two cartons of semi-skimmed for Smoky and me, plus fresh bread.

When I enter the driveway at Kiwi Crescent, I see Smoky sitting on the windowsill.

'Well, how did you get on, Ros?' Mrs Phillips calls to me from her side door when she sees me getting out of the car. The dear old lady was a good friend to Gran, and she has looked after Smoky while I've been away. He can get in and out via the cat flap on the back door but needs someone to put out his food and water.

I move nearer the fence as I know Mrs Phillips is hard of hearing. 'It was a great course and well worth attending. Has Smoky been alright?'

'Absolutely fine. He gave me a nice welcome each time I went into the house and he ate all his food and drank plenty too. I saw him quite often sitting out on your back lawn in the sun and when it got too hot, he moved under the shade of the trees.'

'Yeah, he's a bright cookie is Smoky. Thanks for looking after him, Mrs P. He hates it in the cattery.' Delving into my carrier bag, I give her the souvenir tea towel of Wanganui I'd bought for her.

'Oh, you didn't need to do that, Ros, but thank you for your kindness. He's no trouble and I enjoy his company. See you later,' she says, and goes back indoors, leaving me to enjoy a welcome home from my furry friend.

I check my mail-box and take the contents with me into the house, where Smoky comes towards me and rubs himself against my leg. For once, he doesn't seem to be in a huff because I left him; instead he seems pleased to have me home again.

I unpack and put the washing machine on. Then I have dinner, after which I open my mail. As ever, much of it junk and there are a couple of bills, but the remaining envelope intrigues me. Postmarked Wellington, my name and address is typewritten, and inside is a Valentine card. There are the usual hearts and flowers on the front, and inside the message is displayed in an unusual manner. Every word in the message has been cut separately out of a paper or magazine and stuck on to the paper with adhesive. There is no signature or handwriting, which keeps the sender anonymous.

I stare at the card for a long time, then shake my head. 'It has to be Leggat,' I mutter to myself, before throwing the offensive item into the garbage bin.

CHAPTER FIFTEEN

The morning of my return to The Post is wet, with my wipers working overtime during the drive into the city. Rain is slanting down in sheets as I get out of the car.

Halfway across the car park my mobile rings, and I hook the handle of my umbrella under my chin while I trawl through my shoulder bag for the phone. 'Damn,' I yell, when the brolly tips to one side, leaving my hair and face exposed to the heavy rain. Next thing my folder lands upside down in a puddle. I pick it up and dash into the building, the sodden papers stuffed under my armpit.

By this time the caller has rung off and I head immediately for the ladies' room, where I hold the soaked papers under the hand dryer for a while, hoping that the words haven't run. I re-comb my hair, then check the missed call, deleting it when I see an unfamiliar number on the screen.

'How was the seminar?' Ted asks, as soon as I enter the office.

'It was great, really worth going to.' I open my umbrella and sit it on the carpet beside my desk. I barely have time to sit down and sort out my papers when Charlie buzzes me to come in and see him.

He's drinking a coffee when I go in, with the rain still battering against his window and running down the glass like a monsoon.

He points to the coffee percolator to offer me a drink.

I shake my head. 'No thanks, too soon after breakfast for me.'

'So, tell me about your time in Wanganui?'

'I wasn't sure what to expect, boss, but I think the information I got from the seminar should help to improve my writing skills.'

He smiles. 'I'm glad to hear it, Ros, considering what it cost the company to send you there. I know Simon would have liked the chance, but I decided you'd get more out of it.'

'The talk Jason Hughes gave on interview techniques was particularly inspiring. He really held the audience and his humour made sure what he said wasn't boring.'

'Yes, Jason's an excellent speaker and tutor. I trained him you know when he first started in journalism.' This Charlie says with well-deserved pride.

'The other session on research was also worth attending. Susan gave us a handout which I'm sure will be helpful to me. And I found the workshops interesting.'

'Great. Give me a written report on your findings, Ros.'

'Will do, Charlie. And here's my expenses form,' I add, sliding the form I'd completed last night across the desk.

He pulls the form towards him. 'Fine, I'll go through it before I authorise the expenses. Just in case you've put in a huge drinks bill,' he says, giving me a wink. 'By the way, how was the hotel? It's the first time we've used it.'

'Excellent, no complaints. The food was super and plenty of it.' Our conversation is interrupted when Charlie's phone rings. He presses the accept button and when the caller answers, signals to me that he wants to take the call.

When I return to my desk, Ted peers over the top of his specs at me, his eyebrows raised. 'Was that Charlie grilling you about the seminar?'

'Yep,' I reply and collect up my almost dry notes. 'Think this lot should keep me on the right track.'

'You're keen, Ros, I'll say that for you.'

I make a face at him and switch on my laptop.

CHAPTER SIXTEEN

Simon stuffed the notes he was going to work on over the weekend into his backpack and got up from his desk. He loved the shorts and t-shirt weather and didn't relish these colder autumn days or, even worse, the thought of winter ahead. 'Are you guys ready?'

Matt switched off his laptop and threw his clutter into the desk drawer. 'Yep, can't wait to get that glass of Foster's in front of me.'

'Are you joining us in the Green Man, boss?' Ted asked, when Charlie came out of his office to leave some letters in the mail tray.

'Not tonight, guys. Karen wants to go late night shopping, and she'll nark at me all evening if I'm late getting home to pick her up.' He looked at the empty desk. 'Ros not going with you?'

Matt shook his head. 'She's meeting some friends for a meal tonight.' Ros had joined them on occasion but more often than not she had other plans. He liked it when she came along but guessed it must be boring for her, being the only female staff member.

When they arrived at the pub, Matt bought the first round of drinks. He and Ted started a discussion about tomorrow's rugby match against South Africa, while Simon lapsed into his own world for a time. His thoughts went back, as they often did, to how he was going to win Ros over. She rebuffed every advance he made to her. This hurt, as he wasn't used to girls rejecting him, but he wasn't prepared to give up yet.

He looked up when Matt nudged his elbow. 'Sorry guys, I was miles away.'

Ted grinned. 'We noticed. We were trying to decide if our boys will win the day tomorrow? What d'you think?'

'I think there's a good chance, the way they've been playing recently. They've definitely upped their game since Watt was taken on as fly-half.'

Matt nodded. 'He's doing a first-class job. Bet it'll be a full house tomorrow.'

Simon drained his glass and laid it on the table. 'I won't be able to come to the match tomorrow. I'm going to the races at Trentham; Gavin's a member there and he gets us vantage viewing seats in the enclosure. The hospitality in the Members' Club is pretty good too.'

'Is that Gavin, the vet?' Matt asked, scratching his nose.

'That's right, he works in a surgery on Hobson Street but also does some work for the farming community. Gives him a variety of household pets and livestock to deal with. I don't go with him to the races every weekend, just now and again. The last time I went to Trentham, I met Ros and her pal there.'

'Yeah, I remember her telling me. I'll get the next round in.' Ted got to his feet, leaving the other two to continue their discussion about the races.

'Thought you'd gone home,' Matt said, when Ted eventually came back.

'Kev's the only one serving at the moment. Think he could do with an extra pair of hands.'

'Probably like all establishments these days, cutting down on the wages bill.' Matt downed half of the contents of his glass in one go, then let out a loud belch. 'I needed that.'

'What, the belch or the lager?' Simon countered, straight-faced.

'Ha-ha, very funny. My brother bought the latest model of Toyota Corolla last week and he likes it,' he said, giving a second, quieter, belch.

Ted grimaced. 'Can't see me getting a new car any time soon, not unless The Post gives us a massive increase in salary. Anne usually has mine spent long before it's in the bank.'

Matt winked. 'Why do you think I've remained single for so long?'

Simon bought the third round of drinks and their conversation moved on to the latest weekly fire drill that was taking place at The Post.

'It's pretty important to get it right, with us being on the twentieth floor,' Ted said.

Simon nodded. 'I always find it a pain when we have to head out of the building on fire drill, especially if I'm in the middle of an important draft. But I guess I'd feel differently if it was a real fire.'

'We just have to think of the Twin Towers,' Matt commented. 'Scary or what?'

A short time afterwards the karaoke started. By this time the pub was filling up, folks ready to set their weekend off with a kick.

Ted pulled on his jacket. 'Sorry to break up the party but think I'll head off, guys, before the noise level increases.'

'Suits me,' Simon said, and Matt nodded in agreement. They drained their glasses and headed for the exit.

***

Linda held the spaniel firmly but gently on the table, stroking him while Gavin administered the injection. The dog whimpered but because of the sheet draped over his eyes, he didn't see the syringe going through the thick coat on his back.

Gavin placed the syringe back into its metal tray and put it over on the sink.

'Well done, Rusty.' He praised the animal and patted the top of his head.

In response, Rusty licked his hand.

Linda called Mrs Mullin in. 'All done,' she said, to the anxious owner and lifted the dog down off the table on to the floor. Mrs Mullin bent down and fondled her pet's ears. Rusty wagged his tail and pressed his wet nose against her face. 'Thanks so much, Docs,' she said, looking first at Linda and then at the back of Gavin's head.

Gavin turned round from the sink, where he was washing his hands. 'He seems to be responding well to the treatment. I think one more injection in two weeks' time will do. Flora will see to that for you on your way out.'

Mrs Mullin put on Rusty's lead and he scampered at her side out of the consulting room, his tail going like a windscreen wiper.

Gavin pulled off a sheet of paper towel and dried his hands. 'You sure about tomorrow's clinic, Linda?'

His colleague smiled. 'Of course, Gavin. It's time you had a Saturday off. Are you going to the racecourse?' Linda peeled off her green coat as she was speaking and changed into her outdoor clothes.

'Yes, Simon's coming with me.'

'Okay, have a great time. See you on Monday. Bye.'

'Bye, Linda.'

With Rusty being the last patient, Gavin settled down to get his paperwork up to date.

About half an hour later, Flora peeked round the surgery door. 'That's everything ready for tomorrow, Gavin. Do you need anything else before I leave?'

He smiled at his loyal receptionist, who'd been with him since he'd started up the practice. 'No, Flora, you get away home now and I'll lock up.'

Gavin completed his write-ups and changed his clothes, ready for going out. He frowned when he thought about Simon, who'd seemed a bit down in the dumps recently. He hoped a visit to Trentham would be good medicine for whatever ailed his cousin.

Although Simon hadn't discussed it with him, he felt sure it was to do with that girl, Ros, who worked in The Post. Simon had always been a wow with the ladies, so this feeling of rejection had hit him hard.

'At least I don't have that problem,' he muttered, as he double checked that all the lights and equipment had been switched off. Gavin had known since the age of fourteen that he was homosexual and, although he wasn't in a relationship with another guy, he had plenty of good mates, both straight and gay.

He turned the key in the front door and strode towards his car.

CHAPTER SEVENTEEN

I adjust my paua shell pendant, a good match for the dress I'm wearing, taking care not to pull too hard and break the fine chain. I hate when the clasp works its way round to the front; maybe I could fix the clasp to the back of my neck with sticky tape, I think idly. I discard that idea when I hear the toot, and grab my shoulder bag on my way to the door. 'Be good,' I say to Smoky, who turns his back on me to show exactly what he thinks of me going off to leave him.

Brenda is already in the back seat of the taxi and I climb in beside her. 'Hi, great to see you again,' I say, and I'm still fiddling with the seat belt when our driver heads off to collect our other two friends. In the past one of us has volunteered to drive and curtail her alcohol intake but, in these days of stiff penalties for driving even a fraction over the limit, we prefer to use a taxi.

'I've left John working in the garden,' Brenda tells me. 'He'll cook something from the freezer later.' Brenda and her husband, John, live in Oriental Bay, so she is the first pick-up and I am second. On the way to get the others, Brenda and I chat quietly, mostly about memories from our schooldays at St. Serf's. 'How are your kids doing?' I ask her, when we exhaust that subject.

'Fantastic,' she says. 'Most of them got excellent results in the recent tests. I was so proud of them.' Brenda is a primary schoolteacher and, with her and John being childless, she throws all her energy into her pupils.

When we get to Brooklyn, Elva's waiting outside her house on Ohiro Road. 'Next stop Aitken Street,' she tells the driver, and joins Brenda and me on the back seat. 'I'll text Dee that we're on the way,' she says, and keys in the message, then presses the send button.

At Aitken Street, Dee sits in the front beside the driver. The four of us were buddies from our first days at the school and our friendship has continued right up until now. Despite the difficulty of getting an evening to suit, we usually manage to meet up every few months. Of course, being the two as yet unattached, Elva and I meet on a more regular basis.

At the new Vietnamese restaurant on Waterloo Quay, we are shown to a window table, with a view over Wellington harbour, reputed to be the safest harbour in the world. The late sun is shining straight into the dining room. Our evening is starting well.

Once we're settled at the table, we order two bottles of a local New Zealand rosé and check the dinner menu. The waiter fills our glasses and takes our food order. When I pick up my glass, the rays of the sun strike the decoration on it, causing it to sparkle. I sip my wine slowly, until I get some food inside me.

'Liz and I have booked a holiday to Oz in the middle of June,' Dee tells us. 'I got the chance of a great deal on a trip to the Barrier Reef.'

Brenda lets out a squeal of delight at the news.

'Fantastic, I've been saying to John for years that I'd like to go there. What it is to be a travel agent.'

'Well you gals know that I can watch out for deals for you anytime.' Dee has worked in New Zealand's largest travel company since leaving school and, after a few promotions, is now branch manager.

'A good choice going into the travel industry. Working in the hospital doesn't get me any reduced travel.' Elva giggles. 'Not even a reduction in the cost of surgery.'

Dee downs some more wine.

'You'll remember when I was at school my ambition was to be an air hostess but I'm glad now I took the job in the travel agency. Flying seemed exciting as a school kid but now of course I know it for what it is, a glorified waitress, although better paid.'

'I bet Liz is excited about the trip,' Brenda says.

Dee nods. 'She's been crossing off the days on the calendar since we booked it.' Dee and Liz have been together for two years now. I recall how wary Dee had been of revealing her sexual orientation to us. But we suspected it even at school and are delighted that our dear friend has found happiness with Liz.

We chat as we eat and never run out of conversation. We talk over one another with constant digressing but being female we understand perfectly everything that is said.

'I met Hannah Weiss in the supermarket in Oriental Bay last week. John and I use that store regularly, but this is the first time I've bumped into her,' Brenda tell us, while Dee is re-filling our wine glasses for the umpteenth time. We're already on to our third bottle of rosé by now and we're only at the dessert stage.

Elva screws her face into a question mark. 'Hannah Weiss? I remember the name but can't think of her face.'

Inspiration dawns on me. 'She wore long skirts to school. Overweight, with mousey brown hair and an Alice band.' I'm unable to keep the triumph out of my voice.

'I remember her, now,' Elva chips in. 'She couldn't attend netball practice on a Saturday morning because that was the Jewish Sabbath.'

'She certainly isn't overweight now,' Brenda says, 'I almost walked past her because she was so slim. She looks stunning.'

'And did she recognise you?' Dee asks.

'Yep, it was she who spoke to me first so obviously I haven't changed. She was keen for a good natter, but I could see John was becoming restless so had to cut it short. She was interested to hear that we four have kept in touch and asked me to say hi. To be exact she asked me to say hi to Rosalind, Elva and Deirdre!'

Dee smiles over at me. 'Proper names no less.'

'Cheers, Hannah.' A slightly inebriated Elva holds up her glass to toast our invisible school friend. In our present state, giggly after our wine, we all crumple up laughing, as if it's the best joke we've ever heard. We pay little attention to the looks thrown in our direction from other, more sober, diners.

Dee asks Brenda a question once we've stopped laughing. 'Wasn't Hannah friendly with Gracie Draper? D'ye remember the girl who had loads of boyfriends? She changed them as often as she did her socks.'

'Hannah mentioned her. They still keep in touch and, from the sound of it, Gracie still has a string of admirers.' Our memories of Gracie and Hannah are stopped by the arrival of our coffee.

'So how are things with Leggat these days? Are you two hitting it off any better now?' Brenda asks me, stirring brown sugar into her coffee. I'd mentioned him the last time we all met, saying how I keep my distance in case I'm tempted to punch him.

'Not really. My colleagues go out on a Friday night after work for a drink. I occasionally join them but can't relax when Leggat is there, so was glad to have an excuse tonight.'

'Bet he isn't too popular with the other staff in the office.' Brenda unwraps the foil paper on her chocolate mint and pops the sweet into her mouth.

'To be fair, I don't think Leggat bothers anyone else as much as me. I've disliked him since day one.'

'He does sound like a bit of a know-it-all.' Dee makes a temple of her fingers as she's speaking. 'Talking of which, when I attended my dental appointment last week, the receptionist was so patronising. Anyone would have thought she was the dentist the way she was going on. Absolute pain in the neck.'

We're still discussing the bossy receptionists we've come into contact with when the waiter begins to clear away our coffee cups.

'Can we have the bill, please?' Dee asks.

'Certainly, one moment please.' He returns swiftly and lays the bill, on its metal tray, down in front of her. 'I hope you enjoyed your meal, ladies?'

'Delicious, we'll be back,' Brenda tells him and the rest of us nod in agreement. When he walks away, we split the bill into four and lay the money on the tray. Then we arrange the date for our next get-together, in record time for once.

'It's too early to go home,' Elva announces, when we're standing outside on the Quay. 'Why don't we have a walk along the waterfront before phoning for a taxi?' The sun has gone down by now, but it's still fairly warm, so we take up her suggestion.

Darkness has come by the time we retrace our steps. I stop for a few moments on the quayside, and stare up at the vanilla-coloured moon, looking like a huge marshmallow against the blackened sky, before hurrying to catch up with the others.

CHAPTER EIGHTEEN

On Saturday afternoon I drive to Johnsonville. Instead of focusing on the road, my mind keeps wandering to Leggat. Is he the one stalking me and did he send the Valentine card? A few times, since the card arrived, I've had the feeling of being followed. I never see anyone when I look round, but nonethcless it spooks me.

Despite my fear, I feel that since Elva and I met him at Trentham back in January, Leggat has been less troublesome at work, not flirting with me so openly. It looks like my rudeness at the racecourse, and my indifference ever since, has at last paid off.

I reach Johnsonville swiftly as there's a rugby match on telly so the roads are almost deserted. I pass only a handful of pedestrians, with almost no gardeners at work during the match. I've got no interest in the game, but rugby fans will be glued to the screen, either in their own home or in Wellington's crowded pubs. They want to see the mighty All Blacks take on South Africa. Ted and Matt told me yesterday that they had tickets.

Leaving the Toyota in the high school car park, a shiver runs through me as I make my way to the main entrance. It's chillier than it should be for this time in March and I regret not wearing a heavier jacket. I dread the thought of the winter ahead.

Inside the school, I wave to Tony, the janitor, as I pass his office, the rugby commentator's voice coming across clearly from his radio. From the smile on Tony's face, I guess that our lot are winning.

Johnsonville Creative Writers' Group meets here every second Saturday afternoon. I've been a member for well over a year now and enjoy giving and receiving feedback. As I climb the stairs to our classroom on the first floor it crosses my mind that, of the ten folk on our group register, there are six of us who form the core of regulars at every meeting. I joined the group around the same time that I started at The Post; can never remember whether being a journalist made me start fiction writing or if it was the other way round. Either way I get a lot of pleasure out of my hobby.

Our classroom door is ajar, and Phil Stafford sits alone at the table.

'Hi, Phil,' I say, and take a seat facing him.

'G'day, Ros.' Phil lifts his head from the manuscript he's reading. 'I was making some changes to the piece I submitted.'

Phil works on the Wellington docks, his occupation in keeping with his broad shoulders and legs like tree trunks. His shift ends at midday on a Saturday and, with no time to go home, he comes to the class wearing his work clothes of khaki shorts and vest top. The tattoo on his upper arm depicts a crocodile baring its teeth.

I open my writing case and sort out my bits and pieces to allow Phil to continue with his reading. The noise of traffic reaches me through the open window, and I hear the ring of a bicycle bell in the distance. The room allocated to us is comfortably furnished, with bookshelves along one side of it and a kettle on the table behind the door, which allows us to make tea and coffee. The chairs are upholstered in red leather and the table seats six of us comfortably. If any more than six members come, then we push two tables together.

My thoughts are interrupted when Natalie Dent comes in, swinging her car keys round her finger. 'Hi, guys,' she greets us and dumps her voluminous bag on to the table beside me. I give her a smile and Phil makes do with a quick nod.

'You all right for a pizza after the meeting?' she asks me, keeping her voice low so not to disturb Phil.

'Sure thing.' Nat and I often go for something to eat after the class, depending on her shifts as a midwife at Wellington General. 'How's Oscar?'

She beams at the mention of her German Shepherd. 'He's in fine fettle, had a romp in the garden before I went to work and another quick outing when I came off shift.'

'Were you on an early shift today?'

'Yep, started at 6 am. Within my first hour on duty, we had two deliveries, a boy and a girl.' Her eyes are bright with happiness and I think once again how suited she is for midwifery.

'Will Oscar be alright until you get home? I mean, with us going for pizza.'

'He'll be fine. I'll give him a proper walk when I get home from the Pizza Parlour.' She rummages in her bag and finally brings out a pen which she lays on the table beside her notepad, one with elephants on it and the slogan 'Save The Elephants'.

'Another of your campaigns?' I ask, pointing to the pictures. I always tell her I think she joins in with every march, sometimes without even knowing what they are protesting about.

She chortles and nods. 'One of the many, kiddo.'

'How's the story coming on?' I ask her. Nat writes a mean short story, with wonderful twists in the plot, so different from my feeble efforts.

'It's taking shape,' she begins, and before she can go any further two more group members arrive. Lauren Hammersley comes in, followed closely by Marcus Wyatt. He dwarfs Lauren, who is a small, slim girl, and works as an office clerk in the city centre. Lauren takes the seat facing Nat and slips her jacket over the back of her seat before sitting down.

Marcus struts across and opens the window wider before joining us at the table. His black hair is gelled and his pin-striped suit immaculate. I notice he takes his usual seat at one end of the table, as if presiding over the group. Having his own law firm, Marcus is used to being in control, and his behaviour doesn't appear to change when he comes here.

'Sorry I'm late, folks,' Justin Grove apologises, as he rushes in, his faded jeans and crushed shirt the reverse of Marcus' clothes. 'I had some parents to see this morning and the last interview overran.' Justin's work as a remedial teacher in a city centre high school often makes him late for our meeting.

'No problem, Jus,' I say, as he settles himself at the opposite end of the table from Marcus, who gives me a withering look, as though I've uttered some swear words. I have a strong desire to stick out my tongue at him, but instead choose to ignore him.

Jus looks over at me and smiles his thanks.

'Right, I have your piece on the top of my pile, Phil, so why don't we begin there? We can go round the table in a clockwise direction so would you like to kick us off with your feedback for Phil, Lauren?' he suggests, giving the girl an encouraging smile.

'Oh … right … em … well I really enjoyed your story, Phil,' she stutters, then smiles up at him. 'I think it was clever of you to … em … have a dock worker as your main character.' She stops, blushes and twists her hair round her finger, something I've noticed her doing often when she's giving feedback. She's a lovely girl and an excellent writer, yet seems so nervous of speaking aloud. 'I mean with you working at the docks, you can describe the character and the surroundings so vividly. I like the story being set in the 1860s, when the dockyards around here were thriving and the way your characters speak and act suit the period.' Lauren gets into her stride now and gives Phil some excellent suggestions for ways to improve the chapter of his novel that he's shared with us.

As the session goes on, we continue to give and receive feedback which is beneficial to us all. I try to hide the smile on my face when I have to start the feedback for Marcus on his 'bestseller' that he insists his novel will be but for once he seems to accept my comments without argument.

'Right folks, see you all in two weeks' time,' Jus says, at the end of the meeting. 'Remember and keep going with your story, it's taking shape well,' he tells Lauren, before he leaves the room. The others gather up their books and pens and gradually filter out, leaving Nat and me to take up the rear.

I drive behind Nat on our way to the Pizza Parlour. 'How did you think it went today?' she asks me, once we're settled at the table and have placed our order.

'I'm delighted with all the ideas I received and can't wait to get home to make some alterations to my story. It's amazing how other group members can see glaring errors that you've missed yourself.'

'I think we're probably too close to our own work when we're writing but another member sees it with fresh eyes. And for once Marcus didn't seem too miffed about our suggestions.'

I give her a nod. 'He seemed more subdued than usual. Wonder if he sent something off to a publisher and it was rejected?' I lick my lips when the pizza arrives, and our conversation ceases while we make light work of the food.

CHAPTER NINETEEN

The landline was ringing when Simon came out of the shower. He threw himself down on the edge of the bed and lifted the receiver. 'Hello'.

'Simon.' Charlie's voice blasted into his ear. 'We've had a whiff of scandal from that dockyard company we ran a story on months ago. Can you come and see me the minute you get in?'

The words were said as a command, not a question. Although Simon got on well with Charlie, he'd decided from the outset that he wouldn't like to tread on his editor's toes.

'Sure,' Simon replied, in his most willing tone. 'I recall the company clearly. It was one of the first stories I covered when I came to Wellington.' As he was speaking, he let the towel drop to the floor and used his spare hand to pull on his boxers. 'I remember even back then there were rumbles of discontent among the workforce.'

'Well, I hope this recent information might help to shed some light on exactly what's going on.'

Simon put his foot into a sock and lifted his leg a little to assist in pulling the sock over his heel. 'I've got a couple of interviews to do first thing today but once I've dealt with them, I'll come by your office.'

'Fine,' came the clipped reply before the line went dead.

Simon finished dressing and made up the bed in his usual haphazard way. Pushing his feet into his shoes, he sat down on the bed again and tied the laces. He polished the tops of his shoes with the bottom of the vallance, before making his way into the kitchen.

He put two slices of thick farmhouse into the toaster. The remnants of last night's dinner were still sitting on the table and the dregs of his brandy remained at the bottom of the glass. Promising himself that he would do a blitz of the unit over the weekend, he scraped the left-over food into the recycling bin. He dumped the plate and his glass into the dishwasher, before spreading his toast with butter and locally-produced honey.

Without sitting at the table, he wolfed down his toast. Afterwards, he stood at the window and stared out into the garden, bare of any colour now. It had been a long winter this year, and he yearned for the spring to start. While he drank his strong, black coffee, he tried to figure out where he'd gone wrong with Ros. She constantly rejected his advances of friendship and sent him away feeling well and truly brought down to size.

He brushed his teeth, then picked up his briefcase and car keys on his way to the front door. He was no further forward on how to win Ros round by the time he strapped himself into his Ford Ranger and revved up the engine.

***

I'm relieved when Leggat leaves the office to go and investigate the dockyard scandal.

Because of the short time frame Charlie has

allowed me to write my current story, I stop mid-morning to buy a sandwich and a drink from the delicatessen in the foyer. This will allow me to work through my lunch break. The only drinks they have on offer are fizzy, so I pop out into Cuba Street and get my preferred cordial in the deli close to Alston Tower.

On my way back to the tower, I once again sense my stalker is nearby but as usual when I stop suddenly and look round, I can't see anyone. This really is spooking me out and I still want to accuse Leggat, but I know he's down at the dockyard.

With Leggat and Matt both out this morning, it's only Ted and me at our desks. Aware that I'm stressed and pushing to finish my story on time, Ted leaves me in peace to get on.

CHAPTER TWENTY .

My phone rings again, the third time within the space of fifteen minutes. On this occasion I don't say hello. There's only the sound of someone breathing, before the click of disconnection. I feel angry but also something bordering on fear. Why is Leggat doing this? I'm sure it's him. At work I give him the brush off when he chats me up, but he refuses to take no for an answer.

These calls can come any day of the week and at varying times, but I've noticed that there's usually more at the weekends. I make light of the calls when I'm speaking to Elva, but in truth I'm afraid to sleep at night. I tell myself that I'm being melodramatic but am sure something bad is going to happen.

Should I confide in Charlie? Or perhaps Ted? But I've no proof that Leggat is involved since the number is always withheld. These calls are made to my landline at home, so the caller has access to my personal details. This thought freaks me out even more. With no proof, the police are likely to ignore my complaints, although I've heard they can intercept any calls to a particular number. Might be worth considering.

Smoky jumps up on to my lap. I stroke him while I stare out into the garden. The summer plants have long since died off, giving way to the autumn blooms. Smoky quickly falls asleep and I drift off soon afterwards. My snoring wakens me up and, when I look at the clock on the wall above the fireplace, I jump to my feet, remembering that Elva will be picking me up in less than half an hour for the cinema. Smoky gives a start and digs his claws into my leg due to his rude awakening. 'Sorry,' I say, stroking him, but he turns his back on me and stalks off, miffed at being disturbed.

Ten minutes later, while I'm waiting for Elva's toot, my mind returns to the nuisance calls. They started back in February, following the Valentine's card I received. At first, I dismissed the card as the work of a crackpot, had a laugh and binned it. Now I'm not so sure it was a joke and am beginning to connect the card with the person who persists in phoning and stalking me.

A shiver runs through me and I decide the next time I receive such a phone call I will definitely contact the police to see if they can put a check on my line.

***

'Wasn't too struck on the plot,' Elva says, when we're sitting in the bistro after the film.

'I found it very poor. The story depressed me, just when I could do with cheering up.'

'Are you still getting the weird phone calls?' Elva asks. She stops speaking when the waiter brings our food.

'Yep, I'm quite spooked by them. Got another three calls today.'

'Maybe you should report them to the police?'

'I've decided to do that the next time he calls. I'm saying he because I've a good idea who the caller is.'

Elva scratches her forehead. 'Do you still think Leggat's behind the calls?'

'I'm sure he is.'

'But couldn't someone else be making them? What about that horrid man, Marcus, in your writing group? Maybe he's been secretly lusting after you?'

Despite my fear, I laugh aloud. 'No, Elva, I'd be the last person Marcus Wyatt would be interested in. He thinks the rest of us in the group are inferior to him. Anyway, there's no way Marcus would be making nuisance phone calls, it isn't his style, believe me.'

'But how well do you know him? Or any other members of the group for that matter?'

'I suppose you're right. I obviously know Natalie Dent best of all. She's the one who writes fantastic short stories. It's true that I only know the other members within the group setting but I still can't see Marcus as a stalker.'

'What about someone else at The Post, other than Leggat?'

I shake my head vigorously. 'No. Ted adores his wife, Anne, and no way would he be stalking me. He's more like a father figure to me. Matt's a confirmed bachelor and Charlie is a married man with a family. No, it's definitely Leggat.'

'And you still sometimes think you're being followed?'

I nod. 'Yesterday I was convinced someone was following me on my way to the shopping mall. And even once I got inside.'

'Have you actually seen anyone?'

'No, that's the problem. I sense more than see the person.'

She shakes her head. 'I don't understand it. I still think you should try and get some counselling, Ros.'

'Surely you don't believe that me trying to deal with Gran's death has anything to do with these mysterious phone calls. Unless you think it's all in my head.'

'No, the calls are obviously happening. But, even so, maybe there's a link. Oh, I don't know, the whole thing's odd.' When our meal arrives, Elva changes the subject.

By the time we leave the bistro, my mood has lifted, despite the heavy rain waiting for us outside the cinema.

CHAPTER TWENTY ONE

I have to fight against a high wind on my way to The Lavender for lunch. When I get there, I see Elva hurrying towards me from the opposite direction. I grab her by the arm when she is almost blown off the kerb into the path of a passing car.

'Thanks, Ros. Thought I was going to be late,' she says, trying to catch her breath. 'Mr Henderson needed me to type a couple of urgent reports before I went for lunch.'

'What's that boss of yours like? Seems to think you should jump to attention every time he snaps his fingers.'

'No, Mr Henderson's always grateful for anything I do for him,' she says, fiercely loyal as ever. 'He's in theatre this afternoon so wanted to sign the reports before he started.' She wrinkles her nose and laughs. 'He's a sweetie though, a sort of old school type of guy.'

'A dinosaur you mean.' I push open the café door and she follows me inside.

Brenda and Dee arrive together, just after we've bagged a window table.

'Hi, girls,' I greet them and push the used soup bowls on to a nearby empty table. Brenda takes the seat beside Elva, while Dee plonks herself down next to me. She and I have our backs to the wall, a picture of

Wellington Harbour hanging above our heads.

We've been having so much trouble trying to get a night to suit us all that we plumped for lunch this month instead. This week, being a school holiday, means that Brenda can join us.

We fall silent while we all consult the menu.

'Think I'll have a panini with bacon, brie and cranberry.' I close the menu and sit back until the others make their choice.

'So, what's new?' Dee directs her question to us all once the order has been given.

Brenda shrugs. 'John and I are having a new bathroom fitted so my weekend was spent clearing up after the workmen.'

Elva makes a figure of eight with the salt and pepper shakers. 'Mum decided to have the living room painted so I spent most of the weekend helping to move furniture and making tea for the decorators. Nikau as ever was away doing something with his mates. His excuse not to help. I wish Mum didn't hoard so many ornaments. They take an age to wash and dry.'

I nod and give her a sympathetic smile, glad that Gran had been a minimalist. 'Did you not see Adam over the weekend then?' Elva has an on/off relationship with Adam, but she told me a couple of months ago that she fancies him big time.

As always when Adam's name is mentioned, Elva blushes. 'Their team was playing in a match in Auckland on Saturday.'

'Did they win?' Brenda and Dee ask in unison.

'No, and they spent that evening and most of

Sunday drowning their sorrows. I think they were well hungover when they returned to Wellington on Sunday night.'

I've not yet met Adam, but Elva has shown me photographs. He looks pleasant enough but it's obvious that rugby is his life. He's built like a typical All Black too. He doesn't seem like a guy committed to their relationship, so I hope he won't hurt Elva who, although she tries to hide it, is a sensitive soul. My musing is interrupted when Leigh brings our food, the delicious smell tempting our taste buds. We get stuck into our meals and afterwards sit back, our hunger satisfied, to enjoy our coffee. The four of us sit for a time in comfortable silence, the way good friends can. Brenda is first to speak again.

'Did you two get the balance of your holiday paid?' she asked, her eyes taking in Elva and me at the same time.

'Yep,' I answer her question first, 'and we can't wait to go.'

Now we're into October, we leave for the north in around six weeks' time.

'What about Leggat?' Dee asks me.

'I still can't stand him, but he continues to try and chat me up at every opportunity.' I drain my coffee cup and use my spoon to polish off the chocolate dredged on the top.

'And then there's the phone calls and the Valentine card,' Elva reminds me and the other two want to hear about that.

'What is it about him you don't like?' Brenda

asks, when they've heard what's been happening.

'I can't put my finger on it, but I disliked him from the word go. He comes across as someone who loves himself and swaggers about as if he owns the place.' I stop speaking and turn to watch a couple with a young child taking up residence at the next table, with Leigh bringing over a highchair for the little girl. The kid looks across at me; she gives a toothless smile and I wave back to her.

'Perhaps he wants to impress you while deep down he's covering up his shyness. There are people like that.' Brenda returns to our conversation and pushes her empty cup into the centre of the table beside mine.

'It's possible, although he doesn't seem the shy type.'

The little girl at the next table drops her toy rabbit on to the floor. Elva stretches out and picks it up, and from then on our attention falls on to the child and away from Leggat.

CHAPTER TWENTY TWO

I'm feeling sad today, the first anniversary of Gran's death. She was so fit for 77, but the fall downstairs was her undoing. I'd have wagered anything that she had many more years of life ahead of her and her death is so hard to come to terms with.

I sit down at the kitchen table, glad I have a day off from work to attend my first appointment with Dr Tyler at half past three. Strange it should have come for today, Gran's anniversary. Elva has badgered me for months now to go for bereavement counselling and, after one really bad weekend when I hit the bottle big time, I made an appointment with my GP. I told her I didn't want to take tablets and instead she referred me for 'talking therapy'. Right now, I'm fighting against the desire to have a glass of wine to calm me because I don't want the therapist to smell booze on me. Instead I make a mug of strong, black coffee.

My tears well up and run unchecked down my cheeks. I remember every last detail of that day, and don't think it will ever leave me. The ward staff were so kind and caring to Gran, but the Consultant told me that many elderly people develop pneumonia while recovering from a broken hip. It was of little comfort at the time but, looking back, I'm grateful that Gran wasn't left to suffer pain or had to battle cancer. I do still miss her though, and wish she'd walk through the door right now and call out, 'Ro-os, you home yet, sweetheart?'

I glance up at the kitchen clock. Half past ten, which means it will be about half past one in the morning in Scotland. I decide to email Aunt Viv; it doesn't matter if it's the middle of the night because email doesn't mean wakening her out of her sleep.

The very thought of sending it makes me feel better, and I know Aunt Viv will be sad like me today.

Dear Aunt Viv, I begin typing and give her my news. I keep the email upbeat and cheery and that makes me feel better. I decide not to mention the anniversary of Gran's death. Aunt Viv will understand why I'm emailing today.

By the time I press the send button and close down the computer, I'm smiling again.

***

Just before half past three, I stand outside the clinic in Clifton Road. If I were a smoker, I'd be having a draw right now. After long resistance, I'm finally here and I'm proud of that.

The building has a most unprepossessing frontage, although the graffiti on it is quite artistic. The sad and neglected appearance continues once I'm inside the building. The lift also looks dilapidated and unloved, so I plump for the stairs to the second floor.

When Dr Tyler comes to meet me in the reception area, I find her a well-turned-out woman, in her middle fifties I reckon, with a gentle handshake and a welcoming smile. The room she ushers me into is Spartan, with only a badly-scratched table and two spindly chairs in the way of furniture. There's a picture of sunflowers on the wall, or, more accurately, a poster of sunflowers in a cheap plastic frame. The clinic is run as a charity, so I guess they won't have the money to do the place up.

The counsellor puts me at ease straight away by offering me a tea or coffee. I refuse this, but ask for a glass of water, which she brings me. She takes her seat opposite me, a notebook and pen in her hand, and begins by saying, 'I always like to keep these sessions on a first-name footing so, if you've no objection, I suggest you call me Marion and I'll call you Rosalind.'

'That's fine, but I'm known as Ros.' I almost add to my friends but, although Marion Tyler couldn't be looked on as a friend, it seems right than she uses the shortened version of my name. I try to stop myself from picking at my fingernails, something I've done since childhood when I'm stressed. During the worst of these times, I've even made them bleed.

She notices my behaviour but doesn't comment. 'Right, Ros, can you tell me how coming here today makes you feel?'

When I don't reply, she reads over my GP's referral letter and tries another tack.

'I know you were close to your grandmother and you must miss her a lot. Do you want to talk about your feelings regarding her death?' When I don't answer immediately, she goes on. 'Let me assure you Ros, that anything we discuss in our sessions together, stays between us. Everything is confidential and will go no further.'

'Today is the first anniversary of her death.' My voice comes out in a squeak. I take a drink of water and swallow it slowly. 'I miss her like crazy and it's affecting my sleep. I have constant nightmares and am exhausted next morning.' I stop for a moment and take a breath. Once I start to speak to her, it all tumbles out and I find it hard to stop. But I don't mention my problem with Leggat; time enough for that in another session. One problem at a time, I tell myself.

She waits until I draw to a close, then asks another question. 'Would you like to tell me something about the dream you have. Does it frighten you?'

I shake my head and raise my eyes to hers, the first time in the interview so far. 'It isn't scary, and in a way easy to understand. Gran appears and beckons to me. I run towards her but each time I get near, she is enshrouded by a thick mist, then it clears, and she comes again but the same happens when I get close to her. The dream keeps recurring and when I waken up my pillow is sodden, and I'm out of puff with running.'

'A separation dream is common following bereavement and not too unexpected. The dream should vanish with a little more time, once you begin to be more able to live with your loss. Would you like to tell me something about your gran? Help me to feel I know her?

This is easy and all my memories of Gran flood out.

We go on to discuss other aspects of what I'm feeling, and I cry a lot during our session. Marion discreetly slips a box of paper tissues across the table to me and I use them freely.

'You've created a lovely picture for me of your gran,' Marion says, her tone gentle. 'What about your parents?'

'They died young, in a train crash in Britain.' I stretch for the hankies again and weep copiously as I tell her what I remember about life with my parents and how Gran became a second mother to me after they'd gone.

'Yes, I can see how close you and your gran were, which makes grieving for her even harder to deal with.' She smiles. 'Who do you resemble most? Mum or Gran? That is, I'm assuming she's your mum's mother?'

I nod. 'I've often been told I look like Mum but when I look at old photographs, I see myself more like Gran. And I think in nature we're quite similar.' Once again, the tissues are needed and by now the wastepaper bin beside me is half filled with damp hankies. But I'm feeling more comfortable and relaxed with Marion.

'Can you square it with your boss to meet me at the same time next week?' Marion asks, when the session comes to an end. I can't believe I've been with her for an hour.

'Yes, he knows my GP has referred me to you, although he hasn't said to other staff members about my attendance, for which I'm grateful.'

'Good,' Marion says, and marks the appointment in her diary. 'Would you like a card with the date and time?'

'No,' I say, as I'm zipping up my parka, or anorak as Gran would have called it. 'I've always had a good memory for dates.'

She sees me to the exit, and, once out on the street, I blow my nose and hope my eyes aren't too red-rimmed.

By the time I get home I'm relieved from having unburdened myself.

Smoky sits on my lap and purrs when I pet him, then follows me into the kitchen while I put out his dinner. When the phone rings, I wonder if it's another weird call but when I answer, I hear Elva's voice.

'How did you get on at the clinic today?'

'Dr Tyler is very nice. She asked me to call her Marion and she's using my first name too. Says she likes that, as it makes the interview less formal.'

'So, do you think speaking to her will help, Ros?'

'Well, so far so good and I do feel some relief from talking about things with her. She wanted to know all about Gran and asked me about Mum and Dad too.'

'I thought it would help. Always better to speak to a stranger than a friend or relative. Is she going to see you again?'

'I'm seeing her again next week. Don't know how long she'll want me to attend.'

'I suppose until both you and she feel you've turned a corner in the grieving process.' Elva laughs. 'Gosh I sound like I know what I'm talking about when of course I don't, but it's great that you feel a benefit from attending.'

'Yes, maybe this counselling lark isn't as silly as I'd thought.'

We chat on for a bit longer until Mrs Kahui calls to Elva that the film they're planning to watch is about to start.

'See you soon,' I say, as we hang up.

***

Following her interview with Ros, Marion wrote up her notes. As Ros had been her last patient, she drove from the clinic to the supermarket. The store was a 24 hour one, so she didn't have her usual hectic race round the aisles, but could search the shelves leisurely and, in the process, bought far more than she'd meant to.

I fall for it every time, Marion thought, a wry smile on her face as she made her way to the check-out.

When she arrived home, Marion parked in the driveway. She opened the boot, then rang the front doorbell to alert the family that she was home and would welcome some assistance with the shopping bags. Her student son, Ben, appeared at the door and came over to where she stood at the car.

'I see you've been buying out the store again, Mum,' he teased her, 'I think the retailers see you coming. Bet they rub their hands in glee when your car appears.'

Marion punched his arm playfully. 'Less cheek and more brawn please,' she said, handing him the heaviest of the bags, while she followed behind with the lighter ones.

Her husband Larry was coming along the hallway when she entered the house. 'Hi sweetie,' he said, kissing her on the cheek as he took the bags from her. 'Had a good day?'

Marion followed him into the kitchen and took a seat at the breakfast bar, leaving Ben and Larry to put her purchases into the appropriate cupboards. 'Reasonable day. My last client was a delightful young woman. She's had a rough time of it recently, and I know there's a lot she's not telling me, but I'm seeing her again next week.' Marion kicked off her shoes, letting them drop on to the floor, then swivelled round in her chair to watch Larry load the perishables into the fridge/freezer. She beamed when he lifted a half-used bottle of sauvignon blanc out of the fridge and held it up.

'Can I tempt you?'

'I thought you'd never ask,' she replied and went into the family room where she threw herself down on the sofa and put her bare feet up on the stool in front of her.

Larry followed her into the room, carrying a tray with two glasses of wine on it.

'Where's Abi?' Marion asked, as she downed some wine. 'Needed that.' She sighed and laid her glass down on the tray.

'She's upstairs finishing off her assignment for school,' Larry told her. 'I've got dinner well under way and I said I'd call up to her when we're ready to sit down.'

'You should be taking a leaf out of your sister's book,' Marion told Ben. He was the very opposite of Abi, who was a conscientious student. Despite this, Ben always got excellent results. He seemed to be a natural without excessive studying after school. But on the whole they were good kids and both she and Larry were proud of them.

Larry got to his feet again. 'I'll go and check the veggies and then we'll be ready to eat. Could you ask Abi to come down now?' he asked Ben, who went to the foot of the stairs and called to his sister. 'Abi, grub's up.'

There was no reply, but they heard her footsteps heading towards the bathroom.

Cocooned in the folds of the sofa, Marion lay back and closed her eyes. There was a smile on her face as she thought how lucky she was with her family life. Larry had worked from home over the past couple of years and had found an interest in cooking which spared her having to come home from work and start slaving over a cooker.

CHAPTER TWENTY THREE

Viv was delighted to find an email from Ros waiting for her when she opened her in-box, especially with this being the first anniversary of her best friend's passing. She guessed that was the reason why Ros had decided to message her. Knowing Ros would be feeling down, she decided to reply straight away. It would be the middle of the night in New Zealand, but Ros would get it in the morning.

It'll be good when I get on to Skype, she thought, aware that Daryl was planning to set it up for her. Viv was quite excited, if a little scared, at the prospect of being able to see Ros while they chatted. All this modern way of communicating was beyond Viv, so it was good to know that Daryl would explain it all to her before she started.

She hit the reply button on her laptop and started to type her reply to Ros.

Dear Ros

It was lovely to open your email today, especially as I was feeling a bit down in view of what date it was.

I'm so glad you and Elva have your trip up north to look forward to and it will be here before you realise it. I heard on the news today that it is only eight weeks until Christmas. The time seems to go quicker each year, but I guess that is an ageing thing on my part.

You seem to be enjoying your writing classes and it's such a great interest for you. I had ideas of writing myself years ago but never seemed to get round to it. I look forward to seeing your work in print one of these days and I will be able to boast to my friends about my great niece who is a famous author!

Daryl plans to put Skype on to my laptop. I need to wait until he has time of course because he is very busy with his work. I'm in awe of all this modern stuff so hope it works out.

Hope today hasn't been too stressful for you, Ros, and I know your gran will be proud of how well you've coped without her.

Speak soon.
Love from Aunt Viv
xx

CHAPTER TWENTY FOUR

In Bella Italiana, the waiter shows me to a table and brings a glass of Merlot, while I wait for Nat. I'm engrossed in the story I'm writing when she eventually rushes in, her coat flying open and a very large handbag swinging from her arm.

'Hi Ros,' she says, and stands beside me while she catches her breath. She dumps the bag on the floor under the table, and slips out of her coat. 'Sorry, got caught up at the last minute. One of my mothers, decided today was to be the day. She delivered a gorgeous wee girl a couple of hours ago, a bit early but a good weight and we have no concerns about her. I left mum and baby getting acquainted.'

'What a worthwhile job you have Nat, bringing all that new life into the world.'

'Yes, especially when one of my patients returns for her next pregnancy, and brings her older child to clinic appointments with her. It's marvellous to see the child I helped to deliver when he or she is 2 or 3 years old.' When the waiter brings us the menus, Nat asks for a glass of Chardonnay.

Once our order is placed, we settle back and relax with our wine.

'So, busy as always,' Nat says, nodding towards my notebook lying on the table. 'You're a prolific writer, Ros, and sure to get something published soon.'

I put the book back into my handbag. 'I just look on it as a hobby. I find writing fiction a refreshing change from the non-fiction I do at work.' I scratch my itchy nose, trying to recall if it means I'm going to be angry with someone, or that I will come into money. The latter would be good.

I take another sip of wine. 'Nat, why don't you send off some of these super stories you produce? I'm sure the New Zealand Women's Weekly would snap them up.'

'It's time you see, or lack of it.' She reads my thoughts from the expression on my face and holds up her hands in surrender. 'I know, if I was really keen to get into print, I'd make the time.' She shrugs. 'I'd like to write a novel but don't know if I could sustain something for so long.'

'Would be interesting to see whether you or Marcus produce your bestseller first,' I say, and we both laugh. Then I shake my head. 'Poor Marcus, we do make fun of him.'

'But he leaves himself open to ridicule, the way he struts around, looking down on the rest of us. Thank God Jus is our Chairperson.'

'Jus is a lovely guy. Wonder if Marcus will ever finish his bestseller?'

'Time will tell,' Nat says, as our food is brought to the table.

We continue to chat as we satisfy our hunger and, by the time we leave the restaurant, we are up to date with one another's news.

CHAPTER TWENTY FIVE

'You miss the other guys, don't you?' Ted says, as we face one another across the table at the Green Man.

'Mmm,' I reply, taking a swallow of my gin and tonic. I wonder if he realises how glad I was that Leggat flew to Dunedin after work to attend a wedding there. 'Wonder how Matt's doing in New Caledonia?'

'He'll be having a ball. I've always fancied a holiday there, but it doesn't appeal to Anne, so not much hope of getting there.' Ted shrugs. 'She who must be obeyed and all that.'

I take another drink from my glass. 'You know you love it.' Despite the way Ted sometimes slags her off, his devotion to Anne is obvious for all to witness.

'By the way,' he says, 'Anne and I wondered if you were free next Wednesday evening. We'd like you to come to our house for dinner.'

'I'd like that very much, Ted. I've only met Anne once when she came into the office so it will be great to get to know her better.'

'She said the same thing.' He hesitates for a moment, then brings up Leggat. 'Tell me to mind my own business if you want, but why have you such an aversion to Simon?'

'What do you mean?'

He laughs. 'It isn't too difficult to detect. You have a most expressive face, Ros, and your thoughts are mirrored on it.'

I take another drink and put the glass down on the table, rather more heavily than I intend. 'Have you and Leggat been discussing me, Ted?'

He stretches over and pats my hand. 'Of course not, Ros, he simply said he didn't know why you were so antagonistic toward him.'

I sigh and shake my head. 'Ted, he just isn't someone I can relate to. I find him so damned full of himself and his manner really annoys me.'

'I know he gives that impression, but I think underneath all the bluster he's a pretty decent guy. And I know he's got an eye for you. Maybe if you give him a chance, you could grow to like him better. I'm sure he'd like to be friends with you.'

'You're such a peacemaker, Ted, and loyal to your friends,' I say, smiling over at him. 'But this time you've backed a loser.' Looking at my watch, I push my chair back from the table. 'I'll need to head off now as I want to catch my local supermarket before it closes.'

Ted gets to his feet. 'I need to go myself.' Outside the pub, he escorts me to the bus stop. 'Sorry if I spoke out of turn. No hard feelings?'

'None whatever,' I assure him and put out my hand as the bus approaches.

'See you Monday, Ros, and I'll tell Anne we're on for Wednesday evening.' He waves as he heads off around the corner.

CHAPTER TWENTY SIX

A few weeks later I go into Skype and ring Aunt Viv. Daryl has put the facility on to her laptop, allowing us to speak face to face. We'd made arrangements by email that this time would be convenient for us both.

Sure enough, after a few rings, I hear the click from the other end. 'Hello, Ros,' she says, but there is no picture on the screen. 'How are you?'

'I'm fine, but I can't see you, Aunt Viv.'

There is the usual time lapse until she hears my words. 'I can see you,' she tells me.

'I think your video must be turned off. It's the blue icon at the bottom, first on the left. Looks like a camera. Click on it and the line through the icon should disappear.'

After a short wait her picture appears on the screen. She's wearing a deep blue jumper and her hair looks as if it's been freshly set. 'Hi, Ros,' she says and waves to me. 'I suppose you'll be enjoying lovely weather.'

'Yes,' I reply, waving back. 'What's yours like?'

'Very cold and icy. We're having a really severe November this year.' Aunt Viv shifts in her seat to get into a more comfortable position, ready for a good old blether, as Gran would have called it.

CHAPTER TWENTY SEVEN

Ted looked up when Simon was putting on his jacket. 'Off anywhere exciting?'

'I'm going to interview the lady who is fighting an unfair dismissal case. I'll see you and Matt in the pub afterwards.' Simon hadn't seen much of Ros today as he'd been out all morning while she'd been in the office and she left to conduct an interview shortly after he returned. She barely looked at him these days and her hostile attitude towards him continued. He wished he knew what he'd done to warrant her having such a grudge against him. He'd like to ask her but doubtless she'd bite his head off.

Simon parked outside Emily Weston's house, sure he'd get a good story from her. When he'd contacted the widow to request this interview about her complaint, she'd sounded very much the victim in the story. When she opened the door to him, he held out his identification badge. 'Good afternoon, Mrs Weston, I'm Simon Leggat from The Post. I called you this morning.'

'Come in.' She stood back to allow Simon to enter the narrow passageway, leading to a well-appointed sitting room. She directed him to a sofa in front of the window. 'Take a seat,' she said, then sat down on the opposite end of the sofa, leaving a space between them.

'As I explained, Mrs Weston, I'd like to write a piece for The Post, highlighting the unfair treatment you've received at work.'

From the outset she took control, taking offence at some of Simon's more probing questions. He was disconcerted by this, as he usually took charge of the way an interview proceeded.

It quickly became obvious to Simon that this wasn't the first legal wrangle Mrs Weston had been involved in with employers. After starting badly, the interview continued in a downward spiral until, finding one of Simon's question too intrusive, Mrs Weston got to her feet, scarlet with rage, and ordered him out of her house.

Simon closed his notebook and stood up. 'Apologies, Mrs Weston, I didn't mean to cause any offence by my question.' But the woman remained unmoved and, aware that he'd blown it, he took his leave.

Back in the car he looked at his watch and decided it wasn't worth returning to the office. Instead he drove to the pub, which was almost empty at this time of afternoon.

'Your usual?' Danny, the barman, asked.

'No, I've got the car today, so I'll have a soft drink.'

'What about your mates?'

'They'll be here shortly,' Simon told him, laying the money for his drink down on to the counter. He was sitting at their usual table in the corner when Ted and Matt joined him half an hour later. He noticed that Ros wasn't with them, but he made no comment.

He looked up as Charlie followed the other two into the pub. 'Hi, boss, you gracing us with your presence tonight?'

Charlie nodded. 'Just have time for one. We've got a dance tonight and I've to pick Karen up from the hairdressers in half an hour. Another?' he asked, pointing to Simon's half empty glass.

'A soda water for me thanks, boss. I've got the car outside.'

Charlie grinned. 'Good man, and I should follow your example.'

'Have you been here long?' Ted asked, while the boss was over at the bar.

'Not long. Mrs Weston took offence at one of my questions and showed me the door.' Simon laughed. 'So much for my interviewing skills. I must be losing my touch.'

'I wouldn't worry, mate. You can't win them all.'

Charlie brought the drinks over and for a time the four of them discussed the state of the economy. Soon afterwards they were having a go at the politicians currently in power although they all agreed that their recently elected Prime Minister, Jacinda Ardern, had done a good job since her election. The conversation became quite heated when Simon and Matt disagreed on a recent policy the Government had brought in.

'Keep your voices down, guys,' Ted cautioned, when he noticed drinkers at other tables looking over.

Charlie excused himself shortly afterwards and the subject changed to less serious matters. A few drinks later, when the pub began to fill up and things became a bit rowdy, they made their exit.

***

Simon's landline was ringing when he got home. He raced through to the kitchen and dropped his car keys on to the worktop as he grabbed the receiver. He wasn't surprised to hear his mother's voice as he'd expected she would phone today. The anniversary was hard for them all. He listened patiently as she spoke about farm business. 'Is Dad coping alright today?' he asked.

'I think so. He doesn't say much, as you know, but he's kept himself busy all day. Right now, he's mending the boundary fence while there's still some daylight left. Two of our ewes got into Tom Brown's paddock the other day.'

Simon was aware that his father had never got over the accident. On that fateful day, Jamie had slipped out of the farmhouse without Mum noticing. He was playing in the paddock, running up and down the furrows where the tractor was working. Being a small 8-year-old, Jamie was out of Dad's line of vision at the moment he reversed the tractor.

Listening to his mother's voice coming over the airwaves, the scene flashed through Simon's mind again and he began to shake. The counselling he'd received at the time hadn't made much difference and even now, over twenty years later, he still hadn't come to terms with Jamie's untimely death.

They chatted a bit longer and eventually his

mother let him go. 'Try and come home soon, Son, you know Dad and I miss you a lot.'

'Will do, Mum, I promise,' he said gently, before replacing the phone on to its cradle.

CHAPTER TWENTY EIGHT

Leggat has been working on assignments out of town for the past couple of weeks but today is in the office, photocopying, when I get in.

'Morning,' I say to all the staff in general, and proceed to check my messages on the answering machine.

Once I hang up, Leggat appears behind me. 'How're you, Ros? Did you miss me?' He lays his hands on my shoulders as he's speaking.

'Of course, I cried myself to sleep every night.' My voice is thick with sarcasm, but even as I shrug his hands off, I'm aware that I feel less hostile towards him.

When I was at Ted's for dinner recently, he had a chat with me about Leggat while Anne was in the kitchen so maybe that has made the difference. I'm surprised to discover that I have missed him. Weird or what?

Ignoring my sarcasm. Leggat looks up at the clock above Charlie's office door, and says, to no-one in particular, 'I'm off to interview that woman who has the neighbours from hell.' He grabs his jacket and pushes a notebook into the pocket as he leaves the office.

I look round and watch Leggat's retreating figure and, when I turn back, Ted has a strange smile fixed on his face. But he says nothing and, feeling my cheeks burn, I drop my head and start to type at breakneck speed.

***

Elva is waiting for me in the foyer after work. She'd phoned at lunchtime to suggest we go to hear her favourite group, The Devils, perform at an open-air gig in the Botanic Gardens this evening. We agreed to leave our cars at work and collect them on the way home.

'Love the trousers,' I tell her, giving her a thumbs up. She bought them last time we were at the market; a lightweight turquoise material, with a design of shells and starfish on them.

She smiles and gives me a twirl.

'Did Adam not fancy the concert tonight?' I know Elva is head over heels in love with Adam so am surprised that she didn't ask him to go with her tonight.

'No, rock 'n pop isn't his scene. He's more of a classical geek.'

'Well, his loss is my gain,' I say, as we head along Cuba Street to the milk bar, where we buy some carry-out food and drink. Then, arm in arm, we head along to the cable car. It's great to be with Elva; with one thing and another, we haven't managed to get together for well over a week.

'Have you heard any more from Jill, from the Auckland Gazette?'

'Yes, and she's recommended some places to visit when we're up there.'

'How old is Jill?'

137

'Ages with us. She also invited us to visit her while we're in Auckland.'

We turn into the cable car entrance in Lambton Quay, buy our tickets and board the red car. The slow as treacle cable car I often rode in as a child has been upgraded. On our way up the two-track system, we pass the other car on its way down, and wave to the passengers inside.

When we arrive at the top, music can be heard on entering the Botanic Gardens, although the concert proper won't start for almost an hour. 'Let's have our picnic in the walled garden before we join the concert crowd,' Elva suggests.

We pass the manuka trees on our way uphill and, once we reach the Carter Observatory, we stop to admire the view below us. From our cliff top position, the brightly coloured craft moored down in the harbour can be clearly seen. We stand between two ancient kauri trees, whose trunks are gnarled and cracked, the broken shapes reminding me of pieces of a jigsaw puzzle. Lemon flowers are beginning to bloom on the nearby rautini trees.

Elva nudges me and points towards a number of speedboats. 'See the race going on down there?'

'Yep, think the blue one is in the lead.'

We watch for a few more moments and then make our way into the walled garden. 'This do?' Elva asks, as we come upon an empty bench seat. We are surrounded by a panorama of harakeke flax flowers and red kaka beak. I gasp at their beauty and their perfume wafts towards us in the soft spring breeze.

Picnic over, we stroll on past the Tree House Visitors' Centre and the Cable Car Museum until we come to the open grassland where the stage has been set up for the entertainment. The Devils are singing their first number when we arrive; the area is heaving with spectators and we squeeze into a space in the crowd and claim a spot on the grass.

Near the end of the concert, The Devils perform their latest number. During the rapturous applause that follows, some of the audience, including Elva and me, stand up and cheer. Elva sits down first and as I'm about to do the same, I notice Leggat and another guy still on their feet further along our row. Leggat hasn't seen me, allowing me to study him for a moment. He has an excellent physique, no doubt about that. He's handsome too, with black hair that's thick and wavy, the colour Gran would have called gypsy black. Maybe I'm getting soft or just becoming used to him, but he seems less arrogant these days.

I'm in the process of sitting down when he spots me and, through the mass of bodies separating us, he waves. I raise my hand slightly in return.

I notice that Elva has clocked what happened. 'You don't seem as hostile now,' she whispers, as the opening chords of the next number strike up, 'you warming to him at last?'

'Wouldn't go that far,' I say, then divert my attention to the musicians once more.

By the time the performance is over we are hoarse from cheering. Mingling with the mass, we make our way towards the exit, still singing some of the numbers. Jostled around in the crush, I barely feel the tap on my shoulder before I hear his voice.

'Hi, Ros, Did you enjoy the concert?' I turn around to find Leggat smiling at me.

'Yes thanks, it was great. You remember Elva?' I look towards my friend.

'Of course. And this is my cousin, Gavin Stokes. Ros works at The Post,' he tells his cousin.

'Hi, girls,' Gavin says, lifting his hand in a greeting.

He is at least a head taller than Leggat but not as good-looking or muscly as his cousin. I find it hard to believe that my feelings towards Simon have softened so much.

Drawn along by the crush, Elva and I get the last two seats on the cable car. I look out as car sets off down the track. Leggat and his cousin are standing amongst the people waiting for the next car and they wave to us. I copy their action, wondering if I'm happier to be waving rather than have Leggat sitting beside me. The question remains unanswered until I can sort out my exact feelings for him.

CHAPTER TWENTY NINE

Viv looked up from the novel she was reading when she heard the sound of the key turning in the lock. The family members all had a key to save her the effort of coming to the door when they called.

'It's only me, Gran,' Pamela's voice rang out as she came into the hallway and Viv heard the door closing behind her. 'I got everything on your list,' the girl continued, as she peeked round the living room door on her way to the kitchen to sort out the shopping into her gran's cupboards and fridge/freezer.

Her task completed, Pamela came back into the living room. She laid the supermarket receipt and her gran's change on the coffee table. 'Gran, are you sure everything you needed is on that list? Did you think of anything else after Mum had taken away your list yesterday?'

Viv shook her head vigorously. 'No darling, I have everything I need. And you're an angel to take the time to get my shopping for me.' Her daughter-in-law usually did any shopping if the roads were bad, but as she had other arrangements today, Pamela volunteered to do it.

'No problem, Gran. It saves you having to go out yourself.'

'I'm usually fine to go to the shops but I really don't like walking on icy roads. I think the fall I had when I broke my arms robbed me of confidence.'

'You're very wise. Even young ones like us have to be careful when it's icy outside. It's so easy to slip. Now, Gran, do you want me to make you a cup of tea?'

'Only if you're staying to have a cup with me, Pamela?'

'No, Gran, sorry I can't. I've to meet Norma outside the jeweller's in Nethergate, the one on the corner. I've to get her in ..' and she glanced at the clock on the mantelpiece, 'gosh I'll have to get a sprint on, as I've to be there in twenty minutes' time.'

'Oh, you'll make it in plenty of time. There's a bus due along here in less than ten minutes. So, what are you hoping to buy in town?'

'I need to get an outfit for our office Christmas night out.' Pamela worked in the office of D.C. Thomson, a well-respected publishing company in Dundee.

'And what about Norma?'

'She wants a new dress for her 6th year school dance.'

Viv smiled when she recalled her own school dances and office parties. Although such a long time ago, it only seemed like yesterday. A shadow passed over her face when she thought of her best friend in New Zealand, who'd come with her to these events and who had now passed on. But she smiled up at Pamela. 'I can hardly believe you're both at that stage now. It seems like yesterday you were down on the carpet at my feet playing with your dolls. Anyway, I better let you get off, love.'

Pamela pulled on her woolly hat and mitts and lifted her shoulder bag off the coffee table. 'How's Daryl enjoying himself?' her gran asked, when Pamela stooped to kiss her cheek. He'd been excited when he told Viv last week about his Aviemore trip.

'Mum got a text from him yesterday and he's loving it. They're on the ski slopes by day and in the pub at night.'

Viv chuckled. 'Good for him. Thanks again, darling, and take care on these roads.'

CHAPTER THIRTY

'You be good for Mrs Phillips,' I say to Smoky, as I run my hands over his fur and lay my cheek against his face.

'Smoky and I will get along just fine,' my neighbour assures me, as she takes him from me and gathers him into her arms.

I pull my case behind me towards the front gate and when I look back, she's stroking the top of his head. 'Bye,' I call, as Elva draws up at the gate.

She moves over to the passenger seat and I take her place behind the wheel. I'm driving for the first leg of the journey. 'Imagine, ten days away from routine,' she says, as we drive off in glorious sunshine from Wellington. Excitement is pulsing through both of us at the thought.

'Had a phone call from Mum last night. She's having a great time and wished us both a good holiday. I'm nervous leaving the house at the mercy of Nikau while I'm away. I love my brother dearly but, as you know, he's hopeless when it comes to running a house.' Elva turns towards me and grimaces. 'Fingers crossed he doesn't allow his mates to wreck the house in our absence.'

'You might be surprised at how well he copes when you aren't there,' I suggest.

'Maybe. I'll give us some air,' she says, and

stretches up to open the roof.

'Do we stay on this road for a bit longer?'

Elva looks down at the large-scale map draped over her knees. 'Take the second left from here and we'll be on the highway for Taumarunui.' She sighs. 'The next car I buy is going to have sat nav.'

With the car radio playing quietly, we drive up through Te Kuiti and Te Awamutu, drinking in the glorious scenery as we go. The broom is blossoming in profusion and gives a marvellous splash of yellow against the lush green grass. And, as we are never very far from the ocean in New Zealand, from time to time we get a glimpse of the water.

Just before five o'clock we reach Hamilton, where we have arranged our overnight stop. Elva, who is driving by now, turns into the car park of the Fountain Hotel in Ulster Street, the nymph fountain in the front garden reflecting the hotel's name. 'Looks not bad,' she says, and I nod in agreement. Neither of us has stayed here before; we booked it on the internet so are delighted that first impressions are good.

As we carry our overnight bags towards the entrance, the front door opens and a well-dressed young woman comes out, with her jacket draped over her arm. 'Hello,' she says, and holds the door open for us.

Inside, the proprietor, Mrs Alexander, greets us in the cool, leafy vestibule. The sun's rays, coming through the stained-glass windows on the front door panel, spread colourful patterns across the highly polished wooden floor. 'Did you have a good journey up from Wellington, girls?' she asks us, and immediately her Scottish accent reminds me of Gran.

'You're from Scotland,' I'm unable to resist saying, feeling my eyes mist up.

'Och, I've lived here for over forty years, lass, but you never lose your native tongue, do you?'

'No. My gran was here for years too and her accent never left her.'

'And why should it?' Mrs Alexander's smile encompasses us both and makes us feel like we are being wrapped in a warm blanket. 'Now, if you would just sign the register, girls, then I'll show you to your room.'

'This is lovely,' I say, when we enter the twin room on the second floor, 'and look, Elva, we can see the fountain from the window.'

Mrs Alexander beams at me. 'Glad you approve, lass. Now, if you girls get settled in quickly, there'll be time for you to come downstairs and have a wee cup of tea and a taste of my fruit bread to keep you going until dinner. The meal is at half past seven.'

'Thanks, that's very kind.' Elva unzips her bag and brings out what she needs for the overnight stay. I do the same while Mrs Alexander slips quietly out of the room.

Elva lays out fresh trousers and a top for tonight's dinner. 'Think we'll be well looked after by Mrs Alexander.'

I lay my nightwear on the bed under my pillow. 'Yes, but it's good that it's only an overnight stay, otherwise we'd put on weight with eating Mrs Alexander's home baking. What d'you say if I try and

146

ring Jill Patterson before dinner to arrange when we can see her during our stay?'

'Good idea,' Elva calls over her shoulder, as she disappears into the shower room.

CHAPTER THIRTY ONE

'I'm looking forward to getting to Auckland,' I say to Elva next morning, as she is driving us north, after a huge cooked breakfast that Mrs Alexander insisted we eat.

Elva checks in the mirror, indicates and moves lanes in the heavy tourist traffic. 'Yes,' she finally answers, 'I've always wanted to go there. We were always going to visit the northland when Dad was alive, but somehow we didn't get round to it.'

I sit back in my seat and look out at the well-fed sheep grazing in the fields. 'I expect it'll be more tropical in Auckland than back home in Wellington and warmer too. Think this is the crossroads where we go to the right,' I tell Elva, drawing my finger across the line on the map as I'm speaking.

'Yep, there's the sign for Pukekohe now.' Elva indicates and makes a right turn as soon as the traffic allows.

'How long do you think before we get to Auckland?'

'About another couple of hours, I reckon. Mind you, the roads are better than I'd anticipated.'

We fall silent once more and listen to the radio as we drive northwards. Elva's estimated couple of hours proves correct and we soon see the sign WELCOME TO AUCKLAND.

I trace where we are on the Auckland city map. 'If we drive along City Road and turn off when we come to Bracken Street, it should lead us to our hotel.' We've booked into the Skycity Hotel which, from the pictures on Google, looks luxurious.

Elva looks as impressed as I feel when we drive into the hotel car park. 'Fab,' she says, 'and even better that we got such a good deal on the accommodation.'

'Yep, I don't think we'd have been able to pay the normal price on our salaries.'

The receptionist, Morag, welcomes us to the hotel and sorts out all the paperwork for us. 'Do you want to book any tours while you're here? You get a discount on the fare because you're resident in the hotel.'

I glance at Elva. 'What do you think?'

'It sounds good. After all, we might never be here again.'

I turn back to Morag. 'We were hoping to drive up to Whangarei and visit the Kauri forest and also go to the Meeting House at' …..

'Waitangi,' Morag prompts, smiling at me.

I shrug my shoulders. 'Of course, I should have known the name as we got the history of the Treaty at school.'

'There's a trip going tomorrow that takes you to both the Kauri forest and the Meeting House. Would you like me to book you on it? It will leave from the front of the hotel at 9 am, directly after breakfast. No need to drive and you can relax on the coach.'

Elva throws her hands up in the air. 'Okay,

Morag, you've sold it to us.'

'Great. I'll give you seats near the front of the coach.'

I take my credit card out of my bag. 'Will I pay them on this, and you can give me your half back in cash?'

'Fine,' Elva nods, and wanders over to look at some of the leaflets lying on the far end of the reception desk, while I hand my card to Morag.

CHAPTER THIRTY TWO

'Max is quite entertaining,' Elva says of the driver, when we are drinking a cappuccino in a pavement café in Whangarei during our first stop on the bus tour.

'It's good he doesn't chat constantly. Some coach drivers are a bit OTT with info and jokes.' I check my watch. 'We don't board again for another twenty minutes. There should be time for a walk along the beach first.'

'I don't want a walk, I'd rather have a look around the shops.'

'No worries, you spend the time at the shops while I go down to the beach. We can meet back at the bus.' Decision made, we drain our cups and leave the café.

A short time later I stand on the beach and watch the surf. The wind down here is brisk, and it catches my breath at times. Turning to my left I spot a couple and their three young kids seated further along the beach, a windbreak pushed into the sand beside them for protection. I enjoy the spectacle of two of the children burying the third one in a sand grave, their shrieks as loud as mine used to be when Dad buried me in the sand at Lyall Bay.

Back on the coach, we drive to the Kauri forest. Max drops us in the coach park with instructions when to return. 'You have the option here of a guided tour in the forest or just doing your own thing,' he advises us, 'there are lots of signs to follow to save getting lost. You can consult the map on the leaflet I gave you. And please don't be late back at the coach so that we have enough time for our stop at Waitangi,' he requests.

'Will we wander on our own?' Elva asks me as we stroll with our fellow passengers towards the entrance to the forest.

'Yeah, probably best. Sometimes you can hardly make out what the guide is saying anyway.'

We show our tickets and pass through the turnstile. The forest is huge, and we enjoy exploring its many tracks that criss-cross one another, coming face to face with lots of native flora and fauna in the process.

When we reach the main attraction, we gaze up at the giant Kauri tree, reputed to be the largest in the country, and probably even abroad too. Elva puts her arms as far round the immense trunk as she can. 'Wonder how old you are?' she whispers to the giant.

'And how many stories could you tell us?'

'Spoken like a true journalist.' Elva laughs and takes her phone out of her bag. 'I'll take a picture of you beside the tree, Ros, to show the difference in size.'

'Would you like me to take one with you both in it?' a man's voice enquires. We turn around to face a man and woman coming down the track nearby.

'Yes, please,' Elva replies.

She gives him a smile of thanks when he hands the phone back to her once the photograph has been taken.

At our next stop, the Waitangi Meeting House, Max allows us two hours at leisure. We find The Meeting House well worth a viewing and the Maori Museum surpasses our expectations. The two of us stare for a long time at the Maori drawing called 'The Separation of Rangi the Sky Father and Papa the Earth Mother'.

Elva points to the figures in the drawing. 'You can see the pain on their faces at being pulled out of their embrace. It's strange that Papa is the Earth Mother, the name sounds more like it should be the Father.'

I nod and move closer to the drawing. 'Notice the light appearing between them as they are prised apart to create the earth below and sky above.' We move on to read other Maori Legends, such as Maui, the sun-tamer, and Kupe, the Polynesian explorer.

Before leaving the Museum, we read the interesting legend about Rona, the woman in the moon. The legend says that the moon descended from the sky and carried Rona away as a punishment for her cursing it, leaving her husband and children to mourn her loss.

'Do you want anything to eat?' Elva asks me, when we find a quiet corner table in the crowded restaurant.

'A drink would do me, especially remembering the huge portions at dinner last night.'

'Same here,' she says, and we order a soda water and lime from the bar.

The heat is building up on our return to Auckland and we're happy to sit with a cool drink at the side of the hotel pool.

CHAPTER THIRTY THREE

Jill lets out a whoop of joy as we get out of the taxi. She comes towards me and opens her arms for a hug, then gives Elva a kiss on the cheek. 'So glad you could come, and it's so good to see you again, Ros.' She stands aside and ushers Elva and me up the path ahead of her. 'Door's unlocked, just go in,' she calls to Elva who is in the lead.

Inside her unit, she shows us into her spacious kitchen, where a tall, slim woman stands at the sink washing a couple of mugs.

'This is Hazel, my next door neighbour,' Jill introduces her to Elva and me. 'Hazel will let an electrician into the house tomorrow while I'm down in Hamilton at a friend's birthday lunch.'

Hazel dries her hands on the towel hanging beside the sink before she comes over to say hello to us. 'I'll head off now, Jill, as my washing should be ready to peg out. Enjoy your catch up, girls, and the rest of your trip,' she says to us.

'Have you got my spare keys?' Jill calls after her neighbour.

In reply, Hazel holds the keys aloft and jingles them. 'See you later,' she says over her shoulder and closes the door gently behind her.

There is a tray set with tea things on the white scrubbed table and Jill immediately switches on the kettle 'Take a seat.'

Elva sits down at the table, while I go over to the large window, which runs along the entire length of one wall of the room. From here, there is a clear view of the beach.

'This is a view to die for,' I say to our hostess, my eyes drinking in the scene outside. 'I'd never get any housework done if my window looked on to this.'

Jill checks if we want tea or coffee. 'Do you want to sit in here, or would you prefer we go into the sitting room?'

Over tea, taken in the kitchen at our request, Jill is keen to hear about our trip so far. 'Have you been to the Meeting Place?'

'It was fantastic,' Elva tells her, as she reaches for another macaroon biscuit. 'So much history and the museum and kauri forest were also well worth a visit.'

Jill's smile encompasses us both. 'And what else have you done?'

'We had another day at Cape Reinga and drove along the Ninety Mile Beach.' Jill holds the teapot towards my mug, and I nod. She pours the tea and I add a little more milk. 'Yesterday we had a trip on a catamaran to Cape Brett and the Hole in the Rock,' I continue, stirring my tea.

'See any dolphins?' Jill asks as she tops up Elva's tea.

Elva beams at her. 'We sure did, we saw some bottlenose and some common dolphins. I could watch them all day, they're such fascinating creatures.'

We chatter on and then Jill comes up with an

idea. 'I thought we could have a drive this afternoon and I'll show you some of the sights of Auckland that aren't usually on the coach tour's programme. Then afterwards I'll treat you both to dinner at The Pines, one of my favourite eateries in the city centre. How does it sound?'

I give her a thumbs up. 'Sounds great, Jill, and kind of you to do this for us.'

'No worries. I'll clear these dishes and we can get off,' she says, pushing her chair away from the table. 'And if you girls want to inspect the plumbing, it's along the hall and second door on the right.'

Fifteen minutes later we're driving towards the first place of interest on Jill's tour, with me in the passenger seat beside her and Elva sitting behind me. The afternoon races by and we've built up an appetite by the time we reach The Pines.

There are lots of fish dishes and pastas on the menu but there is a wide variety of other cuisines too.

'This building used to be a branch of the ANZ bank in a previous life,' Jill tells us, once we've ordered.

'The conversion has been done well, hasn't it?' I stare up at the magnificent sculpture work around the cornicing, in tasteful shades of pale blue and gold. Some spectacular chandeliers are hanging from the high ceiling, giving the place a look of opulence. I especially like the way the tables are laid out around what was the tellers' booths, which is now a well-stocked bar.

Over our meal we discuss our jobs, with Jill

interested to hear of Elva's work at Wellington Hospital. I listen, pleased that my two friends seem comfortable in one another's company.

'So, what happens next when you leave Auckland tomorrow?' Jill asks us, during a lull in the conversation.

'We drive down to Rotorua, and visit the Movie Set for The Lord of the Rings on the way,' I tell her, 'then, after an overnight in Rotorua, we will go to Te Puia to see the boiling mud pools and geysers.'

'You'll enjoy that. The geysers are unique to this area. I think the only other ones might be in Iceland. And you'll see all the Maori kids in the mud pools. Tourists throw coins in and the children dive in after them.'

Elva smiles at her. 'I'm particularly keen to visit Rotorua because of my Maori ancestry. My dad was Maori, and my mum is Austrian. When Mum and Dad married, he broke away from his Maori roots as he wanted to become part of Mum's culture.'

Jill waits until the waiter refills our coffee cups before replying. 'So, you say your mum is Austrian but was she born in New Zealand?'

'Yes. My Austrian grandparents, who I remember clearly, came over here after the Second World War. They loved the country immediately, and said many areas, especially in the South Island, reminded them of their homeland.'

'And what about your Maori grandparents?' Jill holds out the plate of chocolate mints to me as she asks the question.

'Sadly, I've never met them, but I'd like to trace my ancestry on that side of the family. I might start the search when I get back home. I think Mum would be pleased to know about Dad's family before she dies.'

'You might find something about them while we are in Rotorua,' I butt in with the suggestion.

'Mmm. Perhaps.'

Jill makes a face. 'Well good luck with that. Maori ancestry can be very difficult to trace because of the lack of written records but hopefully you'll come up with something. If I can help you find anything through the Auckland Gazette, let me know,' she offers.

'Thanks,' Elva says, 'I might take you up on your offer.'

I look at my watch at that moment and am gobsmacked to see it's almost ten o'clock. 'Sorry to break up the party but I think we need to get back to the hotel, Elva.'

'Yes, we've still to pack our cases for tomorrow's departure.'

'Thanks for everything,' I say to Jill, when she drops us off at the hotel.

'Yes, you've been very kind,' Elva adds, 'and you must come down to Wellington soon so that we can return the hospitality.'

'I'd like that very much,' Jill says, and gives us both a hug. Then she gets back into her car and we wait outside the hotel entrance to wave her off.

CHAPTER THIRTY FOUR

'So how did you guys enjoy your trip?' Ted asks me, leaning back in his swivel chair, arms crossed, ready for a chin wag.

I take the files that await my attention out of my desk drawer, and leave them at my side. 'We had a fab time. The scenery in the north is breathtaking and the weather played fair too.'

'What did you enjoy most?'

'I loved the kauri forest, have wanted to go there for years. Rotorua was special for Elva, of course, with her Maori ancestry.'

'When did you get back?'

'Friday night. We left Rotorua after breakfast and took the Thermal Explorer Highway to Huka Falls and then on to Lake Taupo.'

'Taupo's one of Anne's favourites.'

'Yep, it was worth a visit. When we left there, we stopped off in Napier for something to eat and then drove down to Wellington without a break.'

'Hi, Ros,' Les, the mail courier, breaks into our conversation and limps over to my desk. When I first started at The Post, Les told me that his limp was the result of a war wound. Which war he didn't say, but he does look pretty ancient. He lays a couple of envelopes down on my desk, then lifts a pile of packages out of his trolley and sits them beside the letters. 'I don't think people write letters nowadays, all folk seem to do is order from Amazon.' He smiles. 'Enough of my grousing. How was the trip?'

'Great thanks.'

'How far north did you go?'

'We travelled as far north as we could,' I tell him, 'any further and we'd have landed in the sea.'

'But you liked Auckland?'

'Loved it, a beautiful city. Wouldn't mind living there.'

'But you couldn't leave all of us at The Post, you'd really miss us.'

Les pats my shoulder and moves over to Ted's desk, before pushing his mail trolley into Charlie's office.

I smile when I open the first letter on the pile.

'Good news?' Ted misses nothing.

'It's a thank you letter from Sheila Carter of the Community Trust. Because of the publicity my article gave them, they've had some extra funding from the Council.'

'Morning all,' Leggat says as he comes in. He hangs his wide-brimmed sunhat up on the coat rack and pulls off his sunglasses. 'How was your holiday, Ros?' he asks, and smiles at me.

'Great, thanks.' For once I don't mind having a conversation with him and I tell him about our travels. Am I thawing, I ask myself? I certainly don't feel the animosity I did previously. He seems different now, but I guess it's my feelings towards him that have changed rather than his behaviour.

Our conversation comes to an abrupt end when Charlie calls Simon into his office.

CHAPTER THIRTY FIVE

When Simon opened his eyes it took him a moment to remember where he was. Of course he was at home for Christmas. He'd arrived late last night to find that Mum had a banquet of food waiting for him. Having eaten at one of the service stations on the way down from Picton, this had taken the edge off his hunger, but he managed to stuff down some food lest he offend her.

Turning his head towards the window, he lay on his pillow and idly watched the sheep grazing on the hill behind the house. He and Jamie had loved living here at Lime Tree, so named because of the many Mexican limes surrounding the farmhouse. The scene of carnage from the past intruded into his happy mood, but he was determined to quell the sad thoughts. At least for today.

With his bedroom window open, he could hear the sound of his mother moving utensils and dishes around in the kitchen, accompanied by the delicious aroma of a fry up. He did enjoy breakfast at the farm and looked forward to having it served up to him on his visits home.

'How did you sleep, Son?' Yvonne asked, when he joined her shortly afterwards in the kitchen.

Simon yawned and raked his fingers through his tousled hair, then tightened the cord around his dressing gown. 'Great thanks, Mum. Didn't realise how done in

I was last night.'

Yvonne transferred the bacon and sausages on to a hot plate and cracked five eggs into the frying pan, two for each of the men and one for herself. 'It's a long journey down from Wellington. Bound to tire you out.' When the toast popped up, she put in on to the rack and carried it over to the table.

Ron's large, sunburned frame filled the doorway. His black and white collie, Susie, squeezed round the side of Ron's leg and went over to her feeding bowl in the far corner of the kitchen.

'Morning, Son. Hope I didn't waken you when I went out this morning?'

'No worries, Dad, I was dead to the world.'

Ron rubbed his hands. 'Smells fantastic, love,' he said to his wife, 'I'm starving.'

'I'm sure you are, you were out well before dawn.' Yvonne smiled first at her husband and then her son, happy to have them both with her at this Festive time. A cloud passed over her face as she thought of the missing family member, but she quickly dismissed any sad thoughts.

Simon sat next to his dad at the table, with his mother facing him. Next to her, as always, was the place mat and cutlery laid out for Jamie. Despite the years that had gone by since Jamie died, Yvonne still included him in their midst. Simon thought it was a bit spooky but he'd come to accept it over the years. It seemed to bring comfort to Mum and that was all that mattered.

Sitting down with his parents for his welcome

fry up, Simon felt that the only thing to better this was if Ros had been with them. He didn't think there was much hope of that happening any time soon, although he had been aware of a recent thaw taking place in their relationship. The day before he stopped work to come home, Ros told him that she planned to spend Christmas day with her friend Elva's family.

'So how are things at work?' Yvonne asked him, as though she'd been reading his thoughts.

'Fine thanks, Mum,' he said, spreading butter on another slice of toast while he proceeded to tell them about life at The Post.

***

'We can use my car, Dad,' Simon offered that afternoon, when they were getting ready for a barbecue at Beltrees, their neighbours' farm.

'Right, Son.' Ron willingly agreed, putting some bottles of wine into the chiller bag. 'Good on ya, that way I can down a few beers with Wilf.'

Wilf and Moira Stanhope owned a massive property with some 14,000 sheep, much larger than Lime Tree. It felt like the two couples had been friends for ever, and Simon had gone to school with Wilf's daughter, Claire, who was now Assistant Manager in the ANZ bank in Dunedin.

His father got into the passenger seat beside Simon, while Yvonne sat behind them, with the food and wine on the seat beside her. Simon drove along the familiar track to Beltrees, a journey he'd done so often in the past that he could almost do it with his eyes closed.

'Claire came home yesterday. She's managed to get holidays over the Festive period and doesn't go back to work until 2nd January.'

Simon was aware why his mother was talking about Claire. For years she'd been keen that he and Claire would marry. He'd told her that they were just good pals, but she still clung to her hopes.

'It'll be good to see Claire and her parents again,' he replied, attempting to keep his wheels out of the potholes on this country track. 'Time some repairs were done to this road,' he said, 'it's worse than the last time I drove to Beltrees.'

'The Roads Department don't worry about us out in the sticks,' Ron grumbled, 'the government want our votes, and our taxes, but don't give a damn about the state of the area.'

When they reached Beltrees, Moira came out into the yard and waved. By the time they got out of the car, Wilf had joined her. After hugs all round, Moira held Simon's hands in hers.

'Can't remember when I last saw you, Simon. It must be at least a couple of years. Claire's so excited at the thought of spending time with you.'

Simon tried to stop himself from laughing out loud because she sounded so like his mother. He knew that Mum and Moira had both schemed to make Claire and him an item. But they were pals, no more, no less. He could never think of Claire as anything more than a childhood playmate, almost a sister, and he was sure it was the same for her.

'Hello, stranger.' Her voice came from behind

him and when he turned around Claire was holding out her arms to him. They hugged tightly and she clung to him for a few seconds before turning to greet his parents.

'Right, let's go and join the others,' Wilf said. 'The Fergusons and the Martins are with us today.'

'Great,' Yvonne said, 'it'll be good to hear Tom's yarns.' Tom Martin had a treasure trove of anecdotes which he loved to share with his friends.

They joined the party, out on the decking at the back of the farmhouse, and Wilf filled their glasses. Yvonne sat at a table with Freda Martin and Joan Ferguson, catching up with all their doings. The three women, along with Moira, were members of the Women's Rural during the winter time and missed the contact during the summer. Yvonne smiled when she noticed Claire and Simon were together at another table. She sent up a silent hallelujah and left fate to do the rest.

Yvonne broke off from the conversation at one point to catch hold of Moira's arm when she was passing their table. 'I see you have a new home for the chooks,' she said, pointing to the sturdily-built henhouse positioned against the fence. The chickens were scratching around on the ground nearby, scavenging for any tasty morsel they could find.

'Yes, Wilf made it during a quieter spell on the farm.'

'But that's as far as my input goes,' Wilf called from the nearby table where the men were ensconced, 'it's Moira's domain, not mine.'

'But you enjoy the eggs they produce,' Moira countered, laughing. 'Claire's a good help with the chickens when she's home,' she added, looking fondly at the sight of Claire and Simon chatting together. Yvonne saw her own thoughts mirrored on Moira's face, and it felt good to have an ally in the matchmaking business.

'Grubs up,' Wilf, wearing an apron and a chef's hat, called shortly afterwards, and the appetising smells and sizzles from the barbecue confirmed his words.

After their meal, the dancing started. Alan Ferguson had brought along his fiddle and, with accompaniment from Tom's mouth organ, the music started while the wine flowed freely. They took turns to dance in couples, even managing an eightsome reel at one stage.

It was a merry crowd who, reluctantly, made tracks for home, with a promise to meet up again over the coming few days.

'Great day, wasn't it?' Yvonne voiced all their thoughts on the journey back to Lime Tree. She tapped Simon's back. 'You and Claire seemed to be getting on well.'

Simon looked into his driving mirror and smiled at her. 'Yes, we're good pals,' he said, stressing the last word. But she isn't Ros were the words he left unsaid.

CHAPTER THIRTY SIX

I have a late breakfast this morning. Smoky, wearing his crimson sparkly collar he got from Santa, sits on my knee while I drink my second cup of coffee. For the next few hours, we chill out on the deck, my nose in a book while he pursues his favourite pastime of chasing the birds.

At about one o'clock, I stir myself and dress in my new white trousers and dark blue lacy top. I leave out some water and treats for Smoky. Mrs Phillips next door has her sister staying with her over the Festive Season and the two ladies are more than happy to feed him later on today.

I leave at two o'clock and drive over to Brooklyn, listening to Christmas Carols on the car radio. My eyes become moist when I hear a children's choir singing 'Away in a Manger.' The young voices always have this effect on me; whether you are a believer or not their beautiful sound is hard to resist.

I'm staying over at Elva's so that I can enjoy a Christmas drink without worrying about organising a taxi ride home. I've been low in spirits in the lead up to Christmas, my second one without Gran, and am happy to be spending the day with the Kahui family.

The road is deserted as I drive along the coast from Lyall Bay, with the pohutukawas glinting in the sunshine. Most of the traffic lights are at green and the first time I'm stopped on red is just before I take a left turn towards Brooklyn.

As I wait for the light to change, I cast my mind back to Christmas day, 2016. I was still shell-shocked at that time following Gran's death eight weeks earlier. Despite Elva urging me to join them for Christmas dinner, I decided to spend the day on my own at Kiwi Crescent.

It proved to be a miserable time and I wept for hours on end. When Elva invited me this year, I jumped at her offer.

Engrossed in my thoughts, I realise I've missed the traffic light sequence. Fortunately, there are no cars behind me, so I wait patiently for the green light to re-appear. While I'm sitting there, I begin to think of Simon, and I find myself missing him. I must be going soft in my old age, as I'm sure that he won't be giving me a second thought.

'Welcome Ros, so happy you can join us,' Elva greets me at her front door, then stands back to let me enter.

'Happy Christmas, Elva,' I say and give her a hug. I put my parcels, wrapped in bright Christmas paper, on the hall table, ready for the exchange of gifts after dinner.

'Ros, how lovely.' Mrs Kahui's voice reaches me through the open patio door.

Nikau lopes indoors, a cooking apron over his shorts and t-shirt. He plants a kiss on my cheek. 'Good to see you, Ros.' Elva and I follow him out on to the decking and he returns to the barbie to turn the steaks and sausages. My appetite sharpens with the delicious smell of food wafting over.

'It's beaut to join you all,' I say, and take a seat beside Mrs Kahui at the table, where we are shaded by the large kowhai tree. 'It gets lonely in Lyall Bay.'

'Sure it does,' she replies, smiling at me. 'Why would you want to be alone at Christmas? Have a noggin',' she invites me, then pours a large glass of Chardonnay.

'Come and get it,' Nikau calls to us a few minutes later.

We've eaten our fill and I'm drinking my second cup of coffee when the front doorbell rings.

'I'll get it,' Elva says, standing up and padding, barefoot, towards the front door.

'It'll be Adam,' Mrs Kahui tells me, 'Elva said he'd probably call round after having Christmas dinner with his family.'

'Oh good, I'll get to meet him at last.'

'Have you not met him yet?' Nikau sounds surprised.

I shake my head but before I can say anything, Elva comes out on to the deck, followed by a tall, well-built guy, his dark hair greying at the sides. 'It's Adam come to join us,' she announces, unnecessarily. 'Nikau, get a lager for Adam, or would you prefer wine?' she asks her boyfriend.

'Lager's fine thanks, Nikau,' Adam says and bends to kiss Mrs Kahui's cheek. 'Happy Christmas.'

'And to you, Adam,' she replies, then turns to me. 'This is Ros.'

'Hi, Ros,' he greets me and gives me a peck on the cheek too, then he and Elva join us at the table.

'Anyone fancy a walk in the forest?'Nikau suggests, once we've all had a snooze on the deck and have recovered from the large amount of food we've consumed.

'I'm up for it,' I tell him. There is an area of forest behind their house and Elva and I have enjoyed walks through it in the past.

Elva and Adam are keen to join us. 'What about you, Mum?' Elva asks.

Her mother laughs, her ample bosom heaving. 'Not me, liebling, but you four go and enjoy a walk. I'll be perfectly happy here sitting in the shade with my book and my wine. We can all have coffee and Christmas cake when you get back and maybe play a game of cards.'

Although it's late in the afternoon, the sun is still hot and we are grateful to walk under the canopy of trees. Shadows fall across the dried up forest path and ahead of us the branches touch and kiss from their positions on either side of the path. We walk through this cathedral of trees, before beginning our descent to the open valley below.

I have an interesting chat with Adam on the way down and begin to feel I have misjudged him as he seems to be head over heels in love with Elva.

Before we know it, we are rounding the corner into Ohiro Road once more, looking forward to our cake and cards.

CHAPTER THIRTY SEVEN

Viv stood in front of the mirror to put on her new hat, bought especially for today. It was a beret style, with a skip at the front, and she pulled it down at one side at a jaunty angle.

'You'll do,' she told her reflection and went off to the bedroom to fetch her gloves. Just then, the phone rang, and she hurried, as quickly as she could these days, to answer before the caller hung up.

'Happy Christmas, Aunt Viv.' Ros' bright tones reached her from the other side of the world, where it was now late evening.

'And the same to you, Ros. Have you enjoyed your day?' Viv cleared the newspapers off her chair and sat down as she was speaking.

'Very much. I spent the day with Elva and her family. We had a barbie in the garden and a walk in the forest later. What about you, how will you be spending Christmas day?'

Viv laughed. 'Our weather certainly won't allow us to eat out in the garden but I'm looking forward to having dinner with the family.'

'Do you have snow?'

'No snow as yet although there is a forecast of some over the next few days. It's bitterly cold today, with a very grey sky. The opposite of your weather.'

'Never mind, Aunt Viv, you'll enjoy being with

the family. By the way, thank you for the lovely gift and card you sent me.'

'You're welcome, lass, and thanks for yours too. The scarf is gorgeous and the mustard colour matches my new hat. I'll be wearing both today.'

'That's great. I wasn't sure about the colour so I'm pleased it suits.'

Viv heard the latch on the gate open and from where she sat, she could see Daryl striding down the path. 'Here's Daryl come to collect me,' she told Ros, as her grandson opened the front door with his key.

'I'll let you go then, Aunt Viv, and please wish Daryl and the family a happy Christmas from me.'

'Will do, love. That's Ros saying happy Christmas to you, Daryl,' she informed him, when he came into the living room.

'Happy Christmas, Ros,' he called out, loud enough for her to hear.

'Bye and thanks for ringing,' Viv said, before she replaced the receiver.

***

'Thanks, Daryl, I've had a wonderful day with you all.' Viv smiled up at her grandson as he opened the passenger door for her.

'Glad to hear it, Gran,' he said, taking her arm to help her into the house. He waited until she'd switched on the lamps in the front room and put her outdoor clothes into the wardrobe before he left.

Once Daryl had gone, Viv switched on her electric blanket, humming a Christmas carol they'd heard earlier in the day. Her granddaughters had organised an after-dinner quiz, which Viv enjoyed. Her failure about pop groups and modern songs had been offset by her vast historical knowledge. Their team didn't cover themselves in glory, but they hadn't been shamed either.

Instead of a cup of tea before bed, Viv decided to pour herself a brandy and dry ginger. She rarely touched alcohol nowadays, especially not on her own, but she reminded herself it was Christmas, so what was the harm?

Returning to the front room, cosy thanks to the central heating, she settled herself into her armchair. She put her feet up on the stool and spread a tartan rug over her legs.

With a glass in her hand, she leaned back to watch the Christmas day episode of Coronation Street, which she'd left to video while she was out.

CHAPTER THIRTY EIGHT
2018

When I get to the writing group this afternoon, there are eight of us, so we push the two tables together and spread ourselves out. There are the usual six members, plus Pauline, who writes both poetry and short stories, and Harry, who produces some gruesome crime novels.

'Let's start with your piece, Harry,' Jus suggests.

By the time it gets to my turn to comment, most of what I've been thinking about the story has been said. 'I agree with what everyone else has said, Harry, and you certainly haven't disappointed, if you wanted to scare the living daylights out of us. I'd be terrified to go to bed after reading this chapter.'

Harry responds to all the feedback by telling us about some of the next lot of gruesome delights that are in store for us.

'Right,' Jus goes on, 'we'll take yours next, Ros.'

'I found this an excellent opening chapter, really draws the reader in,' Phil says, when he starts off the feedback. 'Nicole is a strong character and I know her already. I don't think Rick's right for her and feel sorry for John's lack of success in winning her over, but I'm sure they will get together in the end. There's nothing I would alter in this chapter and I encourage you to continue with the story.'

Delighted to hear Phil's praise of my work, I scan the faces around the table and see nods of agreement from the other members.

Nat, who's next to comment, looks across the table and gives me a smile. 'I agree with Phil, Ros. You've set the scene well for the reader and the hook at the end of the chapter makes us want to read on.' She has a coughing fit and takes a drink of water before continuing. 'Rick's definitely hiding a secret and I'm keen to find out what it is, but I suspect you'll keep us guessing until nearer the end of the book. I'm not sure about the title 'Cruel Minds' but maybe once we read more it will become clearer.'

'You next, Harry,' Jus says.

Harry grins. 'I suspect Rick has murdered his wife and cut her up into pieces, so hopefully Nicole won't fall under his spell.' Once our laughter has died down at this typical Harry plot, he adds, 'I like your style of writing Ros and think you should continue with the story.'

I receive equally constructive feedback from the others and, to my surprise and delight, even Marcus is supportive of my writing.

'Thank you all for your feedback,' I say, when it's my turn to respond to the crits I've received. 'This is my first attempt to write a novel. It's a first draft and to receive such positive comments will motivate me to continue and I'll submit the next chapter in two weeks' time.' I look over at Nat. 'I'm not too happy about the title either, so it could be changed later. I'm open to suggestions.'

'I'm not sure about Mark's reaction to his step-sister,' I say to Pauline, when I'm giving her my feedback, 'don't you think he'd be much angrier about the way she's treated his mother?'

Pauline nods slowly. 'Yes, I see what you mean. I hadn't noticed that when I was writing it, but now you've brought it up, I think you're right.' Pauline has been missing from the writers' group for the past few meetings and we're all glad that she has returned, especially as she produces some excellent work.

'This is what's great about attending here,' Jus says. 'We all get so much benefit from what our colleagues pick up that we overlook in our own work. Have you got some feedback for Pauline, Lauren?' he asks our youngest member.

'I really liked the piece, Pauline,' Lauren tells her, 'I don't have anything I can suggest to improve it and can't wait to read the next part you send us.' Lauren has gained a lot of confidence by coming to the group and I'm glad to note that she is standing up more to Marcus and his bullying tactics. I wait for him to put in his cent's worth, but he seems quite happy with what Pauline has written.

'Will we go for a coffee?' Nat asks me, when we are all packing up our bags for off.

'Good idea.' Nat and I both find it helpful to exchange our ideas for our stories.

Jus arranges a date for the next meeting then, as a group, we part company at the school entrance. Once Nat and I decide on a coffee venue, I get into my

Toyota and follow her Nissan out of the car park.

CHAPTER THIRTY NINE

I'm checking something on the Internet when Charlie pops his head around his office door and calls to us. 'Simon, Ros, can you both come in here, please?'

Simon carries his paper cup into the room with him and, clicking to come out of Google, I follow him, feeling like a naughty schoolgirl being summoned to the Headmistress's room. Sunlight coming through the vertical blinds covering the large picture window casts a stripy reflection across the surface of Charlie's desk.

Leaning his elbows on the desk, the boss clasps his hands in front of his face and waits until we are both seated before he speaks. 'I want you two to go over to Christchurch and find out about the supermarket scandal there. I've been impressed by your work, Ros, and before I let you loose on your own assignments, you can work with Simon on this one.'

'Thanks, boss.' I've read about the scam and there was a report about it on television the other day. The Farm Steadings Limited, a supermarket chain in the South Island, has been accused of selling offal and other inferior cuts of meat under the guise of top New Zealand lamb.

I throw a swift glance at Simon, who looks happy about the prospect of us going together. Recently I've found him less irritating so maybe working together won't be so bad.

'It's certainly worth a write up,' Simon says. 'My father's angry by what it will do to New Zealand's reputation. Dad prides himself on rearing top quality stock and, along with some of the other farmers in the area, he's put in a strong protest to the Farmers' Union.'

'When do you want us to go, boss?' I'm hoping Charlie will give us time to pack a case and maybe set off tomorrow.

But my luck's out.

'I want you to go today. You couldn't make the ten o'clock ferry but you can aim for the one o'clock.'

I try to remember what clothes are in the washing basket and hope I've got something suitable to wear in the evening. Before I can think any more, Charlie speaks again. 'One car will be sufficient, no point in paying for transporting two cars over on the ferry,' he says, with an eye on the company budget.

'I'll drive,' Simon volunteers before I can reply. 'I'll pick you up Ros in time to get to the ferry terminal for about 12.30.'

Anger rushes through me, feeling that he is trying to control me. I'm about to argue but the boss gets in first. 'Good, that's sorted then. I'll book you both into the Columbo Lodge in Christchurch, the hotel we always use.'

I've no option but to go along with the plan, since Charlie's obviously happy with the arrangement. At least I can relax and let someone else take the strain.

'Find something to make a good headline,' Charlie calls after us, when we are heading back to the main office.

Ted's speaking on the phone when I get back to my desk. 'Where are you off to?' he asks, when he hangs up and sees me collecting my jacket and handbag.

'Christchurch. Charlie will fill you in.'

Simon saunters over. 'Will I pick you up around midday?' he offers, 'then we can have lunch in the ferry café before we buy our tickets.'

'Okay by me,' I reply, and we walk together towards the lift.

***

After my case is packed, I see Mrs Phillips hanging out her washing and call to her over the fence.

'Mrs P, I've to go to Christchurch at short notice, to be exact at lunchtime. I'll be away for two or three days. Do you think you could see to Smoky for me?'

'Of course, Ros, you know I love looking after him.'

'Thanks so much, Mrs P. You're a star. Be back soon, Smoky,' I say to my pet but he turns his back on me. 'That cat's almost human, he knows I'm going off to leave him.'

'Don't you worry, Ros, he and I will get along just fine,' she calls after me, when I go back indoors to lock my case.

***

Simon picks me up at twelve noon. We become caught up in heavy traffic and he turns on the radio to while away the time, keeping the volume low. 'I'd like to meet up with my friend Trev and his wife when I'm in Christchurch,' I tell him. 'Don't want to put you under any pressure to come with me but I'm sure they'd make you welcome.'

'I'd be happy to come.' The cars in front of us move and we head off once more, but very soon afterwards come to a halt again. 'Is Trev the guy you met at the seminar in Wanganui?' Simon asks me, drumming his fingers on the steering wheel.

'Yes. He works with the Christchurch Herald. I think he knows some people you do.'

He stops drumming and looks round at me while we are still stationary. 'Might be interesting to chat with him,' he says, and begins to hum along to the tune on the radio.

'One thing though, Simon, I don't want you to grill Trev about the scandal. I'll be visiting him as a friend, not to get information from him.'

'Message received.'

We put on another spurt, only to stop yet again. Simon groans and shakes his head. 'I'm going to take the next street on the right, think it might be a shortcut to the terminal.'

We reach the terminal with about ten minutes to spare and there is already a long line of vehicles waiting to board the ferry. 'I guess we'd better join the queue,' Simon says, and we drive into our place. 'So much for my idea of eating at the café before we board.'

'No worries, we can grab something on board.' No sooner have I spoken than we sight the ferry coming into view. The vessel draws nearer and its bulk looms over us. In no time, the Silver Streak berths. 'These new ferries are so comfortable,' Simon tells me, 'much better than the old Aranui and her sister ship that used to cross the strait.'

'I've only been on the Aranui once, when I went to the South Island with my gran. I was fourteen at the time.'

On the ferry, we head downstairs to the diner. 'It's too nice a day to be stuck inside,' I suggest, 'what about buying a sandwich and going up on deck?'

Simon agrees and we find seats on the Port side, where we eat lunch. Shortly afterwards, we hear the clatter of the chains being loosened and feel a juddering sensation under our feet as the engine springs into life. The ferry slides away from the dock and gradually picks up speed.

Once out in the Cook Strait, we stand together at the rail, staring at the magnificent scenery of our homeland. I'm enjoying the breeze and notice that some of Simon's dark curls are blowing across his forehead. When a desire comes over me to draw my fingers through his curls, I remind myself that this is work and not a date.

The Silver Streak lives up to its name and we have a speedy and safe crossing into Picton harbour. On the drive through Blenheim and Kaikoura to Christchurch, we make little conversation, instead listening to the radio.

'Will you use your sat nav to find the hotel?' I ask, when we come into the outskirts of the city.

'No need.'

'Of course, I'm forgetting you used to live in Christchurch.'

By the time we draw up in front of the Colombo Lodge, we're both feeling jaded and hungry. Inside, the foyer is cool and inviting. Some healthy looking plants sit on the floor, with a couple on the desk top.

'How can I help you?' the receptionist asks, giving us a friendly smile. From the badge on her smart navy jacket, I see that her name is Mandy.

'We're from the Wellington Post,' Simon says, 'we're booked in for two nights.'

'Oh yes, Charlie phoned me. I've got your rooms ready, they're on the second floor. Dinner will be served in an hour.' She hands us our key cards and we head over to the lift.

'I'll knock your door in an hour,' Simon says, when we reach my room, and he continues along the corridor to find his.

My room is bright and spacious, with twin beds. The French windows are open, the net curtains blowing gently in the soft breeze. Out on the verandah, I have a view over the garden, with a row of tall trees standing sentinel in front of the back fence. Some bright red and purple flowering bushes on either side of the garden completes the feeling of privacy.

Thinking that this room will do nicely, I lay out something suitable to wear for dinner, then make my way into the en suite to inspect the plumbing.

CHAPTER FORTY

Viv climbed upstairs when she boarded the distinctive maroon-coloured double-decker bus in Princes Street. Despite her slow gait and the need of a walking stick, the effort of going to the top deck of the bus was worth it for the superb view along the capital's main shopping street.

Once seated, she turned her head towards Edinburgh Castle, built she understood on the site of an extinct volcano. From her seat on the bus she watched a line of tourists, snaking their way up the winding road. She'd scrambled up there herself as a teenager, past the volcanic rocks scattered over the slope beneath the castle.

Her eyes followed the buildings on the Royal Mile, standing out against the skyline. The road ran from the castle down past the decorative dome of St Giles' Cathedral to the magnificent architecture of Holyrood Palace at the bottom. She'd had a tour of Holyrood last year and enjoyed a wander through the extensive grounds and glorious gardens. Daryl, who'd driven her to the Palace, had treated her to afternoon tea in the Holyrood café after their tour.

Viv loved coming to Edinburgh. Her pleasure over her early visits as a young girl, accompanied by her parents, had never waned and she spent a day in the capital as often as she could. It was easy and inexpensive, thanks to her Concessionary Travel Pass. This pass allowed her to travel free over the length and breadth of Scotland.

This bus, the No 22, took Viv through the old part of Leith, with its built-up streets lined by tenements, the kind of buildings that featured in many of the Rebus books that Viv had read over the years. She'd also enjoyed watching, first John Hannah and later Ken Stott, playing the part of John Rebus in the TV programmes, created from Ian Rankin's books. Later in their journey, the bus went through the more recently built Leith Marina area, where there were sumptuous flats and trendy shops and cafés.

Viv got off the bus at Ocean Terminal, where she trawled her way round the stores until, feeling her energy level drop, she found a window table in her favourite restaurant.

She placed her carrier bag, containing the shoes and matching handbag she'd treated herself to, under the table at her feet. While waiting for her vegetable lasagne to be brought to the table, Viv spent some time on her favourite pastime of people watching. She loved to guess why they were here and where they were going afterwards. In her mind she created fascinating stories about them and often thought she could have forged a career for herself as a fiction writer.

The Royal Yacht Britannia was berthed on the dock below the window. Having been decommissioned some years ago, it was now a popular tourist attraction. She'd been toying with the idea of inviting Ros over for a visit, and it crossed her mind that she could take the girl for a tour of the Britannia.

Since her gran's death, Ros had kept in close touch with her, and Viv hoped she'd take up the invitation to visit. She'd enjoy showing the girl around the Dundee area, as well as some of the places where her gran had lived. She also has some special items belonging to her gran that she'd pass on to Ros.

While Viv was eating her lasagna, she was smiling at the thought of introducing Ros to Daryl, a thought which rekindled the notion of them falling in love. Ever since they were children, Viv had nurtured this hope, and her romantic nature flourished once more.

Aware that there was a bus leaving Ocean Terminal at 3.15 pm, she signalled to the waitress for her bill. She needed to get on her way if she was to catch the 4 pm bus to Dundee.

CHAPTER FORTY ONE

On arriving at the Farm Steadings supermarket after breakfast, Simon parks as near as possible to the building and we walk towards the main entrance.

'Look, over there, near the dustbin,' Simon says, nudging me with his elbow. 'That girl's wearing a supermarket uniform, let's see if she'll talk to us.'

I see the girl standing beside the bin, smoking a cigarette. She tilts her head back and blows rings of smoke into the air above her. It's a long time since I've seen anyone doing that, as most smokers are now on to the new vaping type. The girl's hair is pushed back into a roll, her face framed with wispy strands that have come loose. She's wearing high-heeled shoes with pointed toes; I'm sure they can't be comfortable if she's on her feet all day.

By the time Simon and I get closer to her, she's stubbing out her cigarette end in the tray on top of the bin.

'Enjoying a break away from the buzz inside?' Simon has to raise his voice over the noise of customers entering and exiting the supermarket. He flashes the girl a smile as he's speaking and she grins back, her eyes taking me in too.

'Yeah, it's hectic in the store today and I've been kept busy at the check-outs. Good to get a break for some fresh air now and again.'

I bite back my desire to suggest that she is polluting the fresh air she's seeking. I check her name on the badge pinned to her dark blue uniform. 'Sandra,' I say, just as a woman passes us, pushing a squeaky trolley laden with goods, 'I wonder if we could speak to you about the store's problem with the lamb products.'

Sandra looks uncomfortable and edges back from me. 'I don't know, em, we aren't supposed to speak to anyone about that. Are you from the Press?'

I nod and give Sandra a friendly smile. 'We're from The Wellington Post. I'm Ros Mathieson and this is my colleague, Simon Leggat. We'd be grateful if you could spare us a few minutes of you time?'

'Sorry, but I can't ...' Sandra apologises and begins to turn away.

'But it would just be an informal chat,' Simon butts in. He smiles again and gently steers her away from the entrance where it is quieter. 'I'm sure you could tell us something about what's been happening. Even what you've heard on the grapevine. What harm is there in that?'

'And don't worry,' I assure her, 'we won't mention your name in our report. It's purely a chat, nothing official.'

The idea of being anonymously involved in our reporting seems to appeal to Sandra. Our friendly approach has done the trick and, after only a moment's hesitation, she tells us what she's heard from various sources around the store. With her permission, I record our conversation on my phone.

'Thanks a lot, Sandra,' Simon says, when she

draws to a halt, 'you've been most helpful.'

A worried frown crosses Sandra's face. 'You won't let it be known that I spoke to you? I mean, I wouldn't want my name in the newspapers. I don't think my line Manager would be too happy about that.'

I give her a reassuring smile. 'Don't worry, Sandra, as I told you earlier, we will simply say 'a source at the store told us'. It occurs to me that most of what she told us was just staff gossip anyway.

Sandra nods her thanks and scurries back to her check-out.

'Why don't we buy a coffee in the store café? I suggest, pushing my phone back into my handbag. 'We might get a chatty assistant.'

Simon makes a face. 'I couldn't drink another coffee after the three cups I had at breakfast, but I suppose I could have a cold drink.' The café's quiet and while we're placing our order, Simon makes some small talk with the girl behind the counter.

'Can you give us any information about the lamb scandal at the store?' he says, once he's got her interest.

'Fraid not, the coffee shop is a franchise and we don't have anything to do with the store.'

'No worries.' Simon picks up our tray and we move over to a table at the window.

'Well that was a waste of time,' I say, as we sit down.

'Let's go and see if we can get one of the Managers to open up before we visit the Head Office,' Simon suggests, when we leave the café. We stop at the

Customer Service Desk and Simon speaks to the female assistant on duty. 'Any chance of a word with one of the store managers?'

'I'll find out,' she tells him, and speaks into the store phone behind her.

'Harvey will be with you shortly,' she says, then returns to her paperwork, leaving us standing near the desk.

A few minutes later a tall chap approaches us. I hold my breath. He's a dead ringer for Mark Pietersson, my favourite New Zealand tennis player. 'Hi, how can I help you guys?'

Simon has elected me to turn on the charm, while he records the conversation. But Harvey's not such a pushover as Sandra and clams up when he realises what we're after.

'Sorry, love,' he says, speaking directly to me and ignoring Simon, 'but I'm not prepared to speak to reporters about a matter that is still ongoing. Best you go now,' he adds, indicating towards the exit doors. Although he appears outwardly pleasant, there's a menacing tone in his voice. We take his advice and make ourselves scarce.

Once outside again, Simon frowns and shakes his head. 'Well that's got us nothing, apart from the gossip Sandra gave us.'

'Still, we can make use of some of the things she told us, even though it's all hearsay.'

'Don't think the boss will be too keen on hearsay, think he's looking for some hard facts.'

Simon drives us from the supermarket straight to

the Farm Steadings' Head Office in Bridge Street. On entering, our senses are hit by the smell of polish in the wood panelled foyer. The gleaming tiled floor and marble finished counter adds to the sense of opulence.

'Guess their profits are doing well,' Simon murmurs, as the pair of us make our way over to the reception desk. 'Good morning,' he says to the receptionist, his manner friendly, 'my colleague and I are from The Wellington Post and we were hoping to have a word with one of your senior staff about the recent problem you've been experiencing with lamb products.'

The woman shakes her head and replies in a firm voice. 'I don't think anyone would speak to you about that as the case is still ongoing and has been referred to the Courts.'

'An interview would give your side of the story to the public,' Simon cajoles. 'Might help your case.'

'A moment, please,' the woman says in a clipped tone, and turns her back on us.

I look at Simon and raise my eyebrows, giving a thumbs down as to our prospects of getting the desired information.

He grimaces but isn't for giving up yet.

We can hear the woman speaking on the phone and when she hangs up, she turns around to face us. 'At the moment there is no one from the management team available to speak to you. As I said before, the Courts are now involved in the matter.' Her expression leaves us in no doubt that, as far as she's concerned, the interview is closed.

But Simon's in no mood to be fobbed off so easily. 'But would there be someone in authority who could speak to us tomorrow? We can come back then.'

Sighing, the woman looks at her computer screen. After a few minutes on the keyboard she says, 'I think if you returned tomorrow about 10 am one of the managers might be in the office. But I can't promise he will grant you an interview.'

'That's fine, we'll come back tomorrow. Thank you for your help.' Simon keeps his voice pleasant and his manner affable. When we're walking towards the exit doors, he turns to me. 'Not available my foot, the correct word is not willing.'

We drive to one of the city centre car parks. From there we cross the street and walk along the side of the River Avon which flows through Christchurch. Even though we're well into autumn by now, there are quite a few punts on the river. We watch the spectacle for a time, shrieks of laughter from the occupants of the boats drifting up to us in the still air. I close my eyes and listen to the soft splash of the oars dipping into the water.

'Hungry?' Simon asks. 'What about a snack?'

I nod and look behind us towards the main road. 'I noticed a couple of cafés further along Bridge Street on our way to the car park.'

'I've got a better idea. Why don't we buy a carry-out burger and coffee and find a seat on the riverside. It's warm enough today to eat al fresco.'

'Good thinking. You go and buy lunch while I find a bench for us.'

Simon heads off and I find the ideal spot further along the path from where we'd been standing. I park myself on the seat, shaded from the sun by the overhanging branches of some nearby trees. The riverside's busy, obviously a popular spot for workers to spend their lunch breaks, so I'm lucky to have found an empty bench.

In no time at all Simon appears with lunch, and we people watch as we eat.

'Peaceful, isn't it?' Simon murmurs, tucking into his cheeseburger with gusto.

I've a few crumbs left from my chicken burger, which I toss on to the grass, soon to be scavenged by some bellbirds pecking away at the grass verges. A fight ensues between the two largest birds. 'I adore the bellbird's song. Elva told me their Maori name is korimako,' I say, partly to myself and not expecting, nor receiving, an answer from Simon.

Just then a young couple with a toddler come along the path. 'Birdies, birdies,' the little girl calls out and excitedly claps her hands at the birds, who instantly fly off. 'You've chased the birds away, Yvette,' the child's mother says, while the father holds on firmly to his daughter's reins. 'Hello,' Simon says to the child and she giggles and waves to him. I watch on, smiling.

'What a beautiful little girl, and so full of life,' Simon says, as the family pass by, and a tender look crosses his face.

Out of the blue I think what a wonderful father he'd make. I draw in breath sharply. My God, a few weeks ago I couldn't stand the guy and now here I am almost imagining him fathering my children. Am I suddenly becoming broody?

I'm pulled out of my thoughts when Simon speaks again. 'I wouldn't mind a go on the punts.' We watch a couple of young lads wobbling about as they try to climb out of theirs on to the riverbank.

'May I remind you, Mr Leggat, that you and I are here to work and not to spend our day sailing along the river. Much as it would be nice,' I add. Being here with him has been much more enjoyable than I'd anticipated.

Back in the car Simon plays about with his sat nav. 'We can follow the A253 road that leads to Timaru. I knew this area quite well when I lived in Christchurch and there are quite a number of farms scattered around.' He starts up the engine. 'Eaglemont is one of them, and I think there's a farm called Hilltop or Knowetop, I'm sure it's something top. There are other farms nearby, but their names escape me right now.'

We get back on to the highway and follow the sign for the A253. While he's driving, I google the names he mentioned and ring one of them on my mobile. I introduce myself and have a brief conversation with the farmer.

'So, would you be willing to talk to us about the damage to the New Zealand farming industry caused by this scandal?' He agrees. 'Great, we're on the A253 so we should be with you fairly soon.' I tuck the phone in between my ear and a raised shoulder while I jot down some directions. 'Thanks,' I say, and end the call.

'Sounds like we've cracked it.'

'With Eaglemont at least. The farmer, John Benson, sounds quite keen to talk to us. Says their side of the story hasn't been reported sufficiently so he's pleased to give us his thoughts.'

'Good work.' Simon says, then we lapse into silence to concentrate on the route.

'That went well,' I say to Simon, when we are driving away from Eaglemont after a worthwhile interview with John Benson. While we were at Eaglemont, Mr Benson phoned his neighbour, Doug Watts, at Hilltop Farm and Mr Watts also agreed to speak to us.

Arriving at Hilltop, we are welcomed by Gracie Watts, a buxom, middle-aged lady with a beaming smile. 'Come in and make yourselves comfortable,' she invites, showing us into the spacious farmhouse kitchen, with its wonderful smell of home baking. 'Tea or coffee?' Gracie asks, switching on the kettle as she's speaking.

'Coffee for me, please,' I reply, slipping off my lightweight jacket and hanging it behind my chair. John Benson at Eaglemont is a widower and fairly elderly, so it's good to receive hospitality from this farmer's wife.

Simon smiles at Gracie. 'Coffee for me too, please.'

'Doug is on his way up from the outhouses,' she tells us, placing a plate with a slice of fruit cake on the table in front of each of us.

She's scarcely uttered the words when a tall, bearded man comes into the kitchen. He kicks off his boots and stands them in the corner behind the door.

'Doug, these are the two reporters from the Wellington Post.'

Simon jumps to his feet. 'I'm Simon Leggat and this is my colleague, Ros Mathieson.'

Doug strides towards ·us in his stocking soles, hand outstretched. 'Pleased to meet you. You've done what our local papers have failed to do and come to ask for our opinion on this outrage. We'll be delighted to have our thoughts out there for the public to read.'

Gracie brings over the drinks, coffee for us and tea for Doug and her. She joins in the discussion, agreeing with what her husband is telling us.

On our drive back to Christchurch, I write out some notes, using my tape recording of the conversations as a memory prompt. Both farmers were happy for me to record what they had to say on the matter. 'We can type out our findings back at the hotel before dinner.'

'Yep, and once we've tried to get some comment from the firm's Head Office tomorrow, we can email our report to Charlie. It might be in time to get into tomorrow's late edition, if not the following day.' Simon switches on the car radio and we relax with the music for the remainder of the journey.

CHAPTER FORTY TWO

We arrive at the Head Office of Farm Steadings Limited a few minutes before ten o'clock next morning. Working at the reception desk is the woman that we spoke to yesterday and she has the same look on her face as before. Gran would have described her as a sour puss. On a score of 1-10 for her efforts with public relations, I give her 2, maximum. And I think I'm being generous.

Once the customer she's dealing with leaves, Simon reminds her of our mission.

'I'm sorry but there are no management staff able to help you with your report,' she advises us, without the trace of a smile on her face.

'But you said we would be able to speak to someone about ten o'clock,' I persist, looking at the clock on the wall above the desk as I'm speaking.

'I didn't promise anything definite. And as I told you yesterday the matter is due to come to Court within the next few days.' The narrowing of her eyes and her unsmiling mouth save her having to say that the matter is now closed.

'Okay, thanks for trying.' Simon smiles at the sour puss and steers me away from the reception desk. 'Thanks for nothing,' he mutters, once we're out of earshot.

Over lunch, in a nearby restaurant, we discuss our next move. 'I think we've exhausted every avenue,'

I say. 'Why don't we return to the hotel and I can send Charlie what we have? And then, after dinner, we can visit Trev and Cheryl. And remember, it's ….'

'I know, it's a social call,' Simon finishes my sentence. 'No worries, I won't be asking him anything about the enquiry.'

***

Using his sat nav, Simon drives us from the hotel to Trev's house at Hoon Hay. I haven't met Trev since the Seminar last year, although we have kept in touch by email and I've spoken to both him and Cheryl on Skype.

We park in the driveway and by the time we get out of the car the front door is open and Trev comes out, closely followed by Cheryl. They're both wearing shorts and t-shirt, making me feel overdressed in my blouse and skirt.

'Lovely to see you again.' Trev gives me a hug, before shaking hands with Simon. Cheryl, an attractive woman, almost as tall as her husband, kisses me on the cheek. I recognise her perfume as one from the Jo Malone of London range; the one with the scent of pear and freesia. It's the perfume that Trev bought her in Wanganui on my recommendation.

'Welcome, Ros,' she says, with a beaming smile. Then she turns to my companion. 'Nice to meet you, Simon.'

They lead us through the house and into the back garden, its neatness a testament to Cheryl's green fingers. 'We thought on such a lovely evening it would be good to be outdoors,' Cheryl says, and she directs us to seats on the decking.

'Let me get you both a drink,' Trev offers. 'Is G and T still your poison, Ros?'

'It is indeed,' I reply, and Simon asks for a Foster's.

When Trev returns to the garden, he hands us our drinks while Cheryl lays a plate of nibbles down on the table beside us. 'I know you said when you phoned that you'd be eating at the hotel, but I thought you'd have room left for some of these.'

'Thank you,' I say, taking a vol au vent off the plate, while Simon chooses a sausage roll.

'So, you're down to cover the recent scandal about the lamb,' Trev says, taking a sausage roll before he sits down beside Simon. He laughs. 'For The Post, no less, our great rival.'

'Yes, I guess we're the opposition,' Simon retaliates, smiling as he's speaking. 'Friendly rivals though and we're visiting you as friends, not as opponents. Did Ros tell you I used to work with the Herald here in Christchurch?'

Trev nods. 'She did and I think I actually moved into your job when you left to go to Wellington. I work with Luke Newman who remembers you well.'

Simon puts his glass down while he helps himself to a vol au vent. 'Yes, Luke and I were good mates.'

'Where did you live in Christchurch?' Cheryl asks, joining in the conversation.

'I had a flat in St Albans. Could walk into the city from there, which was handy for work, especially as I was driving an old banger at the time, which was prone to breakdowns. St Albans was also near enough for me to get to the soccer at English Park on foot.'

'So, you're a soccer fan?' Trev leaned over to refill Cheryl's glass.

'Not really. Rugby's my game but I watched some good matches at English Park.'

'So how did your interviews go today?' Trev now asks, looking from Simon to me.

I straighten up in my chair and swat a fly off my forehead. 'Pretty good, although of course it was impossible to get the supermarket big wigs to speak to us. Some of the staff did though, all keen to stress they knew nothing of the fraud.'

'It's a bad day when you can't trust the shops to sell you the best cuts for your hard-earned cash,' Cheryl puts in.

'Mm,' I comment but leave Simon to reply.

He smiles at Trev. 'I promise we won't steal any of your headlines.'

Trev shrugs. 'I doubt I know more than you two do, as things will be kept under wraps until the Court Case begins.'

Simon nods. 'We might well be sent down again to cover the Court Case. Anyway, enough about work, have things settled down in the city again after the 2016 quake?'

The conversation moves on to the effects of the quake and other general themes. It's almost midnight before we realise it. Even sitting out here under the stars the temperature hasn't gone down much.

'Trev and Cheryl are an easy couple to be with,' Simon comments on our return journey to the hotel.

'They sure are,' I agree, then yawn. 'Think I better ask for an alarm call tomorrow to ensure I don't miss the ferry.'

'Same here,' Simon says, as we draw up in the hotel car park and creep silently to the front door, anxious not to disturb any of our fellow guests.

CHAPTER FORTY THREE

'Well, how did it go?' Elva asks, when I step into her car. 'Did you survive your time in Christchurch without punching poor Simon's lights out?'

I draw the car door closed and laugh as I put on my seat belt. 'It wasn't as bad as I expected. In fact, if I'm honest, I found him pretty good company.'

Elva takes the slip road off to the coast and we join a line of traffic moving at a pace that makes a tortoise look like a boy racer. She turns towards me, her eyebrows arched. 'Do I detect a thaw in your relationship at last?'

'Thaw might be too strong a word but I definitely find him easier to be with nowadays.'

'Good. That's a step forward. You were hard on him when we saw him at Trentham last year, although you were much less so when we met him and his cousin at the rock concert.' She glances in her mirror at the line of vehicles behind us. 'I hope half the population of Wellington don't decide to go to Seaport today,' she says, leaving me no chance to respond to her defence of Simon. With the sunny weekend that's been forecast for the city, Elva and I are having a beach day to top up our fading tans from last year's fantastic summer.

'I don't think the beach should be too busy,' I suggest.

'Yeah, you're right. With Seaport being further

out from the city centre, it should be quieter than some of the other bays around Wellington.'

'We're so lucky to have such easy access to the beaches, aren't we? Yippee.' I clap my hands when some of the traffic branches off towards the Highway, allowing us to put on a spurt.

In Seaport, we bag a secluded spot on the beach. The dunes behind, shelter us from any wind. We strip off the tops and shorts we're wearing over our swimwear and cover our skin in a protective screening agent. For a time we sit and watch the fury of the waves crashing in over the rocks, until hunger gnaws and we raid the eski we brought with us. Our hunger and thirst satiated, we lie down on the warm sand and soon doze off.

'When are you meeting Adam?' I ask Elva an hour later when we've wakened and are enjoying another drink.

She yawns. 'We've plenty of time. He isn't due to pick me up until 8 pm.'

'Where are you going for your dance?'

'To Adam's golf club at Lower Hutt.' Elva twists off the top of her water bottle and takes another drink. As she replaces the top, she smiles at me. 'If you and Simon ever get together, we can go out as a foursome.'

'Mm,' I reply, not yet ready to commit myself. 'Think I'll forget about swimming today, too energetic. Will we sun ourselves for another hour before driving back?'

'Yep,' she agrees, and a few moments later,

after a further application of U.V. screen, we are once more soaking up the sun.

'When's your next appointment with Marion Tyler?' Elva asks, when we're packing up to leave the beach.

'Next Friday,' I tell her, feeling the sand in between my toes as we walk, barefoot, up the dunes to the promenade. I dust the sand from my feet before sticking them into my jandals.

We link arms as we head towards the car park. 'Hopefully she'll see an improvement in me this time. I scoffed at the idea when you first suggested it, Elva, but I really feel talking to Marion is helping me. So thanks for keeping on at me to make the original appointment.'

She squeezes my arm as we're walking. 'No problem, Ros. I remembered how much counselling helped Mum when Dad died.'

Back at the car, we throw our belongings into the boot. 'Look at that sky, what a pretty sight,' I murmur and stare at the sun going down over the dunes.

'Yeah, it promises us another fine day tomorrow.'

When we get back to Kiwi Crescent, Elva leaves the engine idling.

'Thanks for driving us today,' I say. 'Do you want to come in for a coffee?'

'No, thanks, think I best get home so I can have a shower and wash my hair before I go out tonight.' She leans over and kisses my cheek as I get out of the car.

'Enjoy the dance. See you soon in the Lavender for lunch.'

'Will do. Hope all goes well with your appointment on Friday.' She smiles at me and moves away from the kerb.

I stand at the gate and wave to her until her red Kia drives round the corner into Dolphin Road and disappears from sight. I feel Smoky's head rub against my leg and he meows. He has a gash on his ear, where some blood is visible.

I lift him up and carry him indoors. 'Smoky, have you and Tiger been fighting again?' Tiger is the cat who lives at No 4 and he and Smoky are deadly enemies. 'You're monsters, both of you,' I tell him, stroking his fur as I take him into the living room, where I have a better inspection of his war wounds.

'You've a nasty gash there. Think we should get you seen by a vet.' The vet I usually attend has retired but I remember that Dee speaks highly of the Hobson Street surgery, where she and Liz take their rabbit when he's poorly.

I ring Dee's direct line at the travel agents. 'Hi Dee, Smoky's been in a fight with the local bully. Could you give me the number of the vet you use in Hobson Street?'

'Poor Smoky,' she says. 'Hold on. Here it is, 2479156.'

'Got it. Thanks Dee and sorry for troubling you at work.'

'No worries. We've had a queue of people all day but in the last hour or so things have quietened down. Apart from Smoky, all well?'

'It is, Dee, take care and say hi to Liz for me.'

'Will do.'

When I phone the vet practice, the receptionist tells me that the Saturday clinic is a drop-in one so I can just drive over and wait for Smoky to be seen. Once he's in his basket on the passenger seat beside me, I weave my way through heavy traffic towards Hobson Street. Apart from an occasional meow coming from the basket, my pet doesn't seem to be in any distress or pain.

When I arrive at the surgery, I look at the brass plate on the front door.

Dr Gavin Stokes BVSc

Dr Linda Hanlon BVSc

It occurs to me that I didn't ask Dee if she would recommend one of the vets so I'll just have to take pot luck.

'This is Smoky,' I introduce him to the receptionist, 'and he's been in a fight with Tiger, a cat who lives nearby. There's a big gash on his ear, and it's bled quite a lot,' I say, pointing it out to her.

The woman fusses over Smoky and takes a few details from me. 'Right, Miss Mathieson, if you take a seat in the waiting room, Dr Stokes will have a look at Smoky.'

There are only about three people ahead of me and we don't have to wait too long until the receptionist ushers us into a consulting room.

'Hello. I'm Dr Stokes.' The vet shakes my hand and lifts Smoky out of his basket on to the table. 'I hear you've been in the wars, Smoky,' he says and examines the cat's ear, then turns to me. 'Not too much damage, but it'll need some stitches.'

Just then the door opens and another vet, female this time, comes into the room, dressed in her greens. She's an attractive girl about my own age, with a figure to die for. 'Do you want a hand, Gavin? I've had a last minute cancellation.'

Dr Stokes looks up and smiles at her. 'You can hold this young man steady while I sedate him. Miss Mathieson, this is my colleague, Dr Hanlon,' he tells me, and she nods and says hello.

I watch Dr Stokes filling the syringe. As I look at him, it strikes me that I've seen him somewhere before.

Once the injection has been administered, the smell of antiseptic hits me when Dr Hanlon begins to sterilise the area. Then Dr Stokes begins to close the wound with stitches.

Halfway through, the receptionist pops her head round the door. 'Gavin, Smoky's your last patient.'

'Thanks, Flora,' he replies, without looking up.

I'm fascinated to see how quickly he works. As he does so, I'm thinking Gavin … Gavin … and then it strikes me that he's Simon's cousin.

'All done,' he announces, and goes to wash his hands, leaving Dr Hanlon to drop the used items into the dustbin.

'There you are, Miss Mathieson, he's good as new again,' Dr Hanlon says, and she gently places Smoky back into his basket. She removes her rubber gloves and strokes his head. 'He's still a bit groggy from the injection but he'll soon waken up.'

'Thank you,' I reply, and I too pat the top of his head. Although sleepy, he lifts his front paw a little and places it across the back of my hand.

'Do I need to bring him back?'

She shakes her head. 'No need, the stitches will dissolve within a few days.'

'What about payment?'

She opens the door slightly and calls to the receptionist, who was passing along the corridor. 'Flora, could you prepare Miss Mathieson's bill please?'

Dr Stokes looks at me again, a puzzled look on his face. 'Miss Mathieson, do you work on The Post?'

'I do and I think you're Simon's Leggat's cousin, aren't you? My friend and I met you at the pop concert with Simon.'

'Yes, I remember. Simon speaks of you often.' He laughs when he sees the concerned expression on my face. 'Don't worry, all good.'

'Okay, thanks for treating Smoky.' I lift the basket holding my pet and follow Flora back to the office to pay the account.

On the drive home, I try to get my head round the coincidence of taking Smoky to Gavin's surgery. Of all the vets in Wellington, I chose him. Fate or what?

CHAPTER FORTY FOUR

After dinner Viv sat down as usual on Wednesdays to watch the double episode of Coronation Street. There was also a double episode on Mondays and Fridays and she either watched it live or recorded it to watch at a more convenient time. She'd been a keen fan of this soap since it started in 1960 and the characters felt like friends by now, especially ones such as Ken Barlow, who'd been in the show since the very beginning. She could never remember the actors' real names but thought of them by the name of the character they played.

Tonight's episode featured a celebration party in the Rovers Return and it finished with a sudden death. The signature tune was still playing, with the credits rolling up the screen, when the phone rang.

'Hello, Gran,' Norma said, 'I didn't call you until Coronation Street was finished as I know how you hate to be disturbed during it.'

'Thanks, darling. One of my favourite characters died at the end of tonight's episode so it cheers me up to hear your voice.'

'I wanted to invite you to the school prize-giving next Wednesday, Gran. Dad will be working down south but Mum, Pamela and Daryl will all be there. Daryl said he'd pick you up in the car.'

'Of course I'll come, darling, wouldn't miss it for the world.'

'Cool,' Norma said, 'hold on a minute, Gran, Mum wants a word with you. Bye.'

And before Viv could respond she was gone.

While she was waiting for her daughter-in-law to come to the phone, Viv thought again how well Norma was doing in her 6th year at Harris Academy. Her granddaughter had come top of her year in most subjects; she excelled academically and in sport. Norma was a gifted artist and could easily have taken that path, but her ambition was to start a Law degree. She'll succeed at whatever career she chooses, Viv was thinking, when she heard her daughter-in-law's voice in her ear and the two of them chatted for five or ten minutes.

When she put down the receiver, Viv headed into the kitchen to attend to her dinner dishes. As she squirted washing-up liquid into the basin, she hummed the hymn tune 'O Love That Wilt Not Let Me Go', one she'd often sung in church. As she was scrubbing the potato pot, Viv recalled reading somewhere that the writer of the hymn, George Mathieson, had lost his sight and his fiancée broke off their engagement, unwilling to marry a blind man. It had been following this disappointment that George was said to have composed the famous hymn.

Her chores done, Viv settled herself in front of the computer. She clicked on to her internet connection and rubbed her face with the heel of her hand while she waited for her email page to open. There were no incoming messages, so she began to compose a message to Ros in New Zealand; something she'd been meaning to do for a couple of weeks now but hadn't so far got around to.

Wednesday, 6th June, 2018
Hello Ros
    I hope this finds you well and still enjoying your work with The Wellington Post. Pamela is still working in DC Thomson, the publishers; she enjoys her work in their Finance Section but I think she'd like to get into the editing side. Pamela's a good writer and I've been encouraging her to try her hand at writing a novel.

    I enjoyed reading your news in your last email, telling me all about your time in Christchurch with your colleague Simon investigating the recent food scandal there. It's terrible nowadays that half the time we don't know what we're eating. It was good that you managed to visit your friends Trev and Cheryl when you were in Christchurch. Was he the man you met when you were at the Conference in Wanganui last year?

    The family here are all well and I've just had a phone call from Norma to invite me to her school prize-giving next week. She's a clever girl and I'm sure will go far in whatever career she follows. At the moment she is keen to become a lawyer but she's young yet so might change her mind at a later stage.

    I'm well and keeping busy as ever. Our Evergreen Club is off for the summer now, although looking at the dull, wet day here it doesn't feel much like summer. I'm going on holiday with three other ladies from the club in July. We are booked into a hotel in Stonehaven for a week. Stonehaven is a seaside resort, north of here and south of Aberdeen. Fingers crossed for sunny, warm weather during the holiday.

Speaking of holidays, a thought has been going round in my head for ages, Ros, probably since I received word of your gran's death back in 2016. I'm so pleased that you have kept in touch with me and I wondered if you'd like to come over here for a holiday sometime, even later this year if you can get time off work. It would be easier for you to come here than me visit you in New Zealand. My days for far away holidays and long journeys are over. I'd love to show you around this area and perhaps take you to places that meant a lot to your gran. Daryl, I'm sure, would be happy to drive us in his car to places that aren't convenient for public transport. Anyway, you can think about it Ros and let me know once you decide.

I see it's getting near my bedtime so I will sign off for this time my dear and look forward to hearing from you again soon.
Much love from Aunt Viv
Xx

Viv sent the email and switched off the computer. She made herself some buttered toast and tea, then watched the ten o'clock BBC news while she had her supper.

CHAPTER FORTY FIVE

On Friday afternoon, I leave the Toyota in the car park at work and set off on foot for my half past three appointment with Marion Tyler. Cuba Street is buzzing with shoppers and tourists and I wend my way through the crowds to Clifton Road.

In the clinic I get a 'hello, Ros' and a smile from Wendy, the receptionist. I like this as it shows that their clients are more than just numbers to them.

Marion collects me from the waiting room. Her hair has been cut in a different style, fuller at the sides, and I think it makes her look younger. When we are seated in her now familiar consulting room, she starts up our discussion. 'So, what's been happening since we last met? Any specific issues you'd like to talk about today?'

I swallow a couple of times and stare at the sunflower picture on the wall behind Marion's head. I want to tell her about Simon, but it takes me some minutes to begin speaking. 'I want to tell you about my relationship with a colleague at work.' I clear my throat. 'At least it isn't that yet ... well maybe never will be ... I'm very confused,' I finish, stumbling to a stop.

Marion nods, her eyes willing me to go on.

That's the encouragement I need to launch into the pros and cons of responding to Simon's advances and how ambivalent my feelings for him are.

Only once Marion senses I've said all I want to for the moment, does she comment. 'I think you might have already made your decision. Our feelings for someone else can sometimes go from dislike to like without us really noticing when the change took place. Do you think this has happened to you?'

I sit in silence for a moment and when I look up, tears are pricking my eyelids.

Marion's face remains impassive.

'I think it might … my experience with Don seems to have me left me … well, vulnerable I suppose, and I'm scared of committing to a relationship with a man.'

Don's name has been mentioned in an earlier session but we skimmed over it. Now I feel ready to speak about him.

'My gran didn't like Don, she felt we weren't suited. But I … I loved him very much.' I stop again and take a deep breath, before plucking up my courage and going on. 'Although we were engaged, Don didn't seem interested when I brought up the subject of our wedding. He kept breaking arrangements to meet me, usually telling me he had to work late. Gran told me I shouldn't trust him but … you see, I loved him so much and didn't want to think badly of him.' I shift in my seat while I'm speaking and stretch out for my glass of water.

Refreshed again, I continue. 'Gran was proved right in the end, although she was too kind to say I told you so.'

I suddenly feel the urge to tell Marion

everything. 'I couldn't relax when I was living with Don. He blew hot and cold and sometimes he treated me so well that … well I sort of forgot about the bad times.' By now I'm wringing my hands and I can feel my insides shaking.

'Did he hit you, Ros?' Marion asks, when I stop for a fairly long time.

I nod. 'He did sometimes although he was always sorry afterwards. At the time, I felt as though I … I deserved it.'

Marion waits patiently while I take another drink. She's an excellent listener, but then I suppose that's her job. 'One evening, after Don told me he would be working late, I went to the cinema with my friend Elva. After the film, I went home and … and there was a half empty bottle of wine on the coffee table, with two used glasses beside it. Feeling sick, I crept along the hallway. The sounds coming from our bedroom made me both scared and angry at the same time. I pushed open the door and …'

I force myself to look straight at Marion while I'm speaking and see only understanding on her face. No judgement whatever.

It gives me courage. 'I pushed open the bedroom door and stood, frozen, in the doorway. At first, neither of them were aware of my presence. The woman was the first to see me. I let out a strangled gasp and made my escape, almost tripping up over Don's trainers on the way. I managed to get out of the flat without throwing up and drove erratically to the safety of Kiwi Crescent and Gran.'

By the time I stop speaking, tears are gushing down my cheeks and I'm shaking from the effort of talking about that night.

Marion is jotting down some of what I've been telling her and relief washes over me that I've finally opened up to someone. All my bottled-up emotions and feelings poured out in a waterfall of words.

Marion slips the box of paper tissues across the table to me and fills up my water glass. 'I'm glad you felt able to tell me about what happened. Maybe you've been needing to do so for a very long time,' she says, her voice gentle.

I wipe my eyes and nod in agreement. 'Even with Gran, I held a lot back, unable to put my feelings into words.'

More settled again, I look at my watch and can't believe our hour has come to an end.

'Will we meet again in about two months' time?' Marion asks. 'Would you be happy with that?'

I'm about to say yes when I remember Aunt Viv's invitation. 'My great aunt in Scotland has asked me to go over for a holiday and I was thinking of travelling in early September, if I can get four weeks off work. So I might be in Scotland in two months' time.'

Marion gives me a thumbs up. 'An overseas trip sounds wonderful. You've made great progress during your attendance here and I think a break away from routine would be beneficial.'

She leafs through her diary. 'So, shall we arrange another meeting towards the end of August, prior to you leaving for your trip?'

'Yes, please.'

When the appointment is arranged, Marion walks me to the front entrance.

***

When I walk into the Green Man, my workmates are sitting at our usual table in the corner.

Ted sees me and waves. As soon as I reach the table, Simon is up out of his seat. 'G & T, Ros?'

'Yes, thanks.' I sit down in the chair he's vacated.

No-one asks me where I've been and I'm grateful to Charlie for his discretion regarding my counselling sessions.

We're involved in conversation when Simon brings over my drink. He shuffles another chair from the nearby table, then sits down beside me, pulling his own glass towards him. He smiles at me and I return the smile, finding I really mean it. I feel less hostile towards him and I like it.

'What are your plans for the weekend, Ros?' Charlie asks me, during a lull in the conversation.

'Nothing much. I've had a lot on recently so it will be nice to have more time to chill out.' I hope I sound convincing. Elva is going on a weekend camping trip with Adam and some other friends, so in truth I'm at a bit of a loose end.

My recent chat with Marion about my feelings for Simon is still fresh in my mind and a tremor of excitement runs through me with him sitting so close to me right now.An hour later, when the karaoke begins, we make ourselves scarce.

Back at Lyall Bay, I feed Smoky and prepare my own dinner. He's a bit grumpy because I've been out all day, so I play with him for a short time and, while eating, I watch the early evening news. When an advert for overseas travel appears on the screen, my thoughts return to Aunt Viv's invitation. I decide to speak to Charlie on Monday and ask about the possibility of getting holidays for the month of September.

***

After seeing Ros out of the clinic, Marion completed her notes and left the office.

'Night,' she called to Wendy, as she passed the reception desk.

'Bye, Marion, see you on Monday. Have a good weekend.'

'You too,' Marion called over her shoulder.

When she reached the school playing fields, Ben was waiting outside for her. He dumped his soccer kit into the boot, then settled down in the passenger seat, pushing it back a little to accommodate his long legs under the dashboard.

'Have you been waiting long?'

He shrugged and shook his head.

She indicated and moved out when another driver flashed for her to do so. 'How did your team do today?' she asked, glancing at her son while keeping an eye on the traffic around them.

'We won. St Charles' hammered us last time so good to get our revenge.'

'Great. I wonder what culinary delights Dad will

have for us tonight.'

Ben shrugged again and rummaged in the glove compartment for any nibbles.

'Sorry, mate, you're out of luck. I cleaned out the mess the other day and threw everything into the trash can. Anyway, it would spoil your appetite for what Dad has to offer.'

Larry working from home had proved a benefit to Marion, as cooking was the last thing she felt like doing after a day at the clinic.

'Hi, sweetie,' Larry greeted her, with a kiss. 'How did it go, Son?' he asked, turning to Ben.

'We won, gave them a real thrashing.'

'Well done,' Larry said, giving his son a high five.

'Is Abi studying?' Marion asked her husband, as she slung her handbag over the end of the sofa and took off her jacket.

'Yes, she disappeared upstairs the minute she got in from school. Cramming in as much as she can before the exams next week. Not like some I could name.' Larry sighed and gave a pointed look in Ben's direction.

Ben ignored the jibe. 'Something smells interesting,' he said, changing the subject.

'Pork with mustard sauce, it's almost ready. 'Go and call to Abi, Ben. Come and sit at the table, sweetie, I've got your wine poured.' Larry threw his arm around Marion's shoulders and they walked into the dining room.

CHAPTER FORTY SIX

When I get to the office on Tuesday morning, the place feels chilly. June is always a cold month for us but this year it's been more severe than usual, and it hasn't helped that the office heating has broken down. Roll on the engineer's visit tomorrow, I'm thinking, as I bring an ancient two-bar electric fire out of the storage room. I drag it into the main office and blow the dust away from the bars. Then I plug it into the socket nearest to my desk.

I'm glad I got a thumbs up from the boss yesterday for my four weeks' leave in September because today he is at a wedding. With Ted on leave this week and both Matt and Simon out on assignments this morning, I have the office to myself. I pour another coffee from the machine and type as fast as I can to help keep myself warm. I'm engrossed in the article I'm writing about the new housing at Goose Bay when I hear Simon's voice behind me.

'It's colder in here than it is outside.'

I jump when he places his hands on my cheeks before going to hang up his coat. We're getting on much better these days and I even grudgingly admit to myself that I now enjoy his company. He brings a coffee over and plonks himself down on the edge of my desk to drink it. 'Have you been lonely with us all out of the office?'

'No, it's been very peaceful.' I type on, without

looking up, while he sips his coffee.

'I wondered if you'd like to come with me to a movie sometime. Tonight, tomorrow night or even next week. What d'you say?' he asks.

I don't reply immediately but continue to stare at my screen. The truth is I'm speechless as his invitation has come out of the blue, a bit like Aunt Viv's invitation to visit her in Scotland.

I see he's waiting for my answer. 'That would be nice,' I finally say, 'I'm busy this week so better we leave it until sometime next week.'

'Fine. Would Wednesday evening suit you or will we decide nearer the time?'

'Wednesday would be good.' I smile at him, surprised to find myself quite nervous about our date. I'm not doing anything tonight or tomorrow but need some time to get my head round him asking me. I've been aware from the word go that he fancied dating but since I've given him the brush off so often, I was sure he'd changed his mind about me.

'I must get on,' I tell him, and return my attention to the article on my screen.

'Sure, same here,' he agrees, and saunters over to put his empty cup into the paper recycling bin.

***

Driving home after work my mind is still on next week's date. I can't believe how excited I feel about it. It's the same feeling I had on the ferry over to Christchurch when I'd to remind myself that we were there on a work assignment and not on a date. This time will be different.

When I park the car, Smoky is sitting in his usual place on the window ledge. He's curled himself up into a ball. 'Hi mate. Simon's finally asked me out,' I tell my feline friend, when I go into the front room. He jumps up on to my shoulder to allow me to stroke his fur. Since Gran died, Smoky has been my closest companion and I tell him all my secrets, sure in the knowledge that he won't pass them on to another living soul.

Smoky cuddles into my neck when we go into the kitchen, then he jumps down my back and on to the floor. He meows as he pads over to his food dish, anticipating his usual early evening meal.

Once we've both eaten, I switch on the laptop and sit down. Smoky jumps up on to my knee and then on to the table. He stares at the screen for a moment before walking across the top of my keyboard, leaving a row of question marks and then a series of A's across the page.

I laugh at his antics, sure he's going to start typing one of these days.

When I finally coax Smoky down on to the carpet at my feet, I open my emails. Only a couple of junk messages which I clear and begin to compose a reply to Aunt Viv. I've had a few days to digest her invitation and the more I think about it the more I want to go to Scotland. The longest holiday I could take in one chunk would be four weeks which should be long enough as I wouldn't want to impose on my great aunt for any longer than that. When the blank email comes up on the screen, I start typing.

12 June 2018
Dear Aunt Viv

Great to get your email and hear that all is well with you folks in Scotland.

Before I give you my recent news, I must say a big 'thank you' for your kind invitation to visit you later in the year and, after a few days considering it, my answer is definitely YES.

Yesterday I spoke to my boss, Charlie, about the possibility of getting a holiday from work for the month of September. It wouldn't be worth flying so far for any less than four weeks and you can let me know if you would be able to 'tolerate' having a visitor that long?

I fill her in on some of my recent news, telling her about my night out with Elva, Dee and Brenda last week. Although I let her know that all is well with me at The Post, I don't mention anything about Simon.

'Nearly finished,' I tell Smoky, when he starts meowing for my attention. I wonder if other cat owners are ruled by their pets like I am.

CHAPTER FORTY SEVEN

I'm really cross when my landline rings for the third time in half an hour. 'Who is this? I'm going to report you to the police for harassment,' I shout into the mouthpiece. There is silence for a few seconds and then Elva says, 'Ros, are you alright? Are you getting these phone calls again?'

'Sorry Elva for shouting at you. I've had two calls from a withheld number before yours and thought this was the mystery caller yet again.'

'Maybe you should contact the police. I thought the calls had stopped.'

'They had for a while but recently they've started again from time to time. I'll leave it for another few days and if it happens again, this time I will definitely contact the police to get my calls monitored or even change my number.'

'Do you still think Simon's the culprit?'

'Not any longer. I did think so at first but I'm going to the cinema with him next Wednesday so why would he bother to make nuisance calls to me when we have a date?'

'Great about your date and glad you can rule Simon out although still a worry about these calls. Hope they will stop and you won't have to go to the police.'

'Fingers crossed. Anyway, nice to hear from

you.'

Elva laughs. 'I'd almost forgotten why I phoned. It was to see if you fancied going to the beach over the weekend. Saturday or Sunday would do for me. Adam is playing rugby on Saturday and we won't be going out until evening. I'm also free on Sunday.'

'I've got my writing group on Saturday and afterwards Nat and I are planning to go for a few drinks and something to eat. I've nothing arranged for Sunday.'

'Fine, let's say Sunday. I could pick you up.'

'No, you drove last time Elva, so I'll take the car this time. We can take a picnic with us. Will we set off about eleven o'clock before the beaches get too crowded?'

'Sounds ideal. I'll ring you first thing Sunday morning. Night.'

'Night, Elva,' I say and hang up.

Before going to bed, I check my emails and there is a reply from Aunt Viv, who is over the moon that I'm going in September and she's happy for me to stay for four weeks, or longer if I wish. So now I must start to make enquiries about flights so that I can pinpoint my outward and return dates. It's so exciting and I can't wait to see her and hear all she can tell me about Gran.

CHAPTER FORTY EIGHT

'You miss the other guys, don't you?' Ted says, as we face one another across the table at The Green Man.

'Yep,' I nod. Simon has flown down to Dunedin to attend a wedding and Matt is on holiday. 'Wonder how Matt's doing in New Caledonia?'

'He'll be having a ball. I've always fancied a holiday there, but it doesn't appeal to Anne, so not much hope of getting there.' Ted shrugs. 'She who must be obeyed and all that.'

'You know you love it,' I say, and take another drink from my glass. Despite the way Ted slags her off, his devotion to Anne is obvious for all to witness. How I wish I could find such a relationship.

As though he's read my mind, he diverts the focus back to me. 'You and Simon seem to be getting on better now,' he says, looking at me over the top of his specs.

'What gives you that idea?'

'It isn't too difficult. You have a most expressive face, kid.'

I take another swig of my drink and put the glass down on the table, rather more heavily than I'd intended. 'Have you and Simon been discussing me?'

Ted stretches over and pats my hand. 'Of course not, Ros, I've simply noticed a thaw in your relationship. And I'm glad to see it,' he concludes.

I smile at Ted and nod. 'You're right. I always found him too full of himself but recently have seen a different side to him.'

'Although he gives that impression, I think underneath he's a decent guy and you could do worse than him, believe me.' Ted's knowing nod once more reinforces my feeling that he treats me like he was a pseudo dad.

'Well you'll be pleased to hear that Simon has asked me out and we've made a date for next Wednesday evening.'

'Good on you, kid. I'm delighted to hear that. Don't worry,' he adds, when he sees the look on my face. 'I won't say anything to the other guys until you see how things go.' Ted looks at his watch. 'Right, kid, think I need to make tracks, she who must be obeyed will have my meal ready and I'll be in the doghouse if it's burnt.'

We're both still chuckling as we make our way out of the pub.

CHAPTER FORTY NINE

'What about a jar in the Green Man?' Matt asked Simon on Monday. It was his first day back after his holiday and he and Simon were clearing their desks after work. Charlie was still on holiday and Ted was working out of town.

Simon's head popped up from his position on the floor where he had been switching off his laptop. He got to his feet and rubbed the dust from his hands. 'Must ask Charlie to get that socket moved to a more convenient place. You've to crawl on your hands and knees to reach it.'

'Everyone who's worked at that desk has made the same complaint. And you can't move the desk any further back. But it shouldn't be difficult to sort it. Anyway, are you up for the Green Man?'

'Sure. Maybe Ros will join us.' Simon looked round to find Ros's desk cleared and her coat gone from the rack.

'She left about ten minutes' ago,' Matt told him, 'you were speaking on the phone when she called goodnight.'

***

'Hi, guys, what are you having?' the barman, sporting a thick, red beard, greeted them when they got into the pub.

'Two pints of Foster's, mate,' Matt replied, then turned to Simon. 'Will we eat here and save cooking at home?' Simon nodded and after a quick scan of the pub grub menu they both ordered pie and chips.

'Take the drinks and grab us a table,' Matt said to his colleague, then turned to face the barman once more. 'New here, mate?'

'Started the other day,' the bearded one told him. 'Was working in a pub in Auckland and fancied a change of scenery.' He picked up the twenty dollar note Matt had placed on the counter as he was speaking. 'Keep the change,' Matt said.

'Thanks, mate. I'll bring your grub over.'

While they ate, the two men conversed about rugby and the recent success of the All Blacks. 'With these guys in the team, it's no surprise we're the world's most successful rugby nation,' Simon said, lifting his pint to his mouth.

During a lull in the conversation, Matt gave Simon a questioning look. 'You seem unusually cheerful today, apart that is from grousing about the plug under your desk.' His last words made them both laugh.

Simon stared down at the table, twisting his glass mug between his palms. 'I asked Ros out on a date and she agreed.'

Matt looked surprised. 'Good for you. I know you've been sweet on her for some time. I guess we've all known that, except Ros. What do you think turned the tide?'

Simon laid his glass down and made a temple of his fingers. 'I'm not sure but I've felt her warming to me recently. At least, a bit less antagonistic towards me.'

'I've known Ros longer than you,' Matt told him, 'and I think she had a broken engagement a couple of years ago, which might have made her resistant to forming any further relationships. Perhaps she's got over it now and ready to move on.'

'I hope so. Keep it under your hat meantime, till I see how it goes.'

After they'd eaten, Simon noticed a couple of groups coming into the pub. 'It's getting busy so will we move?' he suggested, 'my round next time.'

'Fine,' said Matt, getting to his feet and pulling on his jacket.

CHAPTER FIFTY

Viv got off the bus in Nethergate, close to the modern shopping centre, and crossed the road to the bakers' in Union Street. You had to go early if you wanted the lovely wheaten loaves they baked on the premises.

Viv sensed a definite spring in her step this morning, due she knew to the email she'd received from Ros, accepting her offer to visit later in the year. She did some further shopping in the city centre and got to The Hungry Horse restaurant in Gellatly Street in good time to meet her friend Nora for lunch.

She and Nora had met at the Evergreen club or, as the members themselves described it, the Silver Haired Brigade. They usually had coffee in The Cherry Tree in Nethergate but had decided today they'd try this recently-opened establishment.

When she walked into the restaurant, Viv was hit by a wall of noise from so many conversations going on at once. Nora waved to her from where she was sitting at a table in the rear of the restaurant. 'Thought it would be quieter for us to chat here,' she told Viv and pointed to the empty tables around them.

Viv slipped off her anorak and sat down facing her friend. 'Good idea. Have you had a look at the menu?'

'Yes, and I liked the sound of the half sandwich and soup deal. Thought I'd have mushroom soup and a chicken and bacon sandwich.'

'I'll try the tuna and sweet corn and lentil soup for me,' Viv said and closed the menu. 'My bus raced along Perth Road today, I seemed to be in town in no time at all.'

'Lucky you. We were held up by roadworks near Blackness Road. We came in at a snail's pace.'

The waitress came over and took their order, then they sat back for a good chinwag.

'So, what's new?' Viv asked her friend.

'Not a lot. Just the usual stuff, shopping and housework,' Nora said, and grimaced. 'I was really looking forward to our lunch today. With such a good breeze, I've left some sheets and towels out on the line, so fingers crossed it doesn't rain before I get home. What about you? Anything interesting to report?'

'I have actually. I invited Ros from New Zealand to come and visit me and I had an email last night to say she's coming in September.'

'That's great. Isn't she the girl whose grandmother was your long-time friend? The one who died a year ago?'

'It's nearer two years. Hard to believe, the time seems to have flown by. But it will be wonderful to see Ros again. I haven't seen her since she was a small child.' Viv leaned back in her chair to let the waitress put her bowl of soup down in front of her.

They chatted on about general matters during their lunch and when they were at the coffee stage Nora returned to the visit of Ros. 'So, what sort of places will you take Ros when she gets here?'

'I'll see where she wants to go, of course, but I'd like to take her to see the Britannia at Leith and maybe she'd enjoy visiting Holyrood Palace and Edinburgh Castle. I wouldn't be able to walk too far but we could take a taxi.'

'That sounds excellent and she may well come with some ideas of her own. I know when my grandson comes over from Australia, he's armed with all sorts of places he wants to visit.'

'True, and of course Daryl might be happy to take us on some outings, places that would be difficult to get to on public transport.'

Nora smiled as she signalled to the waitress for the check. 'Have you still got a hope that he and Ros might fancy one another?'

'Well, it would be nice,' Viv said, evading a direct answer. 'But I suppose I'll have to wait and see. Not that I'm trying to match-make,' she said, her eyes glinting.

'Of course not, I'd never have thought such a thing,' Nora teased her.

They paid their bill and, once outside, decided to have a further look around the shops before going home. An hour later they parted company in the town centre, arranging to meet for lunch again in two weeks' time, just before Ros arrived for her visit.

CHAPTER FIFTY ONE

After feeding Smoky and letting him out into the back garden, I shower and dress, then carefully apply my make-up. I slip my feet into my new bronze-coloured shoes, open-toed with a small heel, and stand in front of the full-length mirror. One stray curl keeps jumping up, so I wet my comb and try to flatten it. The fact that I want to look my best tells me how much my feelings towards Simon have changed over the past eighteen months. I'm as excited as a kid going on a first ever date.

The hot day has turned into a pleasantly warm evening. The weather app on my iPad convinces me a jacket isn't necessary. A quick check that I have everything I need in my handbag, then I look at the clock for the millionth time since I got home from work.

Simon arrives promptly and sounds the horn a couple of times. I force myself not to rush out immediately but let him wait for a few minutes before I leave the house. Don't want to look too keen. When I'm walking towards the front gate, I see him standing on the passenger side of the car, holding the door open for me. 'Hi,' I say, and get into the car, hoping I sound calmer than I feel.

We park outside the cinema complex in Ocean Road. Inside, we study the films on offer and like the sound of a thriller. 'Sounds reasonable,' Simon says, 'will we go for it?'

'Yep, why not?'

While Simon is buying the tickets for us, I look at the boards advertising the 'soon to come' films. My new shoes are pinching big time and I long to get into the darkened cinema where I can slip my feet out of them.

'Screen 7 for us,' Simon tells me when he returns, carrying popcorn and pepsi to enjoy during the film. There are only another two couples in the cinema, sitting down near the screen, so we take seats near the back, with no-one in front to block our view.

Towards the end of the film there is a scary bit that comes out of the blue. When I see the bloated face peering in the window, I let out a scream and hide my face against Simon's crisp cotton shirt. The scene changes but, although I turn round again to face the screen, I leave my head where it is, enjoying the closeness we are sharing. Simon seems to like it too, and his arm tightens around me.

We remain like this until the film is finished.'That was a great story,' I venture, raising my head from his shirt as the credits roll up the screen.

'Yep, powerful stuff. I didn't know too many of the actors though. Let's go and get ourselves a coffee, or would you prefer something stronger?'

'Coffee would be great.'

Simon takes my hand and leads me down the stairs towards the exit. I blink as we emerge into the brightly lit foyer, after the darkness in the cinema.

We drive back into the city and find a cosy café

just off Cuba Street. The side street is quiet, and we park in front of the café entrance.

'The doughnuts look nice,' Simon says, spying them piled up on a plate on the top shelf of the glass display unit. 'What do you fancy with your coffee?'

I draw my finger down the glass front, which gives off a screeching noise as I do so. 'I'll have a piece of that chocolate traybake,' I tell him, pointing to the shelf below the doughnuts. Then, with our tray loaded, we find a table in a quiet corner of the café where we can chat undisturbed.

'Have you always lived in Wellington?' Simon asks, once he has scoffed his doughnut and is drinking his Americano.

'Yep, and I've lived all my life in the one house in Lyall Bay. Apart from a short time,' I add, dropping my eyes to the table-cover. I'm glad Simon doesn't ask anything about that time, as I don't relish bringing Don into our conversation. I look up at Simon and notice on the wall behind him and to his left a smaller version of the Wellington Harbour print that hangs in The Lavender Café.

'You're alone in the house now, aren't you?'

I nod. 'I've been on my own since my gran passed away almost two years ago. My grandparents bought the house in Kiwi Crescent when they arrived in New Zealand from Scotland in 1972. My mother was born in the house a year later and I was also born in that same house,' I finish, popping my last piece of traybake into my mouth.

'I take it then that your mother died before your

gran?'

'Yes, my mother and father were both killed in a train crash in Britain, when they were on a holiday of a lifetime.' Despite the length of time that has elapsed since this happened, the memory of their deaths makes me feel sad.

Sensitive to my change of mood, Simon puts his hand over mine and squeezes it. He smiles and I like how his eyes crinkle at the sides when he does so. Why have I never noticed these things about him, I ask myself? Because you were too busy trying to find fault with him, a little voice in my head informs me. 'What about your origins?' I ask, using my spoon to scoop up the chocolate on my cappuccino.

'Like you, my family came from Scotland. My great-grandparents emigrated to New Zealand from Fife and started a farm in Dunedin, the farm my parents still own.'

'Is it a sheep farm?'

'Dad has both sheep and cattle, but mainly sheep. We've got about 8,000 in total.'

'Did you not want to carry on the family tradition in farming?'

'Not really. Ever since I started at secondary school, I've wanted to be a journalist. I think in some ways my father is disappointed I didn't follow in his footsteps, but my mother has always encouraged me to go after my own dreams.' He plays his spoon around the dregs of his coffee. 'I think my brother, Jamie, might have joined my father on the farm when he grew up if he … he hadn't died.' Simon stops speaking and now it's his turn to look down at his plate, visibly moved by what he's told me.

I slide my hand nearer his, without actually touching it. I hesitate for a moment before I speak. 'Do you want to tell me about it? I'm a good listener.'

'Okay,' he murmurs. Then, slowly at first, he starts to talk. 'Jamie was 8 when he died. I was three years younger so it's all a bit vague although I can remember us playing together in the fields near our farmhouse. On the day of the accident, Dad was in the tractor, ploughing some furrows ready for seeds. Jamie had slipped out of our kitchen without Mum noticing and was running up and down the ruts behind the machine, out of Dad's line of vision.' Simon comes to a halt and stares out of the window, looking as if he's forgotten I'm there. I'm about to speak, when he continues. 'I hear Mum screaming and she rushes out of the house, with me in her wake. Jamie is lying in a furrow, still like a rag doll, with Dad kneeling down over him, howling like a wounded animal. Nothing could be done for Jamie.' When Simon looks up, there are tears running down his face. 'Other than my parents, I've never spoken about Jamie to anyone before.'

'I'm glad you felt able to tell me,' I say, my voice a whisper.

He gives me a ghost of a smile. 'Dad has never got over it. Still blames himself.'

'Yes, I can understand that. It's something you'd never get over. How regularly do you return to the farm?

'I drive down as often as I can. In fact, I'm going down there this coming weekend. With me being the only one they've got, Mum and Dad are always keen to see me.'

'Does your cousin go with you sometimes?'

'Gavin? No, his folks have all died off, so he looks on Wellington as home now. He and his partner have made a good life for themselves, with a wide circle of friends, so there's nothing for him in Dunedin any longer.'

'And his partner? Is she from Wellington?'

Simon puts his coffee cup on top of his used plate and pushes them to the side of the table. 'His partner is male, and yes he was born and raised in Wellington? They met at veterinary college and have been together for about three years now. They both practice as a vet but work in different surgeries.'

'So does the partner not go with Gavin to the races?'

'Tod has no interest in horses. Another coffee?' I nod and he calls the waitress over.

'So, what about your friend, the one I met you with at the races last year?' he asks, when we are on to our second coffee.

'Elva? She and I have been best friends since we met at secondary school. She works as a medical secretary in Wellington Hospital. We have lunch together at least twice a week and sometimes go out at weekends.'

'I remember her as a very pleasant girl,' he says, and I'm grateful that he doesn't bring up how unpleasant I was to him, preferring to forget my behaviour that day.

Our conversation continues easily and by the time we leave the café I suspect that I'm beginning to fall in love with him. This thought is confirmed when we reach Kiwi Crescent and he kisses me goodnight before I get out of the car. My heart is singing when I walk into the house. 'I'm in love, Smoky,' I tell my pet, while I'm stroking him, and he purrs happily.

I have difficulty getting to sleep and when I do finally fall over, Simon's face features a lot in my dreams.

CHAPTER FIFTY TWO

Elva and I are seated near the back of The Lavender, our usual table having been occupied when we got here. Through the open kitchen door, the voices of the waitresses calling out orders to the chef reaches us, plus the clatter of serving dishes and other utensils being dumped down on the metal counters.

'Now I appreciate the table we normally use, up near the front window.' Because of my blocked ears, it sounds to me that I'm shouting. When Leigh brings over a jug of iced water and fills our glasses, I can't hear the jingling of the ice cubes as I normally would.

Elva lifts her glass and drinks. 'So will the two of you drive down to Dunedin on Saturday?'

Unable to totally catch the drift of her words over the din from the kitchen, and with my attempts at lip-reading falling short, I shake my head. 'Pardon?' I ask and point to my ears. 'I've got a build-up of wax in my ears again and had to visit Dr Austin at the Health Centre yesterday. She told me use almond oil drops to help soften the wax and I'm to have my ears syringed in ten days' time. Meantime, I shrug, 'I'm rendered almost deaf.'

Elva grins and repeats her question in a raised voice.

I catch her words second time around. 'No, we're going to leave on Friday after work. I'll pack my case on Thursday evening and take it into work with me.'

Just then Elva directs my attention to the front of the café where the people who were at our usual table get ready to leave. She signals to Leigh that we are changing tables and we move hastily before any other customers arrive.

'What about your car?' Elva asks, once we are settled down and I can hear her more clearly.

'I'll leave it in the office car park over the weekend and we'll use Simon's car.' Although nervous about meeting his parents, I'm thrilled that he has invited me to the farm and can't stop smiling.

'It's fantastic that you've discovered a different side to Simon. I always thought the two of you were destined to be a couple,' Elva says, and sits back when Leigh puts down her plate of lasagna in front of her.

'I don't know if we can be described as a couple yet, but I certainly enjoy being with him and I think he feels the same about me' I feel a blush spreading across my face and concentrate on using my fork to twist some spaghetti against my spoon.

'I'm sure he does. Perhaps we'll get out on a foursome yet.'

'Let's not get ahead of ourselves.' I take my first mouthful of spaghetti.

'Are you seeing Adam at the weekend?' I ask her, when we've finished eating and have been served with our coffee.

Elva nods, spooning brown sugar into her cup. 'We're going for dinner at a posh hotel near Masterton.

There's about eight of us in the group and we're staying over at the hotel after the meal.'

'You're really keen on Adam, aren't you?'

'I guess so. At first, I wasn't sure if he was up for a serious relationship, but as time's gone on, he seems to want us to go out regularly.' Elva shrugs and smiles over at me. 'Time will tell.' When we part outside the café, she hugs me. 'Good luck for your visit to the farm and remember to text or phone me the minute you get home.'

CHAPTER FIFTY THREE

I enjoy the mid-winter sun on my face as I lean against Simon's shoulder and gaze on the beauty surrounding us. Because of my difficulty in hearing at the moment, he's given up trying to speak to me and we're simply happy to be together

We've been up on dcck since the ferry left Wellington and, although the strait has been choppy, I have experienced worse. The sky is beginning to darken now but most of the crossing has been in daylight. The hills of my home city have now been replaced by the more rugged cliffs of the South Island visible in the distance. I can well understand why my country is known as the land of contrasts.

Simon drives us off the ferry at Picton and we follow the coastal route. I'm glad I don't need to navigate. Let's me relax and watch the scenery.

'We can stop in either Christchurch or Timaru for toilets.' Simon turns on the radio and we fall silent. The music is soothing and soon I'm straining to keep awake. Eventually I give in and close my eyes.

I'm startled out of my slumber when Simon turns off the engine. It's dark outside. 'Where are we?'

'In Timaru, we don't have far to go from here. I meant to stop in Christchurch, but you were dead to the world when we drove through the city, so I carried on.' He's stopped at a service station, with both toilets and café facilities on hand. Once we return to the car, we have a clear run to Dunedin and get to Lime Tree around midnight.

Yvonne Leggat greets us in the farmhouse kitchen, a fleecy pink dressing gown over her nightwear. Simon pulls her into a bear hug. 'Hi Mum, this is Ros.'

'Lovely to meet you, Ros,' she says, and kisses my cheek. While Simon closes the back door firmly against the strong wind that has whipped up during the last hour, I strain to hear her and finally resort to lip reading. I warm to her immediately. She has an open, friendly face and her grey hair is tied back from her face with a blue ribbon. A lamp on the coffee table is switched on, with her specs and a paperback, opened at her place in the story, lying beside it.

'I'll put your case into the spare room, Ros.' Simon smiles at me and disappears with our luggage.

Yvonne invites me to sit down while she switches on the kettle. Cocooned in the sofa's big, comfy cushions, I look round the warm and welcoming room. Everything is gleaming and I can almost see my reflection on the door of the dark green Aga. I watch her pour boiling water into the teapot. She doesn't ask if I prefer tea or coffee but I'm glad she makes tea as coffee at bedtime tends to keep me awake.

'Ron is asleep as he will be up at daylight to attend to the animals. Simon can show you around the farm tomorrow,' she's saying, when Simon joins us.

'We'll maybe leave that until Sunday,' he suggests, and sits down next to me on the sofa, the leathery material squeaking under his weight. I stifle a laugh as I'm reminded of the whoopee cushion that someone bought me when I was a child.

'I thought we might visit Queenstown tomorrow. If you'd like to go there,' he says, turning to smile at me.

'You bet I would. It looks so scenic in any pictures I've seen.'

Yvonne lays the tray on the table in front of us. 'Have a biscuit, Ros,' she says, holding out the plate of digestives. 'Yes, Queenstown is spectacularly beautiful; to me it's like Austria, Norway and Scotland all rolled into one. Have you been to the South Island before, Ros?'

'Only as far south as Christchurch. Simon says you've always lived in Dunedin.'

'Dunedin yes and Lime Tree's been our only home since we were married. Ron's grandfather, Simon's great-grandfather, started the farm and in time we took it over. Ron kept hoping that Simon would show an interest in farming, but journalism quashed that idea.' Simon raises his eyebrows at this comment but says nothing.

'Do you come from a farming background yourself?' I ask Yvonne.

'I do. When my parents retired from our family farm, my brother took over. By that time Ron and I were married and were living here. The boys were born here at Lime Tree.' A cloud passes over her face as she says this and I'm sure that she's thinking of her dead son, Jamie. I can only guess at how hard it must be to outlive your child and hope I won't ever have to experience it myself.

When we've finished our tea, Yvonne puts the mugs into the dishwasher and shows me to my room. 'I'm sure you must both be dead beat with the long drive. There's nothing to rush you up in the morning, Ros, Ron won't disturb you when he goes out.'

'Goodnight, Ros. Sweet dreams,' Simon calls to me, winking as he goes into his bedroom across the passage from mine.

***

I'm hit by an enticing whiff of bacon grilling when I make my way into the warm kitchen next morning. Sunshine is streaming in through the window and bathes the kitchen in a soft glow. Yvonne turns around from the stove and smiles at me. 'Morning, Ros, and how did you sleep?'

'Like a log. You were right about being dead to the world. I hope I haven't held you up?'

Yvonne raises her hand, palm facing me. 'Not at all, as I said last night there is no rush,' she says, as she cracks some eggs into the frying pan.

'No rush at all,' Simon agrees, coming into the kitchen behind me. He's dressed in denims and a casual top, his hair still wet from the shower. He comes up beside me and kisses my cheek, the scent of his after shave wafting over me. He steers me towards a chair at the table facing the window, then plonks himself down next to me. There are two place settings on the table opposite us; Simon signals to the one facing me, and I remember him telling me yesterday that his mother still, all these years after Jamie's death, lays a place at the table for her dead son. I told Simon I was fine with this. After all, everyone has his or her own way of coping with bereavement.

'There you are, my loves, get stuck in,' Yvonne tells us, as she places a plate of bacon, mushrooms, grilled tomatoes and a fried egg in front of us.

Simon passes me the toast rack and slides the butter dish towards me. 'These eggs are freshly laid by Mum's hens. You'll find a big difference from shop eggs.'

My mouth waters in anticipation as I spread some butter on to the warm toast. We are drinking our second mug of tea when Ron comes into the kitchen, wellington boots in his hand. He drops them inside the doorway and stoops to pull off his thick socks. His face glows with health from working outdoors.

He removes his hat, revealing his thick hair, dark with hardly any grey showing. Makes him look younger than Yvonne although I reckon they are about ages. 'Welcome, Ros, good to have you with us,' he tells me, and pads over to the sink to wash his hands. 'Yvonne said you were both pretty tired when you got here last night.'

'It was a long journey,' I agree. 'Harder for Simon than for me, because I had a nap in the car.' When Ron turns around to face me, I see immediately that Simon bears a definite resemblance to his dad, more so than to his mother. I wonder fleetingly if the other son, Jamie, had looked more like her.

'Simon is taking Ros to Queenstown today,'

Yvonne tells her husband, as she puts his breakfast plate down on the table. She lays his food at the same place she had used, and I notice that Jamie's place remains there, untouched. I wonder what she'll do tomorrow if all four of us are eating at the same time.

***

Simon puts our picnic lunch and folding chairs into the boot and once we are seated in the car, ready to drive off for our day in Queenstown, he spreads the map out across our knees. 'See, here we are in Dunedin,' he says, pointing to the spot on the map, 'and there's Queenstown.'

My eyes follow his finger. 'Gosh, I didn't think it was so close to Milford Sound.'

'Yes, it's in a very picturesque area of the country, that's why it attracts so many visitors all year round. We'll drive down the coast from here as far as Milton,' he tells me, tracing the route with his forefinger, 'then we turn off and take that road via Roxburgh and Alexandra. When we get to Cromwell,' he continues, and I see the place marked clearly on the map, 'that's where we go on to the minor road to Queenstown. Happy?'

'Very. Especially since you know the road well and I don't need to navigate.'

Simon takes a drink from his water bottle before turning on the ignition. He gives a toot as we drive out of the farmyard and, in the side mirror, I see Yvonne and Ron waving to us from the back door. Susie, the black and white collie I met this morning, barks like mad as she chases the car, ducking and diving to avoid being hit as we pick up speed.

'Susie's a terror,' Simon says, laughing at her antics, 'she loves to play this game with the car but one of these times she's going to come a cropper.' The dog stays outside the gates when we leave Lime Tree, her barks following us as we head downhill. 'The road isn't likely to be as busy at this time of year as it is during the summer months.'

Simon's prediction comes true and after a stress-free journey, I gasp in delight when we reach Queenstown. He pulls into the side of the road and stops the engine, to let me admire the town nestling in the valley beside Lake Wakatipu. I drink in the magnificent view, beauty like never before seen in my lifetime. 'It's breathtaking,' I say, speaking in a whisper, afraid to break the spell.

'Pretty, isn't it?' Simon agrees, and slowly drives downhill into the town proper. 'Let's find a car park and then we can explore the town and the lakeside while the weather is fine.'

***

Yvonne and Ron have the lights dimmed and are watching a movie on TV when we get back to Lime Tree. Straight away Yvonne gets up and switches off the telly. 'How was your day? Can I cook you something?'

'No thanks, Mum. We had a meal before we left Queenstown.'

'Well, let me at least get you a drink. Tea or coffee, Ros, or would you prefer something stronger?'

'No more wine thanks but a cup of tea would be

lovely. Sorry we're interrupting your film.'

'No worries, it was pretty rubbishy anyway.' Yvonne switches on the main light again.

Simon and I sit on the sofa beside Ron, and father and son begin to discuss the recent improvements made to the roads we were using today.

'So, what did you think of Queenstown?' Yvonne asks me once we are all drinking our tea.

I lay my cup down on the coffee table before I reply. 'It's even more beautiful than you described it. No wonder so many tourists flock there.'

Shortly afterwards, Ron begins to yawn. 'Well folks, I'm going to hit the hay. I've got some shearers arriving early tomorrow morning.' Ron had explained to me at breakfast time this morning that he always employed professional shearers as they work so much faster than he can.

Very soon afterwards the other three of us are yawning too, and we drift off to our beds. As I slip between the sheets, I can hardly keep my eyes open.

CHAPTER FIFTY FOUR

'Well, how did it go?' Elva smiles at me, anticipation on her face, when I join her at the table in The Lavender a few days after Simon and I return from Dunedin. 'I got your text to say you'd enjoyed your visit, but I want to hear all the details from start to finish.' Having had my ears syringed the previous day, I can hear every word she says.

'It's such a relief to be hearing properly again,' I tell her and pick up the menu. 'Shall we order first? Then I can fill you in on our weekend?'

Once Leigh goes off with our order, Elva sits back, hands folded on the table, her face expectant. 'Right, start from the very beginning, when you first set off from Wellington.'

I'm only part way through the tale when our food arrives but I carry on while we're eating, with the occasional interruption when Elva asks a question. Once we've exhausted the subject of the trip to Dunedin, I look across the table at my best friend. 'Now it's your turn, what about the posh meal with Adam?'

A happy glow crosses Elva's face and she disappears into her memories of Saturday night for a moment. 'It was awesome, the whole meal from start to finish. We shared the table with a great bunch of guys, Adam's friends and their wives or girlfriends. They were all very friendly towards me and I had a fun time.'

'Sounds great. And how was the meal?'

'Excellent, as was the entertainment afterwards. It was a guy impersonating Elton John and he was fantastic. Oh, and by the way, Simon's cousin, Gavin, was there. The one he goes to the races with.'

'Did he recognise you?'

'No, I wasn't speaking to him but I remembered him from the night we met him and Simon at The Devils concert in the Botanic Gardens. During the evening I noticed Gavin was sitting beside another guy, they looked like a couple.'

'They are. His partner is also a vet, but they work in different practices. I like Gavin, he fixed Smoky up when he got into a fight with Tiger, a neighbour's pet. He was really good with Smoky.'

Elva and I move on to discuss our respective workplaces and this conversation keeps us going until our lunch hour is over. 'Not long now until your trip to Scotland,' Elva remarks as we call for our bill.

I smile. 'Three weeks and four days to be exact,' I tell her, 'I haven't quite got it down to minutes yet.'

Elva puts some dollars on the table on top of mine. 'Your Aunt Viv will be keen to see you.'

'Yes, especially as I was only a toddler the last time she came here. I'm keen to get to know her and to visit some of the places Gran knew when she lived in Scotland.'

'Lunch again later in the week?' Elva asks, when we part company outside the café.

I nod and give her a hug. 'Yep, same time, same

place.'

***

'And how are you feeling now?' Marion Tyler asks me, when I attend my counselling session with her that evening. I like the evening appointments as the clinic is quieter than during the day.

'I'm keeping up the breathing exercises you recommended, and only using medication when I really feel I need it. My nightmares have eased, as have the pounding headaches.' I find it easier to look at her when I'm speaking than I did when I first attended. I guess I'm not so churned up inside nowadays.

Marion clasps her hands together on her lap. 'So, would you say there has been a definite improvement since you first attended?'

I take time to consider this before answering. 'I think so. The future seems a bit brighter.'

She looks at me over the top of her specs. 'And what about your visit to the farm, Ros? How did that go?'

I had told her about my invitation to Dunedin when I phoned her last week to alter the time of today's appointment. At the time we were speaking, I was very uptight about the whole experience. 'It turned out much easier than I'd expected. Yvonne and Ron, Simon's parents, were very welcoming and the visit went off really well. Simon took me to Queenstown while I was there, and I bought a cowrie-shell necklace to take to my great aunt in Scotland.'

I watch as she jots something down on her notepad. Then she looks up. 'And did Simon tell you about Captain Hayes, or Bully Hayes as he was nicknamed?'

'Yes, the same day we were in Queenstown, we drove through the Otago region where gold-mining boomed in the nineteenth century. Simon showed me the site of the Prince of Wales Hotel owned by Bully Hayes, although of course the hotel has been rebuilt and renamed by now. From all accounts Bully had a sudden end.'

Marion nods. 'He's said to have been drowned when the boat he was in capsized. And how about your relationship with Simon? Has that improved too?'

'I'd say it has.' I smile at her and shrug. 'Looking back, I think I gave him a hard time when he started at The Post.'

She waits for me to continue but when I remain silent, she writes in her book again.

'Have you kept up the diary I asked you to write?'

'Yes, I have. I find it quite cathartic.'

'Good,' she smiles once more. 'Well, Ros, I'm delighted to hear how well you're doing, and I think one more appointment is all you will require. What do you feel about that?'

I fall silent once more, trying to decide how being discharged from the clinic will affect me. 'When I started to attend, I felt a real mess, my life chaotic and I was drowning in sorrow over my gran's death. But with the breathing exercises and the other tips you've given me to control my feelings, I think I'm almost able to make a new start.'

'Great. What do you say if I see you again after your return from Scotland, with a view to discharge thereafter?'

When I agree to this, Marion gives me a card with the date and time on it. Then she shakes hands with me and shows me out of the clinic by the side door, as the main entrance is locked up.

CHAPTER FIFTY FIVE

Nora carried the tray over to the table Viv had found for them in a quiet corner of the café where they'd have peace to chat. Viv had already made herself comfortable, with her coat and scarf draped over a spare seat and her walking stick hanging on the back of the chair.

Nora laid their mugs and the toasted teacakes she'd ordered on to the table. 'Isa served me and was saying how nice it was to see us again.'

'Yes, she'll be wondering where we disappeared to. Hope you didn't tell her we've been taking our custom elsewhere.' It was some time since they'd been in this café, The Cherry Tree, as recently they'd begun to frequent The Hungry Horse which was closer to their bus stops. However, with today being so sunny and warm, they'd decided to have a walk down Nethergate to their old haunt.

Nora stood for a moment with her hand on her hips. 'Give me some credit for tact,' she said, laughing as she returned the tray to the counter. When she got back to their table, Viv was singing, 'Mamma Mia! Here we go again,' while she cut her teacake in half.

Nora smiled at her friend. 'That you getting into the spirit of the film?' They'd bought tickets for the film which was showing at the Grange cinema at four o'clock today.

'Hope it comes up to expectations. It's got a lot to live up to.' Viv, an Abba fan, had enjoyed the original version of the show and she wasn't sure how much this new one would appeal. She licked her lips as she buttered her teacake and spread blackcurrant jam on top of the butter.

'Not long now until the young lass from New Zealand arrives,' Nora said, as she stirred sugar into her tea. 'Have you got some ideas of where to take her?'

Viv swallowed a piece of her teacake before replying. 'I have indeed. I know she'll want to spend time in Edinburgh, being the capital city, and I'm sure Daryl will take us a run in his car up the coast towards Arbroath and Stonehaven, maybe even as far Aberdeen. Perhaps we could spend an overnight in the granite city.'

'Do you still have hopes Daryl might fall for Ros?'

Viv sighed and rested her cheek in the palm of her hand, with a dreamy expression on her face. 'It would be nice if that happened but' …. she shrugged … 'we'll see …'

Nora's eyes twinkled. 'It's so romantic, I feel like a conspirator in a secret plot.'

Viv laughed. 'What are we like? A couple of old matchmakers. But back to where I'd like to take Ros. Obviously, there's a lot for her to see around Dundee and maybe a trip over to Fife.'

'Yes, St Andrew's might appeal to her, with the ruins of the abbey. And you can tell her that Prince William and Kate Middleton attended the university there.'

'I thought it would also be nice to let her see where her gran and I shared our flat as teenagers.'

'Was that when you were both working in Glasgow?'

'Yes, we met in the girls' hostel we stayed in on the Clydeside. Then later we decided to get a flat and share the rent.'

'Was the flat near the hostel?'

Viv shook her head. 'No, it was in Rutherglen, a fifteen minute tram journey from Glasgow. We had some happy times there, I can tell you.' She smiled, lost in her memories for a few minutes, before Nora's question brought her back to the present.

'How will you get to Rutherglen?'

'Hopefully, Daryl might drive us there, but if not, we could take the train from Dundee to Glasgow Queen Street Station and then take a train or a bus out to Rutherglen. Come to think of it, that might be best, it would be a wee adventure for us.'

'Sounds like you'll have plenty to occupy the young lass.'

'Yes, she's only coming for a month, so we'll probably run out of time and she won't see half of what I've planned. But it'll be lovely to meet her again, now she's an adult. Last time I saw her she was a toddler.'

'Was that when her parents brought her over to see you?'

'No, once her gran emigrated to New Zealand, she never came back to Scotland again and, although Ros's mum and dad visited UK, they didn't get as far as

Scotland. Sadly, they lost their lives in a car accident in London and Ros was left with her gran back in Wellington.'

'Oh dear,' Nora said, her face clouding over.

'The time I saw Ros was when I visited her gran in Wellington.' She laughed. 'Back in the days when I was fit enough to travel that distance, no need for a stick then.' Viv glanced at her watch. 'Here, Nora, we better be getting along to the cinema. The film starts in about twenty minutes.'

CHAPTER FIFTY SIX

'Time for a break, Simon,' I call to my new housemate, when he carries yet another box into the kitchen.

'Thanks, love,' he says, when I hand him a lager, just as he likes it, straight from the fridge. He holds up his can. 'Cheers, I'm needing this.'

'No wonder, you haven't stopped for hours.'

A couple of weeks ago, I agreed to Simon's suggestion that he move into Kiwi Crescent with Smoky and me. Today is move-in day and this morning I thought that he was never going to stop bringing in box after box, crammed full of books, DVDs, IT equipment, clothes, toiletries and much more. 'I thought it was females who hoarded,' I joked with him.

I sit down beside Simon, and he pulls me close. His fingers caress my arm. I snuggle against him, and next minute Smoky jumps up and spreads himself across our knees, half on Simon and half on me. His look says don't think you're leaving me out. He purrs gently, as though bestowing a feline blessing on the new living arrangements.

'Think you've got a fan there,' I say to Simon. 'He knows you'll be looking after him while I'm in Scotland.'

Simon strokes Smoky's sleek fur and the cat purrs again. 'But are you sure you're happy about me moving in?'

I laugh up at him. 'It's a bit late now to be

unsure. After all your effort with the boxes.' But the cuddle I give him confirms my happiness better than words. We've decided that he will rent out his flat in Brooklyn meantime, until we're certain that the new lifestyle suits us both.

'I suppose since it's almost five o'clock we should start thinking about our stomachs,' Simon murmurs, playing his fingers through my fringe. 'Two options come to mind; we get cleaned up and go out to eat or we phone for a carry-out meal. What'ya think?'

'Mmm,' I say, still feeling that I'm dreaming we are together under one roof. 'I think the second option grabs me more. Just chill out here with our dinner on a bean bag tray and a glass of vino. Heaven, eh?'

'Decision made. Hope you've got some carry-out menus?'

'I have a pile of menus, of every cuisine available. When I've emptied my glass, I'll rouse myself and go and get them. Happy?'

'Ecstatic,' Simon replies and draws me even closer.

***

'So, how did the move go?' Brenda asks, the following evening, when she and Dee, Elva and I are seated in the spacious dining room of the Orpington Tavern in town. Since we didn't book in advance, the manageress can't give us a window table. But the booth she gives us affords us privacy to chat without being disturbed by other conversations going on around us.

Before I can reply to Brenda, the wine waiter, sporting a thick black moustache, saunters over to our table. 'Good evening, ladies. What can I get you to drink?'

I look round my companions. 'Red or white?' Everyone plumps for white and I consult the wine list. 'What about chardonnay, does that suit everyone?' Three heads nod in response to my suggestion. 'Two bottles of chardonnay, please,' I say, and the waiter heads off towards the bar. 'By the way, the wine is on me tonight,' I tell the girls.

Dee waves her hands in the air. 'No, it's too much, we'll share the bill as always.'

But I shake my head and laugh. 'We can share the food bill, but I'll see to the vino. At least Simon will; he gave me some dollars to buy the grog to celebrate us moving in together.'

'That was so good of him,' Elva says, giving my arm a nudge as she's speaking. 'I can't speak for the other two, but I'm very happy to accept.'

The wine arrives and our glasses are filled. Dee raises her glass. 'Thanks Simon,' she says, 'and to the two of you being blissfully happy together.'

Once we place our food order, Brenda asks more about yesterday's move.

'It went quite well but he has such a load of stuff, I don't know where we are going to put it all. I used to think it was women who hoarded, but how wrong I was.'

Afterwards, as we tuck into our starters, the conversation moves round to Dee and Liz's holiday in Japan. 'How did it go?' Elva asks.

'Fantastic. The Japanese are friendly people and

their country is spotless, not a bit of litter anywhere. And of course, the cherry blossom is to die for.' Dee is still describing their trip by the time we start on our main courses and, during dessert, Brenda regales us with the delights, or otherwise, of her caravan holiday with her husband, John.

It isn't until we are drinking our coffee that Dee broaches the subject of my overseas trip. 'You'll be getting excited about your visit to Scotland, Ros,' she says.

'Sure am. Can't believe how close it is now. Think Aunt Viv is counting the days.'

Brenda refills our coffee cups. 'How long is it since you last saw her, Ros?'

'She visited Wellington when I was very small, but I don't remember her. Other than from photographs, that is.'

Elva stretches out for the sugar bowl. 'It'll be lovely for you to see where your gran lived before she came to New Zealand.'

'Yes, that's the thing I'm most looking forward to.'

Soon afterwards the conversation turns to our places of work and when we leave the restaurant, we hail a taxi to take us home. 'Please thank Simon for the wine,' Dee says, when she gets out of the cab first, 'and I'll see you after your trip.'

Elva is second home, and when it's my turn, I say goodnight to Brenda who, as always, is last to be dropped off.

CHAPTER FIFTY SEVEN

'Will we go for a coffee?' Nat asks me, when we are all packing up our bags for off.

'Sounds like a good idea,' I tell her. Nat and I often enjoy a drink together after the writing group, when we exchange some of our ideas for our stories. This is something we both find helpful. And, of course, with just over a week until I go to Scotland, our conversation will doubtless go on to that subject.

'See you all in two weeks' time,' Jus says, as he zips up his writing case.

'I'll give my apologies now,' I say, smiling around the group. 'I'll be in Scotland by that time.'

Jus returns my smile. 'Of course you will, I'd forgotten it was so soon. Have a fab time over there.'

'And you'll have lots to write about for your first meeting back,' Lauren says, as she turns to leave.

'Look forward to reading it,' Marcus adds, giving me a wink, and for once he doesn't sound condescending.

'Will we go to the Johnsonville café?' Nat asks me, as we part company with the others at the main door of the school.

'Yep, that's fine.'

***

'Mum phoned,' Simon announces, when I arrive home from the writing group. 'She and Dad are hoping we will go down to Dunedin before you go off on your trip.'

'I'll be happy to do that. Your parents were so kind to me on my last visit and it would be nice to see them again. Only problem is Charlie wants me to do some overtime to make up for the long holiday I'm about to have.'

'I told Mum that. But I wondered if, instead of the long journey by ferry and car, we fly down this time. We could leave Wellington when we finish at The Post on Friday night and return on the last flight on Sunday evening. Dad will be happy to pick up us at the airport.'

'Sounds good. But we'll have to go next weekend because I'll only have a few more days after that before I leave.'

'Okay, I'll get on to it right now. And what do you say to a drive up to Masterton this evening? We could have a meal at the fish restaurant there.'

'Fab,' I say, as I go to hang up my parka.

CHAPTER FIFTY EIGHT

It's the day before my departure for Scotland and I check for the hundredth time that I have everything I need in my shoulder bag. I go through the items slowly; mobile phone, sterling, tickets, passport, travel insurance, make-up, etc., ticking them off my list. I hear Simon close the car door as I finally zip up my bag again, satisfied I have all I need for the journey.

'Hi, Darling, how's it going?' Simon calls out, almost colliding with me when I come out of the bedroom. He looks secretive, almost shifty, his hand behind his back. With his free hand, he beckons me into the sitting room, where he pushes me gently into an armchair.

'I want to do this properly,' he tells me and I watch, open-mouthed, as he gets down on one knee and holds out a little box, saying, 'I'd be so happy if you, Ros Mathieson, would do me the honour of being my wife?' Opening the box, he holds it closer and I see the ring, a ruby surrounded by diamonds, nestling in the folds of the velvet inlay. He's remembered that my favourite gemstone is a ruby. For once in my life, I'm speechless, and can only gawp in wonder at the beautiful piece of jewellery being offered me. Slowly, almost moving without any effort by me, my left hand extends towards him and he places the ring on my wedding finger.

'I wanted to buy the ring before you left so that you can wear it while you're over there.' He winked at me and grinned. 'Can't have any of the fellas over yonder thinking you are in the dating circles. We can arrange our wedding once you come home again. How does that grab you?'

I nod, then fall into his arms, hugging him tight.

He holds me away from him and stares into my eyes. 'Happy?'

'Ecstatically so,' I reply, holding up my hand to let the stones catch the light. 'I can't believe you've done this. It's so romantic.'

'See, I can be romantic when I want,' he says. 'I suppose we should ring my folks later and let them know. Not that they're going to be anything but delighted about the engagement.'

For the next hour we sit together and discuss our future plans, both of us trying to believe that what is happening is true. When Simon's stomach rumbles, I force myself to my feet and go to rustle up some dinner for us. 'After we've eaten and phoned your parents, I'll Skype Aunt Viv.'

A couple of hours later, having made Ron and Yvonne's day, I press the Skype button on my laptop, my excitement at fever pitch. Between my engagement and my journey tomorrow, I'm on cloud nine. I hear the ringing tone and then Aunt Viv's face appears on the screen, smiling at me. She's wearing a lovely pink flowery top and her hair looks freshly done. 'You look very summery,' I say and, once the time gap has expired, she nods.

'It's been very warm for the past ten days,' she tells me, 'and I'm keeping my fingers crossed tightly that it stays the same once you get here, Ros. Knowing the British weather, it could have returned to winter by the time you arrive, but hopefully not.'

'Let's not worry about the weather, I'm looking forward to spending time with you and meeting all your family members. If my calculations are correct, at the moment it must be about ten o'clock in the morning over there?'

Once again she takes time to hear what I've said, then she nods again. 'I have a note of all the numbers and times you gave me of your flights so that I can follow your journey. Daryl is going to bring me to the airport to meet you when you arrive.'

'Oh, that's kind of him. I guess that means him taking time off work.'

'It's fairly easy as he works free-lance so he can juggle jobs around to allow him time to bring me to the airport. Have you made arrangements for Smoky when you're away?'

'Yes, my friend Simon has moved in with me, so he'll keep Smoky company, and look after the house for me too.' Catching the surprised look on Aunt Viv's face, it occurs to me that I've never mentioned Simon to her before. I'm trying to decide why I called him my 'friend' when Simon glances over from the sofa and gives me a meaningful smile. 'Although he isn't simply my friend any longer, he is now my fiancé,' I tell her. A thrill surges through me when I say the word 'fiancé' out loud for the first time and I hold my hand close to the screen. 'Can you see my ring? We got engaged tonight, before I fly off tomorrow.'

Aunt Viv's face breaks out in a smile. 'Your ring looks lovely, lass. And how romantic.' She carries on telling me of her plans for us during my visit. 'I have lots I want to show you but don't expect there will be time for everything. I know you'll need a couple of days to get over any jet lag when you first arrive.'

'Yes, I do tend to suffer from jet lag when I go on long journeys, but it'll be a good chance for us to stay home and have a natter. What about clothes? Do you think I should bring all summer clothes, or would you recommend some heavier ones too?'

She gives my question some thought before replying. 'Yes, I think you'd be better to put a couple of warm jumpers and perhaps one heavier jacket into your case. Our weather can be unpredictable so better to be prepared.'

'Will do. Would you like to say hello to Simon?'

Her answer comes back to me promptly. 'That would be nice.'

Simon is already on his feet by this time and I vacate the typing chair for him.

'Hello, Aunt Viv,' he says, getting off to a good start. During their conversation, I throw my arms round Simon's neck, seeing the reflection of my brand new ring on the screen. When their chat comes to an end, I take my seat again and Simon returns to the sofa.

'Bye, Aunt Viv,' I say, trying to convince myself that in around 36 hours I'll be speaking to her face to face.

She waves into the screen. 'Bye, love, safe journey,' she manages to say before the picture vanishes.

CHAPTER FIFTY NINE

I'm glad to escape from the lady who sat next to me on the plane, and feel jaded from all the listening I've had to do over the past twenty two hours. The only way I got peace was to feign sleep. Thankfully, I'm travelling business class on the way home, so I shouldn't have the same problem.

After an hour's wait at London Heathrow, I board my flight to Dundee. The journey passes in a flash and, once I collect my case from the carousel, I follow the exit signs. I come through the doors into the main hall, surrounded by my fellow passengers, and the first face I see among the crowd of greeters is Aunt Viv's. She's taller than I'd imagined, and I recognise the blue top she's wearing from one of our previous Skype sessions. Having seen many photographs of him, I know that the young, handsome chap standing at her side is her grandson, Daryl.

For a time, we have to walk with the barrier between us until I get out into the main hall proper. 'Hello, lass, how lovely to have you here,' Aunt Viv says, and gathers me into her arms. 'Daryl here has brought me to pick you up.'

'Lovely to meet you at last, Daryl,' I say, looking up at the tall young man, and he gives me a hug too. Then he takes my luggage trolley from me and starts to push it towards the car park.

'Took me ages to find the trolley,' I tell Aunt Viv, as she takes my arm and we fall in behind Daryl, her stick tapping as we go.

***

'What a lovely room, and a wonderful view,' I say, when Aunt Viv shows me into my bedroom at her home in Farington Street. Some fluffy white towels with flowery satin butterflies on them are lying on the bed for my use.

Daryl carries in my luggage, then says his farewells as he is due to be at his next job in half an hour. After he's gone, Aunt Viv moves over to the window beside me. 'Yes, it's a pretty scene from up here with the Tay winding its way through the fields down there. Sometimes you see a splash when a salmon makes itself visible. The Tay is one of most heavily stocked salmon rivers in the country,' she tells me, the pride evident in her voice.

'What's that bridge I can see?' I crane my neck to try and see the end of the bridge on this side of the river.

'That's the Tay road bridge, it stretches over to Fife on the other side of the river. It was opened back in the 1960s by the Queen Mother. Further up the river is the Tay rail bridge, which was constructed right at the end of the 1800s. Have you heard about the Tay Bridge disaster?'

'Can't say I have.'

'It wasn't long constructed when it collapsed in a gale, with a huge loss of life. Anyway, lass, I'll leave you to sort out your luggage and settle in. I'll go down to the kitchen and sort out something to eat and drink after your journey.'

'Please don't prepare a lot, Aunt Viv. I've done nothing but eat on the plane and would be happy simply with a drink of tea.'

'Okay, lass, I suspect you need sleep more than food right now. Lie down whenever you feel like it. Meantime I'll away and put the kettle on. Will give you a call when it's ready.'

I go downstairs when she calls me. 'I thought you might want to read that while you're here,' she says, pointing to a paperback lying on the table.

I pick up the book and read out, 'A Spider's Thread Across the Tay,' a novel of passion and betrayal, by Mary Edward. 'Sounds a good read,' I say, after I've seen the blurb on the back.

Aunt Viv brings in the tea tray and puts it down on the table. 'Daryl bought it for me on Amazon and I could hardly put it down. The author has cleverly taken the facts of the disaster and woven in a love story. A great mix of fact and fiction.'

'Great, I'll start it in bed tonight, if I can keep my eyes open long enough.'

CHAPTER SIXTY

Aunt Viv pushes the toast rack nearer to me. 'Can you polish off this last slice, lass?'

I'm about to refuse, but change my mind when I remember her home-made marmalade. 'Just as well I'm only here for a few weeks, else I'd be three sizes larger than normal,' I say, as I spread the marmalade on to my toast.

'No way, lass, not with your sylph like figure,' Aunt Viv replies, before going into the kitchen to make fresh tea.

We're having a late breakfast once again, like we've done for the past three days since I arrived in Dundee. Thankfully I seem to be waking earlier in the morning, so I guess I'm almost over my jet lag.

She returns to the dining room, carrying a fresh pot of tea and two clean cups. Once the tea has had time to infuse, she pours it for us. Being a tea bag in a cup person, this is an unusual experience.

'What would you like to do today, Ros?'

Up to now we've stayed around the house and garden or gone shopping. 'I feel in the need of exercise,' I tell her, 'I would like to have a walk across the Tay Bridge to Fife. What did you call the place on the other side?'

'Tayport, a pretty wee village. Yes, you'd enjoy that, lass. I won't come as I'm not up to walking that distance nowadays, but you go and get some fresh air into your lungs.'

'Are you sure you don't mind me leaving you behind?'

She chuckles. 'Not a bit of it, I've lost count of the number of times I've been over there when I was younger.'

'What will you do while I'm gone?'

'I can sit in the garden for a wee while with my People's Friend magazine. It'll be good taking it easy today before Daryl drives us north to Aberdeen tomorrow.' Her grandson has organised his workload so that he can take the day off and he's going to drive us up the coast from here, via Arbroath and Stonehaven, to Aberdeen. I've always heard Aberdeen described as the oil capital of Scotland but, from what Daryl and Aunt Viv have told me, it seems the oil isn't as plentiful as it was previously.

'That was lovely,' I say, getting to my feet and carrying the used dishes into the kitchen, where Aunt Viv washes them, and I dry.

'I'll go and brush my teeth before I set off.'

As I go into the bathroom, I hear her singing along to the radio. The radio station is called Classic FM, and the music is quite highbrow stuff. 'None of that modern rubbish for me,' she always says, with a chuckle.

When I leave Farington Street, I follow Aunt Viv's directions to the bridge and soon I'm strolling over it, using the pedestrian lane. The views up and down the river are breathtaking, and I stop a few times to capture them in my camera.

When I reach the Fife side of the river, I walk towards the Tayview Inn. After being in strong, unrelenting sunshine, the coolness in the dark entrance hall is welcome. It takes a few minutes for my eyes to adjust and, once I do, I notice the receptionist sitting behind the desk, only her head and shoulders visible above it.

'Hello,' she greets me, and takes off her specs. 'What can I do for you?' Her cheery smile is almost as bright as the yellow top she is wearing.

'I was hoping you might be serving coffee,' I say.

'Absolutely.' It's only when she stands up that I see how tall she is. 'I noticed you coming over the bridge and thought you might want some refreshment. Coffee and biscuits be okay?'

'Great, thanks.' My guess is that she's a few years older than myself. 'Is that an Aussie accent?'

'Yes, I'm over from Melbourne on a working holiday. You a Kiwi?'

I laugh. 'Got it in one. I'm from Wellington and I'm visiting my great aunt in Dundee. I was in Melbourne a few years ago for a holiday. Lovely city.'

'It sure is. Although I'm enjoying my time in UK and in Europe, I wouldn't want to settle anywhere but Oz. Would you like to sit outside for your coffee?' she asks, and when I nod, she shows me out through the French doors to a magnificent garden area, where I take my place at a rustic table and chairs. From here, I'm looking straight over to Dundee and the boats on the river appear in miniature from this height up. I'm seeing the river from a different angle than when I was on the bridge. I can't resist using the camera again and I'm putting it back into its case when the receptionist arrives with my coffee.

'What a wonderful view,' I say to her.

'Yes, it is pretty spectacular,' she agrees, and lays the tray down on the table, before returning inside when the phone on her desk rings.

***

Aunt Viv and I wash up the dinner dishes, then sit in front of the television to watch her favourite soap, Coronation Street.

'I don't recognise a lot of the characters,' I tell her, during the break, 'although, of course, down under we're quite a bit behind with the episodes.' I don't follow Soaps at home, but I'm happy to watch this one with her.

'Would now be a good time to phone Simon?' she asks me, once the programme finishes.

I look at my watch and do a quick calculation. 'I think maybe in another hour, but I can use my mobile to call him.'

'No, lass, you can use the landline. It's on the hall table.'

'But you'll need to let me pay you for the call. It costs a fortune to phone New Zealand.'

She shakes her head. 'Not with the phone package I have. I can phone anywhere in the world free as long as the call doesn't last more than an hour.'

'No worry there. With all the fresh air I had on

the bridge today, I don't think I'll last more than ten minutes into the call before I fall asleep.'

An hour later when Simon answers my call, he sounds sleepy. 'Don't tell me I've misjudged the time and wakened you.'

His laugh comes over the line. 'You have wakened me, darling, but only because I had a lie in with no work today.'

'Oh, of course, I forgot it was Cup Day in Wellington. Are you going to the races?'

'Gavin did ask me, but I feel it's too hot, so I declined. Thought I'd keep Smoky company, and do some gardening later when it's cooler.'

'Well, don't work too hard,' I say, and tell him about my walk over the bridge.

'Hope you took lots of pictures.'

'Yes. I'll bore you with them when I come home.'

'Missing you, darling.'

'Miss you too. But I'm going to end the call here, Simon, as we're going to Aberdeen tomorrow and have to be up bright and early.'

'That should be nice,' he says, and we speak for a few minutes more. 'Love you,' he says, before we end our call.

'Love you too,' I respond, promising to speak again soon.

CHAPTER SIXTY ONE

'I have a suggestion for tomorrow,' Aunt Viv says a few days later, when she and I are enjoying tea and toast before bed. I can see the excitement in her eyes, as I wait for her to continue.

'You'll remember I told you I met your gran in the women's hostel in Glasgow.'

I nod, wondering what's coming next, but I don't interrupt.

'After a while, we became tired of hostel life and we rented a flat together in Rutherglen.' She stops, waiting I guess for my reaction.

'Where's Rutherglen?'

'A town only a few miles from Glasgow city centre, where we both worked. There was good public transport from Rutherglen, so it was a convenient place to live.' She falls silent for a moment before dropping in her surprise. 'I thought you and I could take the train to Glasgow and go to Rutherglen. I'll show you where your gran and I worked and where we lived. What do you say?'

'Thanks, Aunt Viv,' I say, my voice husky with unshed tears.

She squeezes my hands. 'Okay, lass, let's get some sleep so that we can be up bright and early tomorrow for our adventure.'

***

'This fair takes me back,' Aunt Viv enthuses, when she and I come out of Glasgow Queen Street railway station the following morning and walk down to George Square.

I take a picture of the sunlit Square, enclosed on four sides by magnificent buildings. Following my gaze, she smiles. 'I think they're superb too. That one, with the war memorial in front of it, is Glasgow City Chambers. You can do an interesting guided tour round the building, free it is too, but I don't think we'd have time to do it today if we also want to get to Rutherglen.'

'No, I think we'll forget the tour, although I'm sure inside will be fantastic. Those are lovely buildings facing the City Chambers.'

'Yes, some of them have been bank headquarters, now converted into restaurants. And these buildings across the Square facing us included at one time a Post Office and a Tourist Information Bureau.'

The two of us cross the road when the lights turn green and begin to walk across the Square. 'Am I walking too fast?' I slow down to ask, sensing Aunt Viv is hobbling a little.

'A wee bit,' she tells me. 'Let's take a pew for a few minutes,' she suggests, sitting down on one of the many benches spaced out across the Square.

'Who are on the statues?' I ask, slipping off my back-pack and joining her on the bench.

'I used to know, lass, but I've forgotten a lot of them. Over there in the far corner,' and she points to one of the sculptures, 'that's James Watt, the inventor of the steam engine. And the two on horseback, that's Queen Victoria and Prince Albert. There's also a statue of Robert Burns, Scotland's national poet, but I can't remember where it is.'

'I remember having to learn Robert Burns' poem 'Tam o' Shanter' at school in Wellington. Gran had to help me with pronouncing the Scottish words.'

'Of course, New Zealand was settled by lots of Scots so I expect they will be keen to keep the Scots language going in the schools.' She chuckles. 'To be honest, I think a lot of people in this country have the same problem understanding the poem as you did.'

After a short rest, we get up and walk past the war memorial, towards Ingram Street and from there down to Argyle Street. This is a busy shopping street, pedestrianised so you can walk about without having to watch out for traffic. We stand in the centre of the wide road and Aunt Viv points out a large department store with DEBENHAMS written on its frontage. 'That's where your gran and I worked all those years ago.' She speaks almost to herself, lost in her memories. Then she shakes herself back to the present and speaks to me. 'It was called Marshall's back then and was a high-class establishment. I worked in the haberdashery department and your gran was in the office on the top floor.'

'And how far from the hostel was this store?'

'Come and I'll show you.' She links arms with me and steers me past the St Enoch Centre and St Enoch Underground down to the Clydeside. Standing with our backs to the river, she points out the spot where the hostel had been. 'It's been demolished long ago, of course.'

She goes back into her memories, and then speaks again. 'The residents were all female. There was a strict rule that no men were to be brought into the hostel and anyone found with a lad in their room was sent packing.'

'That sounds so weird. Almost Dickensian.'

'Aye, they wouldn't get away with that rule nowadays, but we were real innocents in those days. Let's go to Kimble's for coffee,' she suggests.

Back at the St Enoch Centre, we ride on the escalator up to the café.

From our window table, we have a view over St Enoch Square. 'There was also St Enoch railway station when we lived here but the building was razed to the ground to make way for this modern shopping mall. Such a shame, as it was a beautiful building.'

'But it's the same everywhere, planners pull down fabulous buildings and throw up shoddy ones in their place.' I sit back to allow the waitress to lay our tea and scones in front of us.

On leaving the café, we board a train at Argyle Street station. With the journey being partly low level, it's nice to come back into bright sunlight once we reach Rutherglen. It's only a five-minute walk from the station to Main Street, although we take a bit longer because of Aunt Viv's poor mobility. She's a stalwart though and doesn't complain.

We cross the road at the traffic lights and stand in front of the Rutherglen shopping arcade. 'See that grey building over there, next to the red sandstone one.'

I shade my eyes from the strong sun with my hand. 'The building with the number 197 on the front door?'

'Yes. If you look up to the oriel window on the top floor right,' and, seeing my eyes rest on the window in question, she continues. 'That was our front room in the flat, the bedroom and kitchen were to the back of the building. In these tenement flats we didn't have a bathroom, there was a communal toilet on the stair landing.'

'Did that mean you shared your toilet with other families?' I wrinkle my nose as I ask the question.

'Yes, lass, that's the way it was, and tenement dwellers thought nothing of it. It's different now though and the flats all have bathrooms fitted.'

'What's that building along there, the one with the clock tower on it, and the Union Jack on its flagpole?'

'That's Rutherglen Town Hall.' She's barely said it, when the clock strikes three. 'I think we better head back to Glasgow to catch our train home. We don't want to land ourselves in the teatime traffic.'

***

When we board the Dundee train, we are lucky to get a seat facing one another with a table between us. Aunt Viv immediately drops off to sleep and I sit back with 'A Spider's Thread Across the Tay.'

She wakens up as I get to the last page in the novel. 'That was a wonderful story, I didn't want it to end,' I say, laying the book down on the table.

'Glad you enjoyed it. And when we get home,

I'll give you the sequel called 'Broken Threads'. A lot of that story is set in India.'

'Sounds super. But I might not have time to read it before I leave.'

'No problem. You can take it home with you. In fact, you can take both books and pass them on to your pals.'

'Thanks, Aunt Viv.'

We fall silent for a short time and I'm the one who breaks it.

'How long did you and Gran live in Rutherglen?'

'We lived there almost two years before I married Dave, and then he and I went to live in Giffnock on the south side of Glasgow.'

'Was Gran in the flat longer?'

The train comes to a halt at Perth and we watch some passengers getting off and a couple of backpackers boarding before resuming our conversation.

'Yes,' Aunt Viv tells me, 'she stayed for about six months on her own and then later with her first husband.'

I gasp, wide-eyed. 'You mean Grandad wasn't her only husband? She'd been married before?'

'Your gran had two husbands before she married your Grandad.'

'Oh my God, I never knew anything about that. Did you know her husbands?'

'Yes. Her first husband worked in Marshall's store beside us. It wasn't a happy marriage and your gran didn't love him.'

'Oh heck. And was her second marriage better?'

'That was a real love match but sadly he died in an accident.'

By this time the tears are running down my cheeks. 'Poor Gran, no wonder she never spoke of her life in Scotland.'

'Her happiest times were at my parents' farm in Ayrshire. Mum and Dad loved her like a daughter, and she became part of our family. My parents sort of adopted her, we all did really, my two sisters and myself as well.'

'Thank goodness, otherwise I don't know how she'd have survived. Did she tell you anything about her own parents?'

'Not a lot. She was secretive about that part of her life. What I do know, and it's very little, is that her dad was killed at Dunkirk during the Second World War, and she was raised by her mother and a stepfather, who I suspect was cruel to her. Her mother died when your gran was 18, and that's when she came to Glasgow.'

Seeing how distressed I'm becoming, Aunt Viv ends the conversation. 'I think we'll leave it there for the moment, lass, and get some shut eye. We've got another forty-five minutes before we get to Dundee.'

She leans back against her head rest and is soon fast asleep again. Although I close my eyes, I can't sleep. I'm too churned up over what I've discovered about Gran's previous life.

***

'Am I glad to get home, lass,' Aunt Viv says, once we're back in Farington Street. 'I've enjoyed my day, but it's been tiring.'

Seeing how swollen her ankles are, I insist that she sits on the settee with her feet up on a stool while I make us both some supper.

Once in bed, even though I'm exhausted, I can't get to sleep, unable to stop thinking about Gran's childhood.

CHAPTER SIXTY TWO

'A letter for you, lass,' Aunt Viv says, and smiles as she hands me an air letter. 'Wish we could still get these, but the Royal Mail have done away with them, making us use writing paper and envelope and then having to wait in a queue in the Post Office to buy a stamp. So much easier when we could simply drop the air letter into the post box.'

'It's from my friend Elva,' I say, when I see the familiar writing on the front.

'Here, use this.' She hands me a silver letter opener, which was lying on the sideboard. 'I'll away and make us a coffee while you're reading your letter.'

I've digested all Elva's news by the time Aunt Viv returns with the tray, which she puts down on the coffee table.

I groan when I see the plate with some of her delicious home baking on it. 'I'll never diet while I'm here,' I say, as I help myself to a piece of millionaire's shortbread.

'Oh, get away with you, lass, you certainly don't have to worry about your weight. Anyway, what about your friend, is she okay?'

'She is, and also her mum and her brother. Elva's looking forward to hearing all about my trip when I get home.'

'You're very close to Elva, aren't you?'

'Yep, it's a bit like Gran was with your family. Elva's family have adopted me.'

'And very nice too. Mind you, once you and that young man of yours tie the knot, you'll be building your own family.'

Her words, that young man of yours, make me smile. It's the sort of thing Gran would have said.

'Could I email some of my pictures to Elva? That is, if you don't mind me using your computer.'

'Of course I don't mind. In fact, why don't you do that now while I switch on the washing machine? We can get the clothes out on the line while there's a good breeze.'

'Are you sure I can't help?

'No need, lass. There's nothing to do other than press a button. I'll have a read at the newspaper while the clothes are washing.'

'Okay, thanks,' I say, and make my way into the bedroom where the computer is housed.

CHAPTER SIXTY THREE

'I can't believe I need to begin packing today. It seems like yesterday I was organising my luggage to come here.'

Facing me across the breakfast table, Aunt Viv nods. 'It's been so lovely having you to stay, Ros.' She sighs. 'I'm going to miss you, lass.'

I lean across the table and hold her hand for a moment. 'I'll miss you too, but I hope I'll be back again in the next few years, maybe with Simon this time.'

'That would be nice. But just ignore me being sad; I've always hated goodbyes.'

'We'll make it a quick goodbye at the airport and you'll have Daryl with you to drive you home.'

'That's true,' she replies, and smiles once more. 'Now, lass, is there anything you'd like us to do today? You don't need to begin packing until this afternoon.'

'You told me about the new V & A museum that opened last week. I'd like to go there, if you feel up to it.'

'I certainly would. My neighbours two doors down were there last week and said they'd enjoyed the experience.'

I take the last piece of toast from the rack on the table and spread it with marmalade. 'I googled the V & A the other day and there's a Rennie Mackintosh room on display. I love his work.'

Aunt Viv lifts her hand and taps her forehead, a

mannerism I've become familiar with over the past four weeks. 'I remember seeing that on TV. It was the furniture from a room in Miss Cranston's tearooms in Glasgow, which was demolished. It lay in storage for years and has now been re-assembled in the V & A.'

I start to gather up the breakfast things and carry them into the kitchen. 'Are we on for it, then?' I call over my shoulder.

'We sure are.'

Back in my bedroom, I comb my hair and tidy myself up for our outing. I'm glancing through my pictures on the iPad when Aunt Viv pops her head round the door. 'Pleased with your photos?' she asks.

'Yes, come and see this one,' I say, holding out the iPad.

'That's lovely, lass. Where did you take that?'

'In that lovely park we visited, off Kingsway.'

'Oh, Camperdown park. Yes, that was a lovely outing and now you have a picture to remind you of it. Now, if we get our skates on, we could catch the eleven o'clock bus.'

***

I'm packing my case, ready for tomorrow's departure, trying to convince myself I've been over here for almost a month. I'm sad about leaving Aunt Viv as I've had an awesome trip, seeing so many beautiful places, including today's visit to the V & A. But I've missed Simon like mad. It will be fantastic to see him again. We've kept in touch by email and Skype, but nothing beats face to face contact.

I leave my nightwear out of the case and put on the new outfit I bought in Debenhams the day we were in Glasgow. I'm wearing it as a dress, although you can wear the skirt and top as separates. I want to look nice when I go out for dinner tonight with Aunt Viv and the family. I can fold my new clothes into the case when we return from the restaurant.

I'm laying the case on the carpet at the side of the bed, when Aunt Viv calls me from her bedroom on the other side of the corridor. 'Ros, could you help me with this necklace please?'

'Sure.' I go into her bedroom, spacious and bright, with a large bay window.

'Thanks,' she says, once her necklace is fastened.

I'm almost at the door when she calls me back. 'I've been keeping something for you Ros. If you take a look in the back of the wardrobe over there, you'll find the box.'

Intrigued, I go over to the heavily carved oak wardrobe standing in the corner beside the window.

I open the wardrobe door and kneel down. Reaching to the back, I pull out an old shoe box. The layer of dust on the top shows the contents haven't been looked at for a long time. I take my handkerchief out of my skirt pocket, and wipe away the dust.

Aunt Viv pats the space on the bed beside her and I carry the box over and sit down. 'Your gran and grandad stayed with us for a few weeks back in the seventies,' she explains, 'it was after they'd sold their house in Glasgow and before they left for their life in New Zealand. This box was left behind by mistake and when I offered to post the diaries that were in the box, your gran told me to throw them out. I decided against that, in case she changed her mind in later years.'

Inside the box are a number of diaries, or more precisely old jotters. The edges are quite crumpled and one jotter has a corner of the cover missing. A quick glance through the jotters reveals that they seem to be from the 1950s and 1960s.

'Have you read these?'

The old lady shakes her head. 'No, I haven't. Despite us being best friends, there were some aspects of your gran's life that I wasn't privy to. I always felt she was harbouring a secret, but I couldn't guess what it was.' She stops speaking for a moment and stares out of the window, with a faraway look on her face. 'When you wrote with the sad news that your gran had passed away, I did then consider reading them. I decided against this though because I wasn't sure I wanted to know what they contained.'

She pats my arm, then leaning her hands on the mattress, pushes herself up from the bed. 'You can discard the box and squeeze the diaries into your case, Ros. Now, I suppose we should be getting our coats on as Daryl will be picking us up in the next ten minutes or so.'

'Thanks, Aunt Viv, I'll treasure them.' I give her a hug and take the box to my room. Deciding against putting the jotters in the case, I place them in my hand luggage instead.

CHAPTER SIXTY FOUR

'Your drink, Madam.'

I remove my reading glasses and slip a bookmark in at my place in 'Broken Threads' before I close the novel. The smiling air hostess lays the silver tray on the table at my side.

'Thank you.' I glance around the other passengers sharing my peace and space on the aircraft, and I'm thankful that Simon persuaded me to travel business class. After all it has been a trip of a lifetime, and the luxury away from the crush of economy class has been worth every cent.

The tonic water fizzes when I twist the cap off the bottle and pour its contents into my gin. Pushing some loose strands of hair away from my face, I lean back against the padded headrest to savour the smoothness of the liquid as it slips down.

My visit to Gran's homeland has held many wonders. I felt at home the minute I stepped on to Scottish soil, the similarity of the scenery so like that of my native New Zealand. It confirmed what Gran had told me on the very few occasions when she spoke about her life in the old country as she called Scotland.

When my glass is empty, I go off to freshen up. The facilities here are luxurious compared to economy class; cloth towels and luxury hand cream.

I take the first of the diaries out of my hand luggage. I'm so glad Aunt Viv didn't destroy them. I open the earliest diary, with 1956 written on the front cover. Inside the cheap, soft-covered notebook, Gran has written a new date at the top of each entry.

I begin to read the familiar handwriting, not spidery as it became in later years, but strong and bold with the confidence of youth. All the entries are fairly routine until I come to a date in March, where Gran writes about sitting at her mother's bedside when she died. The words are poignant, and I can feel her pain. Here she is, writing about my great-grandmother, and I don't even know her name. How I wish I'd asked more questions when Gran was alive. Perhaps Mum knew something of Gran's early life but, if so, she kept it to herself. With Mum passing away at such a young age, it's too late now.

When the hostess arrives with my next meal, I close the notebook. I feel ready for a break anyway. Once my tray is taken away again, I lower my berth into the sleeping position. I check my watch which I moved on to New Zealand time earlier in the flight. Right now, it's just after noon in Wellington, so we should land on time around four o'clock. Simon will be at the terminal waiting for me; my heart flutters at the prospect. I hold out my hand and stare at the engagement ring, the diamonds that surround the ruby glinting in the overhead light.

I switch off the lamp at my side and put on my eye mask before drifting off to sleep.

CHAPTER SIXTY FIVE

Simon couldn't believe how churned up inside he felt about Ros returning today. Unable to settle to anything, all he could think was that she'd be home in less than two hours. He was desperate to hold her in his arms once more.

He put out some food for Smoky, who'd come in after some early morning wanderings. He was pleased that the cat didn't appear to have been on a killing spree today, recalling the remains of a bird's torso that he'd presented to Simon yesterday.

'Ros will be home today,' he said, and the cat peered up at him as though he understood every word.

Once on the freeway, Simon made good progress. The sun shone brightly from a cloudless sky, as though, like him, it was welcoming Ros back to her home city. He arrived at the airport with lots of time to spare. He went straight to the Arrivals board and saw that Flight NZ1482 was scheduled to land on time.

His heart was pounding and his throat dry as he wove his way through the crowd gathered in the waiting area. He chose a spot close to the barrier and wedged himself in beside the handrail leading from the arrivals door. His palm was sticky with sweat and he wiped his hand on his shorts. His stomach churned and he felt nauseous with the excitement of seeing her again. He was determined that they'd go together on any future trips. They'd be arranging their wedding on her return, and he couldn't wait to settle down to life together as a married couple.

The screen showed that her flight had landed, and shortly afterwards the exit doors opened and passengers began to spill through, many of them pushing trolleys laden with luggage. He moved even closer to the barrier and rocked from foot to foot, his eyes firmly on the doorway.

***

When we land and the fasten seat belt sign has gone out, they let those of us in business class off the plane first. Yet another advantage over economy passengers.

My case is one of the first to arrive on the carousel and I push it towards the green nothing to declare lane. When I get to the exit, the doors are open, and I walk towards the ramp leading down to the arrivals hall. I glance round and straight away see Simon waving like mad, a huge grin on his face.

'Simon,' I call, and our hands touch over the barrier, as we gaze into one another's eyes. With excitement mounting, I get to the bottom of the ramp, and find him crushed against the barrier. I fall into his outstretched arms and we hug, so tightly I can hardly breathe. 'I'm never going to let you leave me again,' he whispers, before his lips find mine for a passionate kiss; together on our own island, we ignore the jostling crowd around us. Eventually we come up for air, still with our eyes locked together.

'I guess we'd better get ourselves out of here,' Simon says, his voice hoarse with emotion. He takes my case and forges a path through the vast crowd, with me following in his wake.

***

When the car comes to a halt in the driveway at Kiwi Crescent, I jump out, drinking in my familiar surroundings. I walk round to the boot, where Simon is lifting out my luggage, and hug him again. 'It's wonderful to be home. Aunt Viv was so kind to me and it was lovely to be with her, but this is where I belong.'

I pick up my hand luggage and Simon throws his arm around my waist and pushes my large case at his side as we make our way into the house, where Smoky is waiting for me in the hallway. Dropping my bag on to the floor, I bend down and scoop up my furry companion, rubbing his face against my cheek. He meows his welcome and climbs on to my shoulder, his tail waving about and brushing against my face.

'Do you want me to make you something to drink?' Simon ruffles the fur on Smoky's head as he's speaking.

'No thanks, darling. I've done nothing but eat and drink since I left Scotland.' I put Smoky down and he pads away to the kitchen.

'I'll put your case into the bedroom meantime,' Simon says, and he picks up my hand luggage at the same time. I slip off my jacket and hang it in the hall cloakroom, then follow him along the corridor to the bedroom.

I look around, admiring my familiar possessions. The window is open, and the drapes are blowing in the light breeze coming through it.

'I'm impressed by how tidy it is.'

'Just as well you didn't see it yesterday. I did a blitz on the place this morning.'

He comes over and takes me into his arms and we kiss once more. We are standing at the edge of the bed and Simon looks over at the window and then back at me. When I nod, he moves over and closes the vertical blinds, before pushing me gently down on to the bed.

CHAPTER SIXTY SIX

Simon and Matt are both at a Union meeting this morning, and with Charlie and Ted also out of the office, I'm here on my own. With all the buzz that usually goes on when we have a full staff, I'm enjoying the peace and quiet.

I finish my first draft of an article Charlie has asked me to do and leave it on Matt's desk for him to proofread. I search in his desk drawer for a paperclip and, unable to find one, I try the one below. After staring at the drawer's contents, I let out a gasp.

Slowly I lift out some pieces of paper and lay them on the desk; all random words cut out of newspapers and magazines. In addition, I see a message typed in bold, large lettering and recognise it as the one that was in the Valentine card I received from the stalker.

By now my head is bursting with confusion. Good God, Matt is my stalker, and for so long I'd blamed Simon. My first reaction is to confront Matt when he returns to the office, and tear a strip off him for putting me through such fear and anxiety. My second is that I need a coffee to calm me.

I drink my coffee and try to get my head round what I've just found. I never suspected Matt of being anything other than a decent guy and it strikes me now that, while I thought of him as a confirmed bachelor, he probably yearned to be in a relationship. His stalking of me was purely a fantasy, as I could never have considered him any more than a work colleague.

My anger begins to drain away, as slowly the realisation that he meant me no harm hits me. He would never have hurt me, but I think was too shy to tell me how he felt. I'm sure he would be embarrassed if Simon and the others discovered what he'd done.

Anyway, I think, now that he's aware that Simon and I are together, there will be no more phone calls or stalking.

I close the drawer and return to my own desk.

Shortly afterwards Simon and Matt come back into the office, and they tell me what transpired at the Union meeting.

***

After work I do some shopping. The prices are cheaper at the supermarket in Cuba Street than they are at our local shops in Lyall Bay.

When I get home, I unpack the bags and go into the conservatory where Smoky is reclining happily on the two-seater settee, basking in the sunshine coming through the glass roof. This is his favourite position in the late afternoon, and he purrs contentedly as I stroke the top of his head.

'That's me finished my first week back at work,' I tell my pet, as I squeeze on to the settee beside him and he climbs on to my knee.

It has taken me almost a week to get over my jet lag and today is the first time I'm feeling back to normal.

Simon has gone to The Green Man with Ted and Matt, so we won't eat until he comes home about eight o'clock. Our arrangement is that I do the cooking during the week and he is our chef at the weekend, unless we are out for dinner. Seems to be working so far and we haven't had any major arguments over the rota.

I lift Smoky off my knee and go to switch on the oven. While it's heating up, I prepare the meat in the casserole dish. Then while the meat is cooking, I peel potatoes and sit the pot on the hob to simmer slowly until dinner time.

When the vegetables are prepared, I make a coffee and settle down beside Smoky once more, with Gran's diaries in my hand. I have read some more entries since I arrived home but usually only do so when Simon is out. The entries are too personal to share, even with him, just yet.

The entries are mainly about Gran's work in an insurance company, but I hold my breath when I read an entry in July.

Wednesday 18th July 1956
Dear Diary,
I got away safely while B was sleeping following a nightshift. Very relieved, don't want to see him or that town ever again. Even writing this makes me shudder.

Glasgow seemed the place to come as Mum was born here. Wish I'd asked her where in the city she lived but too late now. I miss her more than words can say.

My room in the hostel is drab but hope not to be here long. I'm trying to think like Scarlett O'Hara and say 'tomorrow is another day.'

Who is B, and why did Gran have to leave home and find lodgings in Glasgow? I move on to the following day's entry.

Thursday 19th July 1956
Dear Diary,
The woman who dealt with me in the Ministry of Labour this morning was a bit abrupt. I suppose she has so many clients that we are all just numbers to her. She did say they would contact me with details of any suitable jobs that become available. I will also keep my eyes on the newspaper adverts. I can check them in the newspapers available in the library to save money. Hope I find a job soon before the money I've saved runs out.

I went into the same café as yesterday, Luigi's in St Enoch Square. I ordered a plain cookie and a cup of tea as that was the cheapest thing on the menu. The waitress recognised me and it felt good, like I had a friend.

I put my mug down and lean my head against the back of the sofa. I try to keep calm, but it's difficult when reading Gran's words. I never for a moment imagined she had anything but a happy life when she lived in Scotland. Since her mother is dead by this stage in the diaries, and she was still living with B, I think he must be her mother's second husband, the stepfather Aunt Viv mentioned.

I take another drink and force myself to read on. Scattered throughout the mundane, some of Gran's words make me sad. The Ministry of Labour woman kept her promise and Gran started working in a tobacconist's shop quite close to the hostel. She appears to get on well with the manager and her fellow assistant, but she is still lonely and not coping with life in a large city.

She writes in September that she is experiencing suicidal thoughts. I gasp as I read about her walking on to a bridge over the River Clyde, with the idea of throwing herself into the water below. A woman with a dog walks past her and she stops to speak to Gran; although the woman is unaware of it, she saves Gran's life, as the interruption stops her from carrying out her plan.

Halfway through November Gran records that she has taken an overdose of pills and is found in her bedroom at the hostel by a member of staff. She survives the attempt, but the overdose is serious enough to warrant hospital treatment.

Tears are pouring down my face by now, but I have a compulsion to continue with the diary entries, no matter how distressing. Just when I'm about to close the diaries and have a break from all the sadness, I come across a more uplifting entry.

Monday 26th November 1956
Dear Diary,

Started working in the office of Marshall's department store in Argyle Street today. Like my job in the tobacconist's, I can walk there from the hostel and save on travelling expenses. I am also earning a better wage there than I did in the tobacconist's shop.

Viv told me about the vacancy as she is a sales assistant in Marshall's. I met Viv in the hostel and we've become good friends. She's my first friend since coming to Glasgow. Hope this is the start of a better future for me.

I echo Gran's sentiments and dry my eyes, so happy to find that she has made a friend in Aunt Viv, who has helped her find a job. Now I can't stop myself from reading on. I leaf through fairly quickly until I get to Christmas day.

Tuesday 25th December 1956
Dear Diary,

I can scarcely believe I'm here at Fairfields with Viv and her family. Sheena and Charlie are such caring people, and they've made me really welcome, as have Viv's twin sisters. Viv is going to give me a tour of the farm later.

I'm off to bed now after a wonderful Christmas day, enfolded by love. Charlie lit the fire in the bedroom for me and Sheena has put a hot water bottle into my bed, so I'm sure to be snug and warm.

When the timer on the oven reminds me the meat is cooked, I close over the diary and carry my empty mug into the kitchen. I mash the potatoes and have just lifted the casserole out of the oven, when I hear Simon's car in the driveway.

CHAPTER SIXTY SEVEN

Simon whistled as he weeded round the flower beds. He'd tidied the garden regularly while Ros was in Scotland although there hadn't been so much growth at that time of year. Now that spring was here, grass and flowers were springing up again and he'd plenty of tasks that needed attending to.

Simon had missed Ros more than he'd expected, and the time apart had confirmed in his mind that he wanted to be with her. He hoped she felt the same; he thought she did, but Ros wasn't someone who showed her feelings overtly. A bit reserved and kept her thoughts close to her chest. He knew she was well through reading her gran's diaries, but she hadn't told him anything of their contents. He'd decided not to pry, but to wait until she was ready to divulge the old girl's secrets.

'Simon, coffee,' Ros called from the patio door, holding up a mug.

'Excellent.' He laid the trowel down on the path and left his muddy boots outside the back door. He dusted off his sweatshirt and jeans with his hands and went, stocking-soled, into the house. Washing his hands at the kitchen sink, he joined Ros in the sitting room, where his coffee was waiting for him. He took a sip of the strong, black coffee, and sighed. Just as he liked it.

***

Elva and Adam are standing outside the Queen's Theatre, sheltering underneath a golf umbrella, when we get there.

I pull the hood of my parka further up to protect my hair from the sudden deluge. 'Sorry. We had difficulty finding a car park space.'

'Used a hotel car park, hope I don't get a ticket,' Simon says, as we go into the foyer.

We're barely settled in our seats when the overture begins and the theatre quietens. The Wellington Symphony Orchestra play for a time before Frank and Michelle, two of the Strictly Come Dancing professionals, waltz on to the stage. This is one of three performances they are giving in New Zealand and we've been looking forward to the show for months.

The next couple of hours whiz by as we are captivated by the music, dance and costumes. The entire audience stands up as one, applauding Frank, Michelle and the rest of the cast, at the end of the performance.

'There's a bar across the road,' Adam says, when we near the theatre exit. 'Will we go there for a nightcap?' The rain has eased while we've been in the theatre, but under the lamplight raindrops still glisten on the pavement.

'That would be a lovely ending to the evening,' I reply. 'It's okay, I'll have a soft drink and drive us home,' I add, when I see Simon is about to decline the invitation.

Adam rubs his hands together, when we get into the bar. 'Right, what are we all going to have to drink?'

Over our drinks, the two men become better acquainted and find they have a number of interests in common.

'We must do this again soon,' Elva says, when we return to our respective cars.

***

'I'm ready to hit the hay,' Simon says, once we get home.

'Same here.'

Simon uses the bathroom first, while I hang up my coat to dry and push some old newspaper into my damp shoes.

By the time I've cleaned my teeth and returned to the bedroom, Simon is sound asleep. I slip under the sheets beside him but, after lying awake for an hour, I get up and return to the living room.

I make myself a mug of drinking chocolate and sit down with Gran's diaries.

A lot of what she writes is about her work and is pretty ordinary, so I skim through these parts. I notice the name Steve Dixon features quite often. She writes that he works in the storeroom of Marshall's. Reading between the lines, it doesn't sound like Gran cares much for him, although he seems to fancy her.

Then an entry dated November 1957 catches my attention. As with the earlier entries, Gran has obviously written up her diary in bed before going to sleep.

Friday 22nd November 1957
Dear Diary,

Writing this before I put out the lamp. I was dreading the dance tonight. Was scared that Steve Dixon would get ideas that I wanted to be his girlfriend. I only went with him to the dance to please Viv who's been a good friend to me. Viv was going to the dance with Dave from the carpet department and she was keen that Steve and I make up a foursome.

Sheena made a dress for Viv and one for me and what a wonderful job she did. I felt like a million dollars in my dress.

The evening turned out much better than I'd expected. The Plaza is a beautiful ballroom, with a magnificent marble fountain in the middle of the dance floor, and I confess I even enjoyed dancing with Steve. But when he tried to kiss me in the close when we got home, I found that a step too far. I know my rejection wounded him and embarrassed Viv, but the thought of letting a man kiss me revolts me. How I hate B for making me like this.

My tears are flowing freely again when I get to the end of this entry, partly tears of joy that Gran has had such a happy time at the dance but also of sadness that she had been put off men by the actions of her ghastly stepfather. He has obviously abused poor Gran, which horrifies me.

My thoughts move to my time with Don and his treatment of me, and a further flood of tears begin. Strange that I, like Gran, experienced something that put us off men for a long time.

CHAPTER SIXTY EIGHT

Nora waved to Viv from the table she was sitting at in The Hungry Horse. She stood up and started to speak as her friend neared the table. 'Lovely to see you again, Viv, and I'm so looking forward to hearing about the time you spent with Ros.' She opened her arms and gave her old friend a welcoming hug.

'It seems ages since we last met.' Viv draped her coat over the spare seat and laid her umbrella on the floor under the table.

'And so it is. Ros was with you for four weeks don't forget. I waited until yesterday to phone you, as I knew you'd want a rest after all the travelling about.'

'Thanks, Nora. That was thoughtful. But I'm well rested by now and raring to go.'

As they were eating, Viv went over the outings she'd had with Ros, including their visit to Glasgow and Rutherglen, with Nora hanging on to every word.

Nora wrung her hands in excitement when her friend was speaking about showing Ros the flat in Rutherglen.

'She must have been so happy to see the flat. Was she asking you loads of questions about that time in her gran's life?'

'Yes, and I think she was thrilled to hear about our lives at that time.'

By the time they reached dessert, Viv had come

to the end of her stories. 'Now it's your turn, Nora, tell me what you've been up to since we last met.'

'Compared to yours, mine is very ordinary. Mainly shopping and housework although my nephew, Graeme, took me out for a drive one day last week.'

'Lovely, where did you go?'

'We went to Perth and had a tour round Scone Palace. It was years since I'd been there.' She went on to tell Viv about the wonderful guide they had at the Palace and repeated some of the interesting facts the lady had told them of the history of the place.

'And how is Graeme doing? And his family?'

'He's great. Had a promotion at work a few months back. The kids are so grown up now, the youngest of the three is now a teenager. Can't believe where the years have gone.'

'Was it very sad saying goodbye to Ros when she left?' Nora asked, when they were enjoying a coffee after their meal.

Viv nodded. 'It was, especially as there's no guarantee I'll see her again,' she said, her voice choked with emotion. She fell silent for a moment and looked down at her empty cup, turning it round in her saucer. Nora said nothing and waited for her to continue.

'Before she left, I gave her the diaries I had in the wardrobe. You'll remember the ones I told you about?'

'I'm glad she's got them. She'll be able to read them when she feels ready.' Nora glanced at her watch. 'Good Lord, Viv, look at the time. I'll need to get to the supermarket so that I catch the four o'clock bus home.'

***

Viv made herself a cup of tea when she got back to Farington Street and sat down with it to watch her favourite quiz show 'Pointless'. She dozed off about three quarters way through and missed the last ten minutes.

By the time she wakened, it was almost seven o'clock, and 'The One Show' had started. Still feeling full from her lunch, she decided to skip dinner and instead switched on her laptop.

She cleared the junk messages from her email, then pressed compose.

My Dear Ros

Thank you for letting me know you had arrived home safely and your darling Simon was waiting for you at the airport.

By now you will have finished your first week back at work and I hope you didn't suffer too much from jet lag. It always used to take me the best part of a week to get over a long plane journey.

The house has seemed so empty without you Ros and I'm missing your company. However, all good things come to an end and we can only hope that we meet again in the not too distant future. You know you're welcome here anytime, Simon too.

I met my friend, Nora, in town for lunch today and she was keen to hear about our time together. It was good to see her as we hadn't met for over a month, so we had a good catch up over lunch. We went to The Hungry Horse, you might remember I took you there when we were in town?

Have you started reading your gran's diaries yet? I hope they will help you piece together your gran's life when I knew her. Also hope there won't be too much sadness.

Take care lass and I look forward to hearing from you soon.
Much Love from Aunt Viv.
xx

CHAPTER SIXTY NINE

Today I'm meeting Elva for lunch in Oriental Bay. We're going to try out a new seafood restaurant we've discovered there.

Simon went out early this morning to go duck shooting with Matt from the Post and another couple of mates. Somewhere towards the east coast I think he said. He won't be home until late this evening and has promised to bring us a Chinese carry-out.

I put away all thoughts of the housework I should be doing. Instead, with a couple of hours to spare, I nurse a mug of coffee while I continue to read Gran's diaries. I greedily drink in all that my dear gran has experienced during her early years in Glasgow and before I know it, I've moved on to 1959. By now I know that Viv and Dave are married. Gran was their bridesmaid and Dave asked Steve to be his best man. Because Steve is head over heels in love with Gran, and no doubt with some encouragement from Viv, Gran convinces herself that her feelings for Steve are sufficient to allow her to accept his proposal of marriage. She is living in the Rutherglen flat alone now that Viv has moved out and needs someone to share the rent with her, so this sways her decision. I have the feeling she knew from early on she'd made a terrible mistake.

Saturday 12th December 1959

Dear Diary,

The wedding yesterday was a happy occasion, but in bed last night I couldn't respond to Steve's advances. I made the excuse I had a headache but I know he wasn't convinced.

I don't know why I agreed to marry him. Viv says Steve and I will make a good life together and I hope she's right. I hope in time that I'll come to love Steve. I want my marriage to be like Viv and Dave's but I can't trust any man not to hurt me.

Aware that time is marching on for my meeting with Elva, I allow myself another half hour with the diaries. I finish 1959 and move on to 1960, then an entry early in January leaves me shell-shocked.

Thursday 7ᵗʰ January 1960
Dear Diary,

How could B have found out where I live? What rotten luck that, when he was made redundant, he found a job in Rutherglen. I've not mentioned him to Steve and pray that they never meet. Oh God, why did he have to come here of all places? The thought of him terrifies me but I'm trying to keep calm, so Steve doesn't suspect anything.

I'm still finding it hard to be a proper wife to Steve. When we have sex, I try to make out I'm happy about it, but I'm sure he knows my heart isn't in it.

I close the diary and think of how scared Gran must have been when she wrote these words.

***

I see Elva's red hatchback when I drive into the restaurant car park.

'Hi,' she calls to me, when I go into the dining room. 'I've started already.' She lifts the bottle of non-alcoholic wine out of the ice bucket and pours some into my glass.

From the extensive menu, I decide on Blue Cod and Elva plumps for Snapper.

'When did you get here?'

Elva switches her cutlery round. Being left-handed, she always does this. 'Only about five minutes before you arrived. How are you going with your Gran's diaries?'

'I've got as far as 1960.' I've told Elva some of the details from the diaries but haven't said anything to Simon as I'm not sure how much interest they'd hold for him.

I turn the stem of my wine glass slowly between my fingers as I go on. 'I was shocked to discover in the last entry I read that the horrid stepfather has turned up in Rutherglen where she lives.'

'Oh my God, that's awful. Has he come to her flat to pester her?'

'I haven't got that far yet. I ran out of time this morning. She's married to Steve by this time, so I don't know what's going to happen.'

'Gosh, your gran had quite a life, didn't she?'

I shrug. 'Yet she never once told me anything about it. I think she was too embarrassed to talk about the things that happened to her back then. Thank goodness she met my Grandad and found happiness with him.'

The waiter comes over with a basket of delicious looking bread for us.

After our meal, we enjoy a walk along the bay, the happy cries of the bathers reaching us on the prom.

Back home, with Simon still away, I settle down in the garden with the diaries. I start from where I left off and I'm finding it compulsive reading. Even though some of the entries pull at my heartstrings, it's good to know what happened in Gran's early years.

Sunday 13th March 1960
Dear Diary,

I took the bus to Bonnycross today. I didn't want to ever see that town again but, when B turned up on my doorstep threatening me with violence, I had to go. I knew he worked in Rutherglen from Monday to Friday and went back to Bonnycross at the weekend. I needed to confront him and warn him that, if he came near me again, I'd report him to the police. I couldn't face telling them about his abuse, because of all the questions I'd have to answer. But I wanted to frighten him with the thought that I would go to them.

The street was deserted when I got there. I'd worn a headscarf and my sunglasses so no-one would recognise me. There was no reply when I rang the bell and, when I went round to the back of the house, the door was lying ajar. The minute I walked into the kitchen, I smelt gas. Benson was on the floor and the gas was switched on but the ring unlit. The smell was overpowering and I stumbled outside once more.

I stood there in shock. He'd likely fallen on the floor in a drunken stupor, forgetting to light the gas ring, and was probably dead by the time I found him. I realised this was my chance to be rid of him for ever so, after a moment's indecision, I got on the bus and came home to Rutherglen, having touched nothing in the house.

I have consoled myself that I didn't harm him, he'd gassed himself. That means I'm not a murderer, doesn't it? I just omitted to ring for the emergency services. Oh Dear Diary, sometimes I wish there was no such thing as a conscience.

Still trying to take in what the last entry said, my eyes move on to the following day.

Monday 14th March 1960
Dear Diary,
Two police officers came to the flat tonight to let me know of B's death. I'm not sure how they tracked me down, but they knew he was my stepfather.

I tried to feign surprise when they told me about the gassing. They seem to think it was his own doing, which strictly speaking is true. The way I see it, if I hadn't gone to Bonnycross yesterday, B would still be dead. The police asked me to go and identify the body. I don't want to but felt it best to agree.

Steve was there when the policemen called and he was angry that I hadn't told him about B. He wanted to know more and, when I refused to tell him anything, that started another row and he went out and slammed the door behind him.

Oh God why did I ever enter this sham marriage? It isn't fair to Steve either as he deserves more from me but I just can't be the wife he wants.

I shake my head, my heart aching for the pain Gran suffered. I can't read any more at present so close the diary and start to lay the table for our Chinese meal.

CHAPTER SEVENTY

'Will we eat al fresco or in the dining room?' Simon asks the following afternoon, when we're lying on our loungers on the deck, reading.

I turn my book down, open, on the deck and stretch over to take his hand. 'Maybe better indoors,' I suggest, looking up at the dark clouds that have formed over the past hour.

'Yeah, think that's best,' he says, and kisses me. Then he gets up off his lounger and goes into the kitchen. 'I'll call you when dinner's ready,' he says over his shoulder.

'Great.' I smile in anticipation of my roast duck dinner. I love the weekends when I'm waited on. I'm glad Simon cleaned and prepared the duck, part of the booty he came home with last night, as I couldn't have faced doing that. A different matter when you simply buy the prepared meat and poultry from the butcher's but I'm squeamish about handling the produce Simon brings from his shoots.

When dinner is cooked, he escorts me to the table. 'Will Madam please be seated,' he says, pulling out the chair for me. Then, waiter-like, he lays the serviette across my knee.

I laugh and play along with him. 'To what do I owe this special treatment?'

'Have patience and all will be revealed. Cheers.'

Simon lifts his glass to mine as we are about to sample the duck. Delicious meal over, I'm enjoying my second glass of vino when he unveils his surprise.

'Do you remember after our engagement we discussed the possibility of holding our wedding in the Wellington Arms?'

'Of course I remember. But we know they're fully booked until April.'

Simon beams at me, enjoying keeping me in suspense.

'While you were in Scotland, I contacted them again and they agreed to let us know if they received any cancellations. And a short time ago, while I was preparing our dinner, the Events Manager phoned me to say there is now a slot available for Saturday 26th January. We've to let him know before tomorrow if we want to take this date.'

He grabs me as I almost fall off my chair. 'How lucky are we? Tell me I'm not dreaming.'

He grins. 'You're not, darling. What d'ya think?'

I throw my arms around his neck and kiss him. 'I think it's wonderful. Please phone him back Simon and say we'll take it. In case they give it to another couple.' I clench my hands and take deep breaths, trying to believe this has really happened. 'I can't wait to tell Elva the good news. And we'll need to start looking for our dresses.'

'Right, first things first. Will I phone and say yes to the hotel? Then we can phone Lime Tree to let Mum and Dad know.'

'Do that. I'll clear the dishes away while you dial the number.'

After confirming the date and phoning Lime Tree, we settle down on the sofa in front of the television. Simon draws me closer, and he laughs when I start to panic over all that needs to be done.

Unable to keep the news until I see Elva on Tuesday, later that evening I decide to phone her while Simon is engrossed in a footie match on telly. Propping myself up on a stool at the kitchen worktop, I look out at the view over the bay and key in her number.

'Hello, Mrs Kahui, it's me, Ros,' I say when her mother answers, as though she doesn't know my voice by this time.

'How nice to hear from you Ros. Are you well, my dear?'

'Yes thanks, I'm fine and over my jet lag at last.'

'I always suffer badly when I visit my family in Austria. A moment Liebling, and I'll call Elva to the phone. She's worked on her computer already an hour, so needs a break.'

I find it quaint how Mrs Kahui's native language occasionally alters the word order when she speaks English.

'Hi, Ros,' Elva says, a few moments later. 'How're you?'

'Great and I'm phoning with the news that the Wellington Arms have given us a cancellation date for Saturday 26th January.'

I hold the phone away from my ear when her

excited shriek comes over the line.

'That's tremendous news. We'll need to start looking for our dresses?'

'That's exactly what I said. Maybe we could take a day's leave one day next week.'

'You're on,' she says. 'Ros and Simon have set the date for the wedding,' I hear her say as an aside to her mother.

When I hang up, Simon's eyes are still glued to the television screen. Rather than disturb him, I go into the bedroom and lie on top of the duvet and read more of Gran's diaries. I've learned a lot up to now about her early life, but am keen to find out what happens.

By now I've got to 1964, with much of the entries about work and little else, but one entry has me gasping and clenching my fists.

Sunday 22nd March 1964
Dear Diary,

Yesterday I had a birthday I won't forget. I had a lovely dinner with Viv and Dave and they had a birthday cake for me. Of course Steve had forgotten about my birthday but that was no surprise.

Dave drove me home and, knowing Steve would be holding up the bar at the pub, I went to bed, hoping to be asleep before he got home. But I couldn't sleep and got up around one o'clock to make a cup of tea. Before the kettle had boiled, I heard him coming into the close, shouting out and singing at the top of his voice as he came upstairs. Scared he was going to waken up the neighbours, I put my coat over my nightdress and went down to the top landing to tell him to shush.

Some of the bulbs on the stair lights were out. I stepped forward and put my hand out to tell him to be quiet. This startled him and he staggered back and fell down the stairs on to the landing below. I crept downstairs and stared at him, sure that he was dead. My first instinct was to call an ambulance but I didn't want to be implicated in his fall, so I convinced myself it was too late to save him. I knew he'd been unhappy which had led to an increase in his drinking and gambling. I felt guilty that much of his unhappiness was due to me, but I was sure he'd been killing himself slowly with alcohol. I certainly hadn't killed him, just startled him without meaning to. That's right isn't it? Then why can't I quieten my conscience?

I tossed and turned for a couple of hours, before being wakened at 5 am this morning by two police officers, one male and one female. They broke the news to me that Steve had fallen downstairs and I asked which hospital he was in. Then they told me that he was dead, having been found by my downstairs neighbour who is a bus driver and was going out on early shift.

They asked lots of questions, one of them about why I hadn't reported him missing. I explained that he was an alcoholic who sometimes didn't return home until the following day, and I said that by now we led separate lives although still lived under the same roof. They seemed to be sympathetic towards my situation, and told me that they were treating Steve's death as accidental which, strictly speaking, it is.

They will return tomorrow to take me to the police mortuary to identify his body.

I know I should be mourning his loss but all I can think is that I'm free of him.

I stare at the words on the page, trying to take in that my beloved gran was almost a murderer. From what she'd written, it was obvious that she didn't actually push him down the stairs, but had startled him and in his drunken state he wouldn't be too steady on his feet. The real wrongdoing was in not phoning an ambulance, but I guess she was scared of being involved in his death.

I close the diary and think about how similar my life has been in certain aspects to Gran's. I haven't been sexually abused by a stepfather, or had a drunken husband, but I have suffered physical abuse and unfaithfulness from Don.

CHAPTER SEVENTY ONE

I eat alone on Monday evening as Simon has gone straight from work to his karate group. After the class, he and his fellow instructors go for a Chinese or Indian meal, so I don't have to leave him any food on his return.

My meal over and the kitchen cleared, I check what's on TV. Only one programme worth watching so I put it on to record and return to the diaries.

I race through the years as most of the entries are routine and soon, I get to 1967. I reach an entry where Gran is going to Arbroath to stay with her friend Helen, from Marshall's, and Helen's mum for the weekend. I'm smiling now that I've reached a happier period in Gran's life. At last.

Friday 16th June 1967
Dear Diary,

I had a lovely journey up to Arbroath today. The cottage Helen and her mum are renting is gorgeous and I felt at home immediately.

On the train I sat at a table opposite a chap who was reading. We didn't speak until we were nearly at Dundee, where he was getting off. He had a stunning smile and his voice sounded like James Mason, my favourite film star. A pity I won't see him again.

Saturday 17ᵗʰ June 1967
Dear Diary,

Poor Helen fell when we were on a cliff walk today and is in Dundee Royal Infirmary with a broken ankle. Of all people, the doctor looking after her is called Len Singleton, and it turns out he is the chap from the train. I think he recognised me. It feels unreal. A small world!

As Helen will be in hospital for a few days, I will phone the office and arrange to take more time off to stay with her mum at the cottage. Helen's mum's happy about this – I think she enjoys the company.

We will visit Helen again tomorrow.

Wednesday 21ˢᵗ June 1967
Dear Diary,

Guess what? I've a date with Len Singleton. It feels like I'm writing fiction but it really is true. When Helen was discharged from hospital this morning, she left her walking boots in her bedside locker. I returned on the bus this afternoon to collect them. I was coming out of Ward 14 when I collided with Len in the corridor.

I couldn't believe my luck at seeing him again and you could have knocked me down with a feather when he asked me out on a date on Friday night. Said he couldn't have asked me out while Helen was his patient. Of course I said yes, once I'd recovered from the shock.

Friday 23ʳᵈ June 1967

Dear Diary,

We had a fantastic time tonight. Drove to Broughty Ferry where we ate in a café overlooking the Tay. Then we went to the cinema to see 'The Sound of Music' – wonderful film.

Len and I found we had a lot in common, such as walking and swimming.

It's a delight to read how happy Gran is with Len. She finds him easy to talk to and tells him about her past; her stepfather, Steve, the lot. She doesn't want there to be any secrets between them, but is relieved that he's so understanding about all the problems she's had. Their romance goes along smoothly, and I get butterflies in my stomach when I get to the entry about their wedding.

Friday 26th *April 1968*
Dear Diary,

Our wedding day has finally arrived. What a special feeling, so different from the charade I went through with Steve. This time it's for keeps. I've just wakened up in my bed at Fairfields. I've heard some of the family stirring. Charlie will already be out milking. But Sheena warned me not to get up until she brings me breakfast in bed. She said this is something you must have on your wedding day. What luxury!

Lying here I can see my wedding dress zipped into its plastic cover hanging up on the outside of the wardrobe. I'm so excited about wearing it and to stand beside Len in St Mark's Church in Kilmarnock. Len and his family will travel up from Peebles this morning so I won't see him until I get to the church. Sheena says that's as it should be, says it's bad luck to see the groom until then, but I can't imagine us having bad luck. All I can see is happiness ahead until we're old and grey and our kids have flown the nest.

I race through the time of Gran's life with Len. They are so much in love and I keep waiting to read of them having a child but that doesn't happen. It continues in this vein until tragedy strikes. There is a gap of almost a week with no entries, followed by a very sad one.

Wednesday 31st December 1969
Dear Diary,
My mind's in a fog. I can't get to grips with what's happened. At night when I take the tranquilliser the doctor prescribed it helps me get to sleep. I usually have happy dreams in which Len comes to me perfectly well and healthy as he always was. Then, when I waken, everything floods back; the snow, the crash, the journey to hospital and seeing Len arrive in an ambulance. I think I knew he was dead at the scene but I wanted the ward doctor to tell me I was wrong. Instead he told me I was correct and Len had lost his battle for life.

I miss Len so much. I needed his love and his presence and now without him everything seems meaningless. I breathe, sleep, eat, walk and talk but none of it matters any longer. I feel empty inside and don't care if I live or die. I sometimes wonder if I'm being punished for being relieved at the deaths of Benson and Steve.

My adopted family at Fairfields are very supportive of me and Charlie has even let me have his German Shepherd, Star, as a pet. He has settled in well and I can't imagine being without him now.

By the time I get to the end of this section, I'm sobbing. I can scarcely take in all that my beloved gran had to cope with. It makes my life seem like a bed of roses. I knew from earlier entries how good Viv's family had been and here I read how supportive they still are.

CHAPTER SEVENTY TWO

'I'm surprised how easy it was,' I say to Elva, when we're enjoying a late lunch after our dress-hunting afternoon.

'Yes, I knew when I saw you in that lace dress that we'd cracked it. The others you tried on were okay but none of them could come up to the one you've bought.'

'And with your dark hair you really suit the crimson.' I re-fill our wine glasses and sit back, my smile extending from ear to ear. 'Now we've got the dresses, tell me about your holiday with Adam.'

'We're planning to spend time at the Bay of Islands,' she tells me, 'I think we'll cover some of the ground you and I did on our tour up north.'

'Great. And remember if you get to Auckland, you could pay a visit to Jill Patterson.'

'Yes, that would be good,' Elva says, rubbing the heel of her hand over her forehead. 'I can get Jill's phone number from you in case we do go to Auckland.'

The waitress brings over our coffee. When she moves away again, Elva asks, 'I meant to ask you about the diaries. Have you finished reading them?'

'Not quite.' Feeling a sneeze come on, I grab a hankie out of my bag. Once the sneezing fit is over, I continue. 'I'm quite close to the end now and poor Len has been killed so Gran is distraught.'

Elva picks at her nails. 'I can imagine she would be. What an awful life she had, with all the tragedy that seemed to follow her. I wonder if that was what made her such a strong person in her later years?'

'Could be. When I read about Gran's life it makes me think back to what I suffered from Don. Can't think why I put up with it, although at the time I tried to justify his behaviour.'

Elva pushes her empty cup into the middle of the table. 'Have you discussed Don with Marion at the counselling sessions?'

I don't reply immediately but sit and make a temple of my fingers. 'I have,' I say slowly, 'and she felt that his behaviour was the reason for most of my stress and difficulty relating to other men.'

'Are you still seeing Marion?'

'Yep, I'm meeting with her later today and this could be our last session. Marion thinks I'm ready to go it alone from here on.'

'And are you happy with that?'

'I think so. I feel so different from when I first attended her clinic.'

'Good luck with Marion,' Elva says, when we say goodbye shortly afterwards. 'Let me know how you get on.'

***

Once Marion had shown Ros out, she wrote up her notes, then went into the staff room, where she changed into her new dress. She hummed to herself as she pinned up her hair and put on her make-up. She was so looking forward to her anniversary night out with

Larry. All thanks to Abi and Ben booking them dinner at a top restaurant in town and buying tickets for the orchestral concert afterwards. She and Larry had been fans of classical music since their teens.

Wendy popped her head round the staff room door and smiled at Marion. 'That's me off home. I hope you have a lovely evening. You're looking gorgeous.'

'Thanks Wendy. Can't believe it's thirty-five years since Larry and I tied the knot.'

'Well, have a great time and tell me all about it tomorrow.'

Marion laughed. 'Yeah, I'll bore you rigid with all the details.'

'No way.' Wendy waved and the door closed behind her.

Larry was waiting outside the restaurant when Marion got there.

'You look gorgeous, sweetie,' he said, kissing her cheek.

'You scrub up not badly yourself. Let's go inside, I'm starving.'

'So, how was your day?' he asked, when they'd placed their order and had their glasses of wine in front of them.

'Good,' she said, running her fingers up and down the stem of her wineglass as she spoke. 'I'm delighted that my last client, the girl I told you about who'd lost her gran, is making great strides and has arranged her wedding for the end of January.' Marion often told Larry about clients although never revealed their identities because of confidentiality.

'That's good news, sweetie.'

She nodded. 'Yes, it makes my job worthwhile when I see a success story at the end of my sessions.' She raised her glass. 'To my happy client.'

Larry's glass clinked against hers. 'To your happy client,' he echoed.

CHAPTER SEVENTY THREE

Simon is still in the bathroom and I'm deciding which shoes go with what I'm wearing when the phone on the bedside table rings.

'Hello Cheryl,' I answer when I hear her voice, surprised at her calling so early on a work morning. I freeze at her next words and steady myself against the edge of the table.

'It was over in seconds,' she tells me, her tone unnaturally calm. 'Thank goodness he didn't suffer. He looked so peaceful, Ros, just like he'd fallen asleep.' All this is said in a voice devoid of emotion and I share her sense of shock.

'When did it happen?' I ask when she finally comes to a halt.

'Last night, just as the late news was starting.'

It flits through my mind how unimportant the exact time of death is, but it matters to Cheryl right now. I make a few more feeble remarks of sympathy whenever I get the chance to break into the conversation, all the while trying to get my head round what she's told me.

'Thanks for letting us know, Cheryl. I'll be in touch again very soon,' I promise. Simon emerges from his shower when I'm saying this and his face crumples into a question mark.

Dropping the receiver on to its cradle, I plump

down heavily on to the bed. Simon sits beside me and takes my hand. He rubs my fingers gently, still unaware of what's wrong.

Tears rain down my face and I'm oblivious to the damage they are doing to the make-up I carefully applied earlier. 'It was Cheryl on the phone,' I tell him between sobs, my breath coming in short stabs.

'What's happened to Cheryl?'

I shake my head vigorously and the tears flood out faster. I blow my nose. 'Not Cheryl, it's Trev,' I say, dabbing my eyes with a paper tissue from the box beside the phone. 'Trev's dead. Heart attack. Last night.' I stare at Simon, feeling as if I'm telling him about something I saw in a film. Not real life, surely not, I think. But I know it's true, Cheryl has just told me, hasn't she?

Simon's face mirrors what mine must have looked like when Cheryl gave me the news, and he puts his arm around me. 'I don't think you should come into work today, darling, you've had a dreadful shock. I'll tell Charlie why you're staying at home. He'll understand.'

I don't answer straight away but when I do, I've made my decision. 'No, I can't do that. Charlie is depending on me to cover the political rally in the city today, and anyway I'm better to keep busy. And also, you know we always finish early on Fridays.'

He strokes the back of my hand. I can see he's upset too, as he and Trev had got on well when we visited them in Christchurch.

'I'll go and wash my face and freshen up my

make-up before we leave,' I say, squeezing his hand as I get to my feet. 'You need to get dressed now, Simon, or you'll be late,' I remind him as I return to the bathroom.

We drive to the city in silence, both of us thinking about poor Cheryl. When we reach Cuba Street, Simon drives into the car park and we make our way, hand in hand, to the lift for our journey up to the twentieth floor.

'Hi Ros,' Harry says, and smiles at me, his smile extending to Simon. I think he's happy that we've finally got together.

Jill phones from Auckland just after eleven. 'You'll have heard from Cheryl,' she says, with a catch in her voice.

'Yes, I still can't believe that Trev's gone.' Ted looks at me over the top of his specs and signals am I alright and I nod, trying to concentrate on what Jill is saying to me.

'I want to attend the funeral,' she says, 'and wondered if I could go with you and Simon?'

'Of course,' I tell her, 'do you want to come here the night before the funeral and stay with us overnight?'

'Thanks, Ros. I'd appreciate that. I keep remembering how well we all got on in Wanganui at the Seminar. I feel as though I've known you and Trev forever, even though we've only met a few times.'

'Same here,' I say, then I see Matt coming towards me, carrying one of my manuscripts. 'I need to go, Jill, speak to you later.'

'Sorry to hear about your friend's death,' Matt says, and shows me the changes he recommends I make. I notice that his bad breath is not so obvious today and wonder if someone has told him about his problem.

'Thanks, Matt,' I say, and smile at him. I've never mentioned anything to him or Simon about the card and the phone calls.

At lunchtime I phone Elva to tell her what has happened.

'I'm so sorry. Although I never met Trev, I feel as though I know him and Cheryl from you speaking about them. Will Jill come down for the funeral?'

'Yes, and she'll travel over to Christchurch with Simon and me.'

'That's good. It's better to be with folk when you go to a sad event like that. Hold on,' she says, and I can hear someone speaking in the background. 'Sorry, Ros, I need to go, but we'll talk again soon,' she promises.

***

I'm nervous that evening when I lift the phone and dial Cheryl's number, but I want to honour my promise.

'Hello, Cheryl. Wanted to ring as I was too shocked to take in what you were telling me this morning. Simon sends his love.' I'm about to ask her how she is but I manage to stop myself. What a stupid question that would be; of course she's devastated, what other way could she be right now?

She fills me in on the contact she's had with police and medical people during the day. 'Because it was a sudden death, he was taken to the mortuary, where they did a post mortem. A policewoman stayed with me until it was over. Afterwards, the pathologist told me Trev died of a massive heart attack. He assured me that he wouldn't have known anything about it as it was so quick.' I can hear her sobbing quietly. 'Thank God, I couldn't bear to think of him in pain.'

'Will you let me know details of the funeral, Cheryl,' I ask her towards the end of our conversation. 'We'll come over to Christchurch to be with you at the service.'

She takes her time to reply and her voice is very quiet when she does. 'There won't be a funeral as such, Ros, because Trev has donated his body to medical science. But there will be a memorial service for Trev's life and you and Simon will be welcome to join us for that. It will be some time, months even years, until we get his remains for burial or cremation.' I hear the catch in her voice as she says this, and we draw the conversation to a close.

'We'll definitely be at the service and Jill is going to come with us.'

'That's kind of you all,' she says, before her voice dies away, and we finish the call.

'Trev has donated his body to medical science,' I tell Simon, once I hang up.

Seeing my distress, he holds out his arms and I join him on the sofa for a welcome cuddle. 'That's very noble of him,' he says, playing his hands through my hair.

I turn and kiss him, clinging closer. 'Yes, it's a

wonderful gift for anyone to give.'

We sit together for a long time, staring into the fire, each lost in our own thoughts. At last, realising it is dark outside, I get up and close the vertical blinds before switching on the light. 'I'll make us something to eat,' I tell Simon, and go into the kitchen with a heavy heart.

CHAPTER SEVENTY FOUR

I'm quite pleased that Simon is at a rugby match with Ted and Matt this afternoon, as it gives me some time on my own.

Last week was trying, with our attendance at Trev's memorial service. It was great to see Jill again but unfortunate it was for such a sad occasion. We gave what support we could to Cheryl and the kids and it was wonderful to see how many people came to the service. Shows what a popular guy Trev was, and even a few of his ex-teaching colleagues turned up.

Jill spent another overnight with us here in Lyall Bay before flying back to Auckland. She's looking forward to meeting up with Elva and Adam when they're up north later in the year.

I take the diaries out of the writing desk and carry them on to the deck. I haven't been able to face reading any more over the past two weeks since I had the phone call from Cheryl, but I'm nearing the end now so want to read the final entries.

Last time I had the diaries open I read that Gran had a fall in the garden of the house she lived in with Len, and was rescued by Grandad when he heard Star barking at the garden gate. I turn to the page I finished at.

Thursday 21st October 1971

Dear Diary,

What a week it's been. When I fell in the garden and broke my collarbone, my biggest worry was who'd look after Star while I was in hospital. What a relief it was when Rob Crane told me he was happy to care for Star. Rob's a lovely man and nothing is too much bother for him. Poor Rob, has suffered too as his wife died last year of cancer, and he's been finding it lonely without her. He has been a very good friend to me over the past week, so much so that I find it hard to believe I didn't know him before. Fancy us living in the same road without knowing one another.

I must confess Dear Diary that I have grown very fond of Rob in the seven days I've known him. It's been lovely to once more have somebody I can rely on and tell my feelings to. When Len died, I felt I had died inside too. But I knew I had to keep on living for Len. He was the most unselfish person I've ever met, and he would have wanted me to go on and make a new life. But the thought of loving another man never entered my head. Now I'm not so sure ....

I hurry through the remaining entries, with Grandad's name popping up ever more frequently. A shiver of delight runs through me when I read about Gran and Grandad's wedding day. A quiet affair, with just the family from Fairfields and a cousin of Rob's present.

At last I reach the very last entry. Nothing sad to come this time as I already know the outcome.

Thursday 3ʳᵈ May 1972
Dear Diary,

Another 24 hours until we leave for our new life. Everything's packed up and we are shortly leaving for the airport hotel where we will stay overnight before our flight tomorrow. When Rob sold his house at the end of last year, he moved in with me. Then, once my house was sold at Easter, Viv and Dave offered us accommodation here with them and the kids. It was very kind of them and Rob and I really appreciate it.

It is sad in a way for both of us to make a break from our past homes and spouses, but we are excited about our future together at the other side of the world. Rob has a job arranged for him in New Zealand, and I hope to get work once we buy a house and settle down.

Wish us luck Dear Diary.

I close the diary and sit back in my chair, staring out into the garden.

Simon's a keen gardener and the flowers and bushes look so much tidier since he moved in with me. My gardening prowess is mediocre at best and I lack Simon's little touches to enhance the garden. Gran, I know, would approve of Simon, and I feel sure she'll be looking down on us, smiling, on our wedding day.

Simon appears at that moment and comes out on to the deck to kiss me.

'How did the match go?'

He gives me a beaming smile and throw his hands up in the air. 'Our team won,' he says, his eyes aglow. He looks at diary lying open on the table in front of me. 'Have you read them all now?'

'Yep, it was hard to read of Gran's difficult life in her young years. I'm so glad she found happiness with my grandad and enjoyed her life once she came to New Zealand.'

Sensing my lowered mood, Simon holds out his arms to me and I go into his embrace. Together we go into the sitting room, where we sit down on the sofa.

He cradles me in his arms. 'Want to talk about it?'

Up until now I've only spoken to Elva about Gran's secrets, but I nod and snuggle closer to him. 'Gran didn't ever talk to me about her life before she came to New Zealand. I sensed her reluctance, so I didn't press her.' I take Simon's hand and weave my fingers in between his thicker ones while I stare out of the window once more.

'Want to tell me the sort of things you discovered?' He plays with my hair, encouraging me to continue.

I take a deep breath and go on.

'Gran's father died in the second world war when she was a baby. Her mother brought her up single-handedly until she married again and then Gran was abused by her stepfather.'

A shadow passes over Simon's face as he looks at me. 'Sexual abuse?'

'Yes.'

He shakes his head. 'Your poor gran. That must have messed up her head.'

'It affected the rest of her life. She found it very

hard to trust anyone.'

'I'm not surprised.'

Swinging my feet up on to the sofa, I lay my head on Simon's lap and he strokes my face as I continue to speak of what I read. 'My gran's mother died from tuberculosis when Gran was only 18, and that left her with the horrid stepfather.'

'I take it her mother was unaware of the abuse?' He bends his head to kiss me.

'She knew nothing. The stepfather was devious and waited until his wife was asleep. It seems he threatened Gran with what he'd do to both of them if she told her mother.'

'So, what happened when her mother died?'

'Gran ran away to Glasgow, where her mother had come from. She didn't leave a note to say where she was going. She knew her stepfather wouldn't report her missing as he wouldn't want the police involved, in case his behaviour came to light.'

'And did your gran do alright in Glasgow?'

I close my eyes, fighting back tears. 'It was hard for her at first and she tried to kill herself on one occasion. But then she met my Aunt Viv in the hostel where they both lived. Aunt Viv got Gran a job in the department store where she herself worked. Gran was also invited to spend Christmas with Aunt Viv's family, who treated her like their own daughter.'

'That must have been fantastic for your gran, especially after losing her own mother.'

'Yes, I think Aunt Viv's family were the only people she could trust and with their support she made a reasonable life in Glasgow.'

'And did your gran marry when she lived in Scotland?'

I sit up again and rest my head against Simon's chest, savouring his closeness. 'Yes, Gran did marry. Twice in fact. She sort of landed into her first marriage by default. Her husband seemed to love her madly, but Gran found it hard to return his love. I think what had happened with her stepfather probably made her unable to show her feelings to anyone. It sounds like their marriage was doomed from the start. She did love her second husband. Theirs was love at first sight but sadly he was killed in a car accident. Gran was distraught about his death and I think only her work in the department store kept her from ending it all.'

'And when did your grandad come on the scene?'

'Oh, that was a couple of years after she was widowed.' I laugh for the first time when I'm telling Simon about a story I did know. 'Gran told me once that, although they both lived in the same road, they didn't know one another. It was when she fell in her back garden one day and broke her collar bone that Grandad came to her rescue and phoned for an ambulance. Gran had a dog at that time, a German shepherd called Star, and Grandad took the dog out for walks while she was recuperating. He had been widowed a short time before and was glad of the dog's company. Gradually he and Gran became close friends and they later married. A short time after their marriage they emigrated over here and my mum was born a year later. And the rest, as they say, is history.'

'So, a happy ending.'

'Yep.' I cling to Simon, feeling much better for having shared Gran's story with him.

'I'm glad her life ended well,' he murmurs, rubbing his hand up and down my arm. He stops abruptly, and stares at me. 'It's just occurred to me that I always talk about your gran, but what was she called?'

'Her name was Madeleine, but she always used the shortened version of Maddie.'

'Maddie,' he said, and smiled. 'I like that, seems to suit her somehow.'

I nod, returning his smile. 'What do you say if we go and see a movie tonight? Elva told me about a good one showing at the Roxy cinema. It's a comedy about a community college professor and a grill salesman.'

'Who stars in it?'

'Tiffany Haddish and Kevin Hart. Elva said there were some great punchlines.'

'Sounds like it's just what we need, and we can grab a meal while we're out.' Removing his arm from around my shoulders, Simon picks up his phone. 'I'll check the web and see if I can get the times of that film,' he says, punching in the keys as he's speaking.

When we're almost ready to leave the house, Simon grabs me into a passionate embrace and says, 'I'm so glad you know about her life now.'

'Yes, I feel even closer to her now that I know all her secrets. Whatever the rights and wrongs of what happened in her past, she will always be my wonderful gran, who meant the world to me. And now, Mr Leggat, I can really concentrate on our wedding ceremony.'

'Can't wait,' he says, as he lifts me off my feet and swings me round and round, ending with us both collapsing on to the settee, laughing hysterically.

CHAPTER SEVENTY FIVE
2019

I waken early, while it's still only half-light. Rolling over on to my other side, I can't stop smiling because it's my wedding day.

I push myself up the bed, propping the pillow behind me. I stretch, and place my arms behind my head, listening to the birds singing on the tree outside my bedroom window. It's almost as though they also know this is a special day.

As the daylight strengthens, my eyes fall on to my wedding dress, hanging up on the front of the wardrobe, zipped into its plastic cover. I can't wait to wear it. I like the way the bodice, with its cross-over effect at the cleavage and the straight skirt, enhances my figure. Beside it hangs Elva's crimson bridesmaid's dress.

Under the shower, I think how much I love Simon, unable to understand how I'd disliked him at first. But the shaky start makes our love now even more vibrant, and I look forward to us sharing a wonderful future together.

I've dried myself and pulled on my robe, when I hear the doorbell. Barefoot, I pad my way downstairs to open the door to Elva.

'Morning,' she chirps, almost falling in the doorway to gather me into a tight hug. 'I'm here at your service, ma'am,' she tells me, grinning. 'I'm showered, but haven't eaten yet.'

'Would you like a fry-up, or are we going Continental?' I ask her.

She wrinkles her nose. 'Continental?' When I nod my agreement, she steers me into the living room and pushes me down on to the sofa. 'You sit here and relax, while I prepare brekkie for us both. We can't have you working on your wedding day.'

I don't put up any resistance, and soon we enjoy a leisurely breakfast.

Simon and his parents have gone to stay overnight at the Wellington Arms in Lambton Quay, where we are to be married by a celebrant. This allows Elva and me to get ourselves prepared for the big event.

'I wonder if Simon has eaten yet,' I say, while I'm spreading honey on my toast.

'He'll be fine, and I bet his mother will enjoy fussing over him.'

Elva carries our used dishes into the kitchen and puts them in the dishwasher. She returns in time for another ring at the doorbell. She goes to answer it, and returns with the girl who is to do our nails and apply our make-up. The beautician is finishing her task, when Marion, the hairdresser, arrives. Marion has washed and styled my hair, and is doing Elva's, when the florist brings our bouquets.

'Did you do the table arrangements at the hotel, and deliver the flowers for Simon and his parents to wear?' I ask her, breathlessly.

She smiles and pats my arm. 'Yes, I did, so stop

worrying, everything is under control.'

'Thanks,' I say, and see her out.

'Have a wonderful day,' Marion says, when she leaves shortly afterwards, giving both Elva and me a hug.

The time seems to fly and before I realise it we're getting dressed. Elva puts on her dress first, accompanied by admiring oohs and aahs from me, and then helps me into mine.

'You're so beautiful,' she says, and leads me towards the full-length mirror in the bedroom.

I stand in front of the mirror, while Elva fixes on my head-dress. I'm trying to believe that the vision in white facing me is really myself.

'That'll be Ted,' I say, when the doorbell rings once more.

Ted had been delighted when I asked him to walk me down the aisle.

'After all,' I'd said, 'you've been like a kind dad to me, so you're the person I thought of straight away.'

'Perfect,' Ted now says, as he looks at Elva and me in our finery.

'You're turned out very well yourself,' Elva tells him, her compliment making him blush.

'What about Anne?' I ask.

'She was ready when I left the house. Charlie and Karen are picking her up, and then collecting Matt on the way to the hotel.'

When the bridal car arrives, Ted ushers us in. He sits in front with the driver, while Elva and I share the back seat.

'Excited?' Elva whispers, squeezing my hand.

I nod, not trusting myself to speak, in case I break down and spoil my make-up.

In the Wellington Arms, we straighten out our dresses and check our hair once again. When the musicians begin to play the Wedding March, I enter the room on Ted's arm. He winks at me and we start off down the aisle, followed by Elva, our dresses rustling as we go.

Our guests on either side of the aisle are smiling at us, but I can't take my eyes off my handsome bridegroom, standing in front of the celebrant, with his cousin, Gavin, at his side.

When Ted and I draw nearer, Simon turns around and beams at me. Happiness surges through me, when I stand next to him and he takes my hand.

The End

Acknowledgements

I am grateful, as ever, to Gerry and Elaine Mann of Authorway publishing, for taking on this novel and for the assistance they offer me.

As a member of two writing groups, Strathkelvin and Kelvingrove, I appreciate all the inspiration and encouragement I receive from my fellow writers. But especially I want to thank Pat Feehan, Patricia Hutchinson and Mary Edward for taking the time to proofread the novel and to offer me valuable feedback and suggestions.

It would be remiss of me not to thank Mary Edward for allowing me to bring her novels, * centred on Dundee and the jute industry, into my book.

My thanks to writing colleague, Linda Bell, for her patience in listening to my ideas for the plot of this novel and offering her thoughts about the story line.

Dr Linda Hanlon kindly helped me to set the scene in the veterinary surgery in Wellington. Thank you also Linda for allowing me to use your name for one of my characters, and I hope you like the way I have described her.

*

'A Spider's Thread Across the Tay' by Mary Edward, published 2013.

'Broken Threads' by Mary Edward, published 2015.

Both novels available on Amazon.

Printed in Poland
by Amazon Fulfillment
Poland Sp. z o.o., Wrocław

54427871R00204